Margins

Landry Brennan

To Natalie, Amelia, and Oliver,
for being the very best parts of my story.
And to all the people who never
found their way to the middle of the page.

It makes a difference doesn't it, whether we fully
fence ourselves in, or whether we are fenced out
by the barriers of others?

E.M. Forster, *A Room with a View*

Contents

Chapter One

Alex Ramos picks up his jacket, presses it back down onto the armchair, then stares at it for a minute while he decides what to do.

What he *should* do or what he *wants* to do, he isn't even sure, but there must be some contrast there, even if it's about as distinct as the two shades of gray he's studying with an unnecessary frown. He's been like this a lot lately, probably far too often for him to argue he's on the right side of okay, a constant restlessness leaving him anxious about something he still hasn't seriously considered figuring out. Unfortunately, it puts him in stupid situations like this, where he looks at a goddamn jacket for too long because he can't decide whether he's motivated enough to take a morning walk around the neighborhood.

He should, he thinks. He's actually pretty sure he wants to. And because those two don't always line up quite so neatly for him, the ongoing battles in his head only worsening his inability to take a step in any direction, Alex figures he might as well take advantage of their truce today. He sighs, grabs his jacket from the armchair again, and shrugs it on.

The fog he steps into feels exactly right, and he's almost positive he's not being sardonic about that.

Alex has always loved this one very specific thing about living near the California coast, a light blanket thrown over his home every morning, one that stretches far past his front lawn and onto so many others around him. Even if the sun is certain to warm them later, or maybe even soon, they're all treated to something tender first, and it's why Alex insists on drinking his coffee on the back patio every day. Very little about the world is soft, and he thinks he needs that one routine to help harden him for the rest.

The coffee is gone though, and the fog is still here, and maybe Alex can keep his guard down for a little while longer.

He shoves his hands into his jacket pockets and turns down the street.

It isn't exactly a new thing, going for a walk around the neighborhood, though most of the time he's with Elena, and most of the time they're traveling to and from the park. With Elena at Cassidy's house today, Alex thinks being alone should be an indulgence, but seeking anything quite like that has been a lifelong challenge, and it seems too early or too late to learn something about it now. As it is, Alex is still adjusting to the idea of his wife and kid being together without him, along with whatever other failures made it necessary in the first place, and he only wishes the cool morning air would be enough to help him solve the puzzle before he's picked up half the pieces.

It's far more likely Alex will be stuck making sense of it all when he's locked inside his empty house again, surrounded by a few too many echoes.

The half of the neighborhood further away from the park is less familiar to him, even after having lived here for six years, and Alex decides to go that way because, as long as a few new experiences have been forced upon him lately, he figures he might as well have a choice about one now. Everything is mostly quiet and calm this early, and Alex makes a point of absorbing it all. With a steady gaze, he takes note of the cars resting in driveways or tucked away in the garage, a handful of people out to walk their dogs, two women jogging while they carry on a hushed conversation, and a couple of cats in something of a standoff until Alex gets close enough for them to take their argument elsewhere. When his toe catches on the uneven sidewalk, he looks down at sneakers that could stand to be replaced, moves up to sweatpants and a t-shirt he'll hold on to for too long, and then while rolling his eyes for nobody, he struggles to remember whether he did anything with his hair after he showered that morning.

Vanity isn't a thing for him, blessed with looks that have never required it, but Alex thinks he could work on being a little less of a mess. Maybe he'll find time for that right after he stops wandering around with nowhere to go. Then he sees a sign on the corner—a literal one, not the figurative kind his abuelita loves to pray for—and a tiny smile tilts his head sideways. It's silly, but maybe now he's headed somewhere.

Garage sales have probably been around forever, in whatever various forms, for as long as people have had old stuff to sell to strangers, but there's something that still manages to be warm about them, furniture and art and toys and absolute junk and a touch of humanity being passed from person to person. They're held so close to home, but not quite close enough that anyone gets a real peek inside, and memories get sold to neighbors who can't possibly understand why they matter but want a piece of them anyway. Or maybe that guy around the corner just loves that he can buy old ski boots for next to nothing, but Alex would like to think there's at least a little more to it than that, and he follows the signs now to a house four streets down from his own, in search of something he doesn't even know he needs.

Even at a glance, he's already sure he'll find something that makes the stop worth it.

There's a bunch of lawn and garden equipment and several tools, some disassembled bedroom and living room furniture, a couple of stacks of large blankets and comforters, small kitchen appliances and other household gadgets, jackets and coats and shoes, framed prints and assorted home décor, piles of books, plenty of board games, two TVs and a few other electronics, probably a hundred vinyl records, and a small collection of kids' toys and sports gear. Most of the stuff looks like it belonged to an older man, if Alex wants to do the most basic of profiling, though there's just enough reason for him to be confused about the rest, and he shakes his head when he realizes it doesn't really matter at all.

"Morning."

Alex looks over at two women—mother and daughter perhaps—rifling through the dozens of books, and at a man measuring a small dresser with his hands, then back toward the guy who must be talking to him.

"Morning," he echoes with a nod.

He gets a tired smile from the guy whose hands are wrapped around a travel mug of what Alex hopes is coffee for someone who looks like he needs it, this man ducked into his hoodie like he might be able to sleep there if everyone leaves him alone long enough. He's probably around Alex's age and he's sitting at a card table, notably also for sale, and there's a dog, likely some sort of black lab mix, lying next to his feet and no more alert than his owner.

"Feel free to look around, pick stuff up, ask questions, whatever," the guy tells him. "I put price stickers on some of the bigger things, but you can just make an offer on everything else."

Alex feels the corners of his mouth curl upward, though he eases them into what feels like a more neutral grin. "Too early in the morning to be greedy?"

The guy shrugs. "Not trying to make a fortune here. Mostly just emptying the house."

At the risk of overstepping, Alex is about to ask what prompted the garage sale now, spring cleaning a thing most people did about six months ago, but they get interrupted by a question from Dresser Man, and Alex wanders off to browse instead. He looks through the rack of coats but doesn't think he has a need for anything there, and none of the shoes are quite his style. The vinyls are tempting, at least a handful of them albums Alex already has at home, but he moves over to the games instead, and thinks about buying a couple of those for Elena. Most of them look barely used, and he could say the same for the rest of the kids' stuff nearby, nothing particularly old or worn. He decides to look around a little more before grabbing anything, already accepting the risk of anyone else coming by to take it first, and he makes his way over to the books, Older Woman and Younger Woman busy buying some of the artwork now.

He spots an easily recognizable collection of Stephen King works and skips that because the last thing he needs are more bad dreams, and he brushes past several western novels and a half dozen memoirs out of a general lack of interest. There are some children's books, but he thinks they might be ones Elena has in her closet, and he only gets stuck for a moment when he thinks about the fact that she has two closets now and might want duplicates of a couple of things.

Alex breathes, a weary and hollow thing that lasts long enough for him to get lost and come back again, then he continues looking through the titles in front of him. There are authors he recognizes and plenty he doesn't, but then he comes across another group of books with some of both, all beautifully bound and almost too intimidating to touch. He's gentle then, reaching for a book he read a cheaper version of back in high school, and opens to that perfect used book smell, his eyes fluttering closed before he can think of how silly he might look to anyone else.

"You too, huh?"

The book snaps shut, just barely missing the tip of Alex's nose, and he feels his cheeks grow warm when he looks up at the Hoodie Guy, the garage sale's sleepy host. He looks no more awake now, but his hair is notably wild where it curls around the fabric of his hood, a bunch of blond vines winding toward the sun. Maybe the rest of him will get there eventually.

Alex cocks his head, his free hand scraping through his own dark hair, and whether he'd styled it earlier becomes unimportant now. "Um, what?"

"It's okay. I love the smell of used books, too," Hoodie promises with only the slightest smirk. "See anything you might want?"

And yeah, he does, especially this entire array, which would be an amazing Christmas gift for his soon-to-be ex-wife, even if that's not the kind of thing he's really supposed to be shopping for at all. D. H. Lawrence, Marcel Proust, E. M. Forster, Oscar Wilde, and on and on, probably a perfect choice for Cass, and something she could always pass down to Elena someday.

"Yeah, I mean, a lot of these are in great condition, but I—" Alex makes a face and lets his gaze fall back to the book still in his hand. "I wasn't really planning to stop by, so there would be a limit to how much I can carry home."

"Not a problem. I mean, unless you're just lying about that to get out of buying anything, which is totally fine," Hoodie laughs, the scratchiness of it suggesting that his voice rarely works this hard so close to sunrise. "But if you do want some of these, I've got a bunch of duffel bags around here and you can go wild. Or I'll hold on to everything if you want to pull up a truck like that guy."

He gestures over to where Dresser Man has loaded his new-found treasures into the back of a rumbling pickup truck—in addition to the dresser, it looks like he might've grabbed the bed frame too—but then Hoodie nudges Alex's arm with his elbow, and Alex can only assume he's being teased.

It's been a while since anything in his world has felt quite that light.

"Yeah, no, um, a couple of bags would be great. You can just add them to my tab."

"Nah, not charging you for the bags. Be right back, though."

He disappears into the open garage, and Alex begins to stack all the books he wants to buy for Cassidy, plus a handful for Elena. When Hoodie returns, they start packing them up, Alex careful to keep a running total even if Hoodie doesn't seem all that bothered. And as long as he's got a way to carry everything now, Alex grabs a couple of the board games, too.

"Not enough time to play all the ones we already have, but I guess it won't hurt to have more, right?"

"Hey, if you want to add to your chaos by helping me unload

mine, that's fine by me," Hoodie laughs. "You have kids?"

"Just my daughter. She's nine," Alex answers. "You?"

"Nope, those were here from when my niece and nephew were younger."

They get everything zipped up, and Alex lifts two straps onto his shoulders before looking around to see if there's anything else before he goes, his eyes lingering on the vinyls until his words are quick to make him seem braver than he is.

"Can I give you some advice?" he asks Hoodie.

"Sure."

"Keep all those albums. Or I mean, if they've got terrible memories attached to them, then maybe don't. But other-wise—" he trails off and shrugs, his fingers curled into a fist only long enough for it to feel good when he relaxes again. "I don't know. Music is a big deal and I think it's usually worth keeping if you can. Even if you can get most of it online now."

"Sounds like the voice of experience."

Alex thinks back to all the ways music has hurt and healed him, especially recently. "Yeah, I guess so."

Hoodie frowns. "Slight problem, though. The record player that was inside with the albums broke a while ago, and I don't have one at my place."

"Wait, you don't live here?"

"Oh, no. I wish. No, I'm just helping out. I've got a little condo like half an hour from here. I'd probably take a few more things with me if I had the room to keep them."

Alex nods, aching with the reminder that he has far too

much room. "Well, I'm not really one to be talking then, but a record player isn't hard to get, and you should be able to store the vinyls easily enough. If you decide it's what you want to do."

"You know, you were already my best customer of the day just for buying up all these books," Hoodie says. "But now that you're dispensing life advice, I feel like maybe I should throw in a free coffee grinder or something."

"Okay, first of all, I don't think you can call anyone your best customer when you probably started this thing an hour ago at the most. Second, if you *did* have a best customer, I'm pretty sure it's the dude who just carted off old bedroom furniture for you."

"That guy was grouchy and taking that stuff off my hands was the very least he could do," Hoodie argues. "You're—well, you aren't *grouchy* grouchy. I'm guessing you just need more sleep, more coffee, or more of both."

"Like you?" Alex asks, nodding at the travel mug Hoodie had been clinging to when he first arrived.

"Yes, exactly like me. So maybe I'll give you the coffee grinder and wish you all the best."

Alex laughs. "I've got every possible coffee contraption at home already—part of my ongoing quest to be a little less grouchy, I guess—but thank you. I think I'm all set with these."

"If you insist."

A young couple has arrived, already pointing excitedly at a few different things, so Alex and Hoodie come to an agreement about the price of the books and games quickly enough, and Alex offers some kind of wave goodbye before he turns to leave.

The fog is gone, and every logical part of him screams that it's only because the sun has made itself known.

With the two duffel bags on his shoulders, he doesn't bother taking the long way around the neighborhood like he might have otherwise, content to head directly back home and into the quiet of his house. It doesn't have to stay quiet, though, Alex still thinking about what he'd said about the vinyls, and before he even unpacks the bags, he puts a record on and makes more coffee.

By that afternoon, Alex has accomplished more than he has in a long time, even if none of it is particularly interesting or likely to matter for longer than a day. He gets the house cleaned, which isn't all that hard, but he also gets some of it reorganized, spreading out what he has to help disguise how much is suddenly gone. Or not *suddenly* exactly, not when Cassidy's departure had already been a long time coming by the time it happened, but watching her leave had still taken Alex by some surprise, and he's been ignoring the most obvious reminders of it ever since.

He misses her, or he tries to convince himself he does, but sometimes he doesn't know where the ache comes from and whether her returning would ever have a chance of making him hurt any less. At the end of it all, she just couldn't pretend it would be good for her to stay, and for someone who so often has all the right words, he couldn't argue that she was wrong.

So, Alex has cleaned in between one too-tender memory and another, and he's reorganized until it feels like he's safely reined everything in, and somewhere in between it all, he even remembered to eat lunch. Then fueled by both music and the caffeine he had on either side of some leftover soup, he got caught up on bills and a handful of other things he'd left piled up on the desk in his little home office, and he talked to both Cass and Elena for a few minutes to check in about plans for the upcoming week. After that, he worked out on the second-hand exercise equipment he has set up in his garage, and he took a second shower, and now he's at his kitchen counter, weirdly rested and relaxed and thinking about ordering some Thai to be delivered for dinner.

Being lazy about dinner is nothing new, but it feels different tonight, an active choice to treat himself on a quiet Saturday night and not a default forced upon him by hours of nothing-ness and an inability to do better than that.

It's fine, and maybe even pleasant, until it gets to be just a little bit later. The sun's gone down, and he thinks he's run out of worthwhile household feats, a touch of sorrow returning when he finds himself missing the sounds of his family and wishing they could play any of the games he'd bought that morning. But that's enough, actually, to remind him to get off his ass and sort through the duffel bags he'd set aside earlier. The games are simple, pulled free and added to the shelves containing over a dozen others, as at home here as they might have been at his neighbor's house before. Alex struggles with what to do with the books a minute longer, first separating out the ones he thinks Elena might want to keep here or there, taking a couple he picked up just because he thought he might like to read them someday, then stacking all the beautiful classics he'd like to give to Cass.

He still doesn't know if that's weird, planning a Christmas gift for her, but he has a few months to figure it out and he sighs in an attempt to shed himself of a little of the worry now. His finger runs back and forth over the spine of *A Room with a View*, the same novel he'd opened at the garage sale—the one he'd read in high school and vaguely remembers liking even if that wasn't a thing anyone was supposed to admit at age 15—and he picks it up again now. Alex makes himself comfortable on the couch and pulls the throw blanket from where he'd folded it neatly against the back, and then he carefully opens the book and accidentally smiles at the memory of Hoodie teasing him about the smell of it that morning.

If liking any of it is a guilty pleasure, Alex isn't sure he cares.

He flips through the first couple of pages until he pauses to read "Chapter 1" in a misleadingly modest typeface for a story more resonant than that, and he finds it underlined, the word "perhaps" handwritten in faded ink just next to the printed words. Alex grins, something so softly mysterious about it, and he wonders if this might have been a gift of some kind many, many years ago. A school graduation or a new job or an engagement or marriage or birth of a child. All the possibilities of someone's beautiful beginning are enough to make him happy, and he starts to read.

He doesn't pay much attention to what time it is when he begins or how long he reads before he sees another hand-written note, he only knows he's not all that far into the book when he finds something scribbled into the margin and turns the entire thing sideways so he can read it more easily, though the ink is just as light as the first word he'd found.

E, such a clever idea you've had. Or perhaps it's so many other things I couldn't possibly describe yet, though I want you to know I feel them all the same.

Alex reads it a couple of times before he slows the thump of his heart and rights the book in his hands again, musing about what the message might mean after the hope suggested by the single word he read a short time ago. He already thinks there must be more messages somewhere, though—that it's unlikely someone took the time to write this one note to a person they've called E, and then left it alone from that point forward—or maybe he just always wants there to be more to the story.

He goes back to the novel itself and tries not to get carried away about something done, or not done, long ago.

The book pulls him back in, which is exactly what he needs, and he thinks back to high school, when he first met Cassidy and was somewhere between being a jock and a nerd and nobody at all, enjoying school and pretending not to. In hindsight, Alex assumes he was a lot like other kids, not quite fitting in anywhere and not knowing why, on a constant search for a way to be like everyone else because it was easier than feeling any different. And when it didn't quite work, when even hanging out with Cassidy felt just a little bit off, he always had books to turn to, and everything about being here on his couch now is comforting him in a way he'd almost forgotten.

He reads for a while and gets expectedly drowsy after another half hour or so, figuring he'll get up from the couch soon so he can head upstairs and get some sleep before he has a whole other weekend day to waste tomorrow. Only a couple more pages, just to a good stopping point, and then it's bedtime.

And then there it is again, another message, and Alex feels himself exhaling, having held his breath for a while for a reason he's yet to understand.

E, you were standing so close when you handed me this book today, and then you brushed against my hand with your finger. I hope nobody saw us because I'm afraid it must be so clear what that small touch made me feel, but no matter how scared I am, I hope you do it again. Please do it again.

Alex blinks down at the page for several seconds before he forces himself to look away from a private moment that he can't actually see. Someone wrote about a finger touching a hand and it seems like so much more than that, something intimate shared and meant to be kept from other people's eyes. A young love, frowned upon perhaps. Or something just new enough that it was embarrassing at the time. Maybe the breathtaking sensation that comes with a crush and the butterfly beginnings of something more.

He groans in the otherwise silent room, finding himself a little silly for reacting like he's the one with the damn crush here, but Alex thinks he's always been something of a romantic, and however implausibly, separating from his wife has only made that worse, not better. He pauses for a moment, concerned too that maybe it's none of his business, no matter when these messages were written or where these people are now—if they're alive at all. It's still their story, not his own, only the novel itself meant for his eyes while the rest was for an audience of two. He really isn't sure what to do, but he finds himself reaching for page after page, tender but too curious to stop until he comes to the next one, handwriting filling the margin like it had the others before.

E, I am so scared, so often. I don't know whether this is the right thing to do, but I cannot make myself stop either, if only because it's one more reason to see you, and these books are the only thing we can give each other. I think you must know how much more I would give you if I could.

It wasn't just the newness of a crush, then. There was something keeping these two lovers apart, but the possibilities are probably endless, regardless of when the notes might have been written. People have faced so many struggles for so many reasons, heartache a natural consequence of too much of the past. Alex grabs one of Elena's bookmarks from the basket she keeps on the end table and he makes himself close the book after reading the passage one more time, tossing the blanket aside and pushing off from the couch to stretch before he double-checks the locks, turns off all the lights, and makes his way upstairs to his room.

The book lands on his nightstand, on top of one that's already had a place there for too long, and it's only when Alex is in the middle of brushing his teeth that he realizes something has been missing from everything he's found in the margins so far. And maybe he's just overlooked a couple of pages somewhere, but he doesn't think so, and he hurries to finish up in the bathroom so he can get back to the book just to study it one more time. He can't let himself get too involved in this love story, but he wants to know.

The embossed cover of the book has become familiar to his hands, and he's careful as he flips through the pages he's already read, then Alex moves ahead to the next couple of messages he can find, intrigued when he confirms what he was sure of a minute ago.

Every one of them is addressed *to* E, but Alex can't find anything *from* E.

Not a back and forth then? Unrequited love? Something still too forbidden to make it any further than the margins of a novel? Were the margins acting as a diary of sorts, all these confessions meant for nobody to see, maybe especially the one person addressed in each one?

His head tilts sideways, as though the new angle might help provide an answer, but he's so tired, and whatever else he's missing, Alex can't keep going right now. Besides, there's one person who might be able to help him tomorrow, if he just happens to be back to hold another garage sale for all the Sunday morning neighborhood shoppers. One person who might recognize the handwriting and know exactly who E is, and who may laugh at the idea that there is any mystery to be solved. One person who probably deserves to know about this anyway, since the books may have belonged to a family member and should probably be returned instead of being pored over by a stranger.

Alex nods to himself and sets the book back down, crawling into bed and promising himself he won't spend all night obsessed with a novel, or the love story hidden inside.

He'll try to find Hoodie in the morning.

Chapter Two

Alex is an early riser and always has been, he thinks. He's so rarely at peace with himself, even when there's no reason to keep up a fight, and maybe that's the first thing to rouse him each morning. But also, there's something about the quiet of those early hours that lures him out of bed for a few tender moments, a gentleness that carries him into a difficult world, and even he has to let a few battles go while everything around him is still waking up.

Once he's out of bed on Sunday, Alex takes a longer shower than usual, treating himself to an extra daydream or two because it's the first morning he hasn't dreaded in a while. Most other days remind him that little family routines have been traded for solitude he never asked for and doesn't particularly want, but he can sit with that now—or stand, he supposes—and let the scalding water course over him while he thinks about the book and the written messages and what Hoodie might be able to tell him about where any of it came from.

Who might have written those notes, and whether E might have known about them at all.

Alex throws on jeans and a hoodie of his own, and he

actually does something with his hair this time, then he grabs the book from his nightstand and jogs downstairs with more energy than he should have before his regular two cups of coffee. Once he's surrounded by the scent of freshly ground beans and a hint of the cinnamon he adds as a treat, he makes himself a quick egg and cheese sandwich, the closest thing he's had to a real breakfast in a while, his stomach growling at the very thought of being treated right. As he eats on his back patio, he looks down at his mug and wonders for just a moment whether he should make some coffee for Hoodie, too—whether maybe that might be the kind of thing one neighbor would do for another. He's terrible at this actually, unsure about how to show up in these random social situations, so much of his life narrowed to work and family and the day-to-day built around those a long time ago.

Maybe bringing coffee would be weird. Alex doesn't even know if Hoodie will be at the house. Inside or out.

He's hopeful, mostly because it seems like garage sales are often a two-day event around here, and even if Hoodie doesn't have one planned, he may still need to take care of whatever he's been taking care of at a house that isn't his. Then again, he hadn't seemed like a morning person, and Alex showing up so early may be stupid.

Alex rolls his eyes as he finishes his breakfast and stares across his backyard. He has a lot of dumb questions about things that don't matter, but there's something at the far back of his mind wondering when he'll start asking all the harder questions about the things that do. He knows Cass has always stopped short of asking them herself, and he's curious about whether there's any time left to force her to scream something out loud. She's never been the cowardly one, and if Alex won't reduce all of their problems to a couple of very simple words, he thinks someone should.

Suddenly close to being frustrated again, by his own inaction as much as anything else, he walks back into his house and locks the rest outside.

It's still early, but there's no reason he can't go out now, Alex perfectly content to walk around for a while if there's no sign of Hoodie yet, or ever. The fog remains as heavy and as welcome as always, and Alex tucks one hand into his pocket and holds the novel in the other as he begins to walk. It's hard not to hurry, even if he shouldn't be in a rush for anything today, so he focuses on the fresh air and the dew on the grass and he takes as many deep breaths as he can. It's only when he turns the corner a few streets down, and sees a garage door open, that all the calm gets a little caught in his chest, Hoodie in the middle of setting up a table in the driveway.

Alex's grip on the book tightens.

"I have to say, only the very best customers come back on day two," Hoodie says when Alex is close enough to hear. He hasn't fully turned away from the table though, and Alex can't figure out how long ago Hoodie had spotted him, the question leaving his cheeks to grow warmer than the cool morning should allow. "Although if you're here to return something, I have to say it'll knock you down a few spots."

"No, I'm—I mean, maybe, but not exactly—not like that," Alex stumbles, curious when he looks toward the street and back to Hoodie again. "Did that guy come back to return the bedroom furniture?"

Hoodie's head falls back as he laughs, and Alex is treated to the sight of an easy joy he envies from a few feet away. "No, but if you're worried he has a chance of catching up to you, you're welcome to help me get all this stuff set up. I'm running a little behind this morning."

"Late night?" Alex asks, finding a shelf inside the garage, right next to the same black lab mix he'd seen yesterday, and putting the book there to keep it safe before he crouches and lets the dog check him out. Alex wants to know his name, but hasn't even found a way to ask for Hoodie's yet, so he scratches behind the dog's ears, then stands to pull another folding table out and snap the legs into place.

"Yeah, actually. I'm a bartender, so—"

"Occupational hazard."

"Exactly," Hoodie says. "You look very awake, though. Probably not a bartender."

"Nah, just a boring newspaper columnist. Though I guess we both listen to a lot of other people's stories, huh?"

"And some are far better than others," Hoodie jokes. Then he nods to the collection of small kitchen appliances Alex is arranging. "And thank you for helping me with this, but you don't actually have to. I was just giving you a hard time."

"Hey, no, I don't mind. And I—I'm Alex, by the way. Alex Ramos. I mean, I guess introductions aren't required garage sale etiquette, but now that I seem to be a regular here—"

"Oh, shit, sorry. Yeah, hi—" Hoodie says, wiping his hands on his jeans before he reaches out for a handshake. "Guess you take me out from behind the bar and I forget how to talk to people. I'm—"

A shout comes from across the driveway, a woman there far too excited about a couple of the coats she's found on the rack, and she's waving at Hoodie for some help, distracting them both. Hoodie's mouth is still open like he's about to laugh or apologize, and Alex just shoos him away.

"No, go, I'll get the rest of the stuff set up for you. Looks like you might be able to get an extra buck or two out of her if you turn on some charm."

Hoodie starts backing toward her. "Hey, I have plenty of charm all the time."

Alex thinks he's probably right, though whether he tends bar because he's charming or whether he's charming because he tends bar is anyone's guess. He turns around and busies himself with the little left for him to do, noting that the vinyls are nowhere to be found, which means they were either sold yesterday, or Hoodie had taken his advice. When Alex is done, he leans up against the side of the house, and Hoodie helps Coat Lady and a couple of other early arrivals. It's another few seconds before the dog wanders out and sits next to Alex, calmly curious and content where he can watch whatever's happening, both of them straightening a little when Hoodie returns.

"Welcome back," Alex says. "She tip you well?"

"They usually do," Hoodie replies with a wink. "But yeah—sorry, I'm Elijah Caplinger. Or Eli, I guess."

"You guess?"

"I—I don't know why I said Elijah. Most people call me Eli."

"Okay, sure," Alex says, nodding slowly. "But what do you prefer?"

There's a long pause and a head tilt that probably serve as enough of an answer, but Alex waits anyway, eternally patient with everyone but himself. And maybe sometimes that patience becomes stubbornness or a martyrdom he never sees coming, but for now it's easy to keep his stare soft until Hoodie—or Eli or Elijah—speaks up and saves them both the trouble of wondering why Alex needs to know anything more about a stranger's name.

"Elijah, actually. I prefer Elijah, but it's—I don't even know why I introduced myself that way. It's been a while since anyone called me that."

"Well, *Elijah*, thank you for accidentally telling me the truth."

"Another occupational hazard for both of us, maybe," Elijah huffs. "Too much honesty."

"I don't know. Sometimes it's just the right amount," Alex argues.

"Sometimes," Elijah agrees. "And I assume Alex is short for

something that you don't like?"

"I don't hate it, really, but yeah, it's short for Alexander. Much to my grandmother's eternal disappointment, I'm not an Alejandro, though it's never stopped her from calling me that when she's mad."

"Does that happen often?"

"More in the past several months than the rest of my life combined, I think."

Elijah's face twists into a laugh and a frown all at once. "Interesting. Here I was convinced that you're the kind of guy who's never done anything wrong."

It's a joke and not—hence the laugh and frown, Alex supposes—and he brushes all of it off with a shrug. "Jury's still out on whether returning to a stranger's garage sale was the right thing to do."

"Mmmm, maybe that means it's time for you to tell me why you came back. I assume you don't actually want a refund on the book?"

"Ha, no, I don't. But I—can I ask you a few other questions first? I know that sounds weird, but I promise I'll explain after."

Elijah's eyes narrow, though he doesn't look all that bothered. "Is this gonna be off the record?"

"Off the—" Alex chokes a little and shakes his head. "No. I mean, yes, off the record. I'm not—this is personal, not a—I'm not writing about you or anything."

"Hmmm, wait a second. You seem surprised by the very thought of that, and I don't know whether I should be offended. Random garage sale dude who doesn't own a record player isn't enough of a story for you?"

"Random garage sale dude with a dog, even," Alex says, nodding down at the dog who got bored with their conversation and dropped back down to sleep. "Maybe I'll reconsider. Pets can be a hell of a hook."

There's another wave from someone looking for help, so Elijah just chuckles and walks away, Alex left to wonder if he's being ridiculous about everything. He bought books at a garage sale, and sure, there are some interesting notes written onto some of the pages, but those messages are so old and may have nothing to do with Elijah, and either way, not everyone is going to be as caught up in someone else's love story as Alex is amid the loneliness of his upcoming divorce. He can't imagine Elijah will be mean about it—the guy seems easygoing and like the most he'll do is poke a little fun at Alex for swooning over a few inked words. Still, maybe it was a mistake to show up here, and maybe there's enough of a distraction right now that Alex can just grab his book and leave without it being a bigger deal than that.

He slips into the garage to pull the book down from the shelf, and only glances over to where Elijah is closing on the sale of a TV that Alex is surprised made it to day two. Then he spares a smile for the sleeping dog, makes his way down the driveway, and turns up the sidewalk to retrace his steps back home.

"Hey, no, Alex, wait," Elijah calls from behind him a few

seconds later. "What happened?"

Alex sighs and turns where he is, Elijah already several feet away from his own garage sale, his hood falling back from his head for the first time since they met. The sun is finally pushing past the morning clouds, and it helps make Elijah's blond curls brighter, and Alex sort of wonders how many people reach for those curls without permission. He's seen it so many times with his daughter, strangers drawn to natural curls and just wanting to touch, forgetting that they belong to someone else and aren't there for their damn pleasure. And on the one hand, he has no doubt Elijah can stand up for himself, tall and broad and halfway between rock climber and surfer, but he wonders if he *does*, the Eli conversation enough to suggest there's rarely a fight for what Elijah wants.

"No, it's nothing," he tells him, stepping a few feet closer so Elijah doesn't have to leave the house any further behind. "I think maybe I was just making something out of nothing. My imagination or whatever. It's probably pretty dumb."

Elijah doesn't move from where he's standing, not for several seconds, but he slides his hands into his hoodie pocket and watches Alex for a while, like maybe he has a whole lot of questions of his own. Eventually he nods.

"I hear a lot of pretty dumb things every night at work, and I'm almost positive that whatever you came back here for isn't one of them." He looks over his shoulder to make sure nobody needs him, then he shrugs back at Alex. "And I'm obviously not gonna make a scene and drag you back, but I'd kinda like to tell you anything you want to know if it means you'd be willing to stick around."

Alex looks behind him, like anyone might need him too, but there's only a quiet street reminding him of his even quieter house.

"Anything I want to know, huh?"

Elijah shrugs again. "Guess we'll find out."

And something about that is already sending Alex down an interesting road, his chest tight with an awareness that Elijah might give too much of himself too easily, when that's something Alex has never been good at. It'll leave them with an uncomfortable imbalance of trust, questions certain to go one way and not the other, unless Alex makes it clear that he can offer a bit of himself too. Regardless of whether it comes naturally to him, he thinks it might be something he'll need to work on soon.

"Okay, I—you're gonna be busy all morning, but I can stay and help if you want, and we can talk in between?"

Elijah's smile is too much for such a small offer, but when he turns around to get back to the garage sale, Alex follows and finds a second folding chair to put behind the card table, the dog coming over to lie next to him and resting just out of reach if he's hoping to be scratched again. The book is in front of Alex now, and he resists the temptation to look for more messages before they have time to talk about it, so he watches Elijah straighten up some of the displays while he greets newcomers, everything getting a little busier as the neighborhood begins to wake up.

"His name's Poe," Elijah says when he returns to the table and gestures to the dog at their feet.

"As in Edgar Allan?"

"Exactly. Figured you might appreciate that given your little book haul yesterday."

"Black dog. Raven might've been a more obvious choice, but Poe is a perfect step sideways. He yours?"

"He is now. Was my grandpa's until he passed away two years ago."

That helps pull at least one blurry mystery into focus. "Sorry to hear about your grandpa. Was this his house?"

"Yep. My brother and his family lived here for a while after he died, but then Austin got a job up in the Bay Area and they moved away, and I've sort of been tasked with getting the house cleaned out and ready to sell."

"You said yesterday that you wished you lived here. Why don't you?"

"Kind of a big place for just Poe and me," Elijah says, and Alex doesn't argue that the dog already puts Elijah a step ahead of where he's at. "There are a lot of memories of hanging out here when I was a kid. Holiday dinners and long summer days and random weekend sleepovers and just—I don't know. All the good grandparent things, I guess? But I'm not sure I could justify the cost of moving in alone."

"So, you're single then?"

"That's what you took away from all of that?"

"That wasn't the point you were trying to make?" Alex chuckles, feeling entirely clumsy even when Elijah doesn't seem to mind. "Seriously though, I can't tell whether that's the kind of thing you'd want to broadcast or desperately hide when you're pulling in all those tips from behind the bar."

"Hide, usually. My track record with relationships isn't fantastic. Lots of tries, lots of failures."

"Ah, well, I just have one big try and one big failure, but it's still probably enough misery to keep yours company," Alex offers, more easily than he might have expected.

"Divorced?"

"About to be."

"And you mentioned your daughter yesterday," Elijah says. "Guess that makes everything more complicated?"

"Eh, I'm not sure any of it has been complicated for us. Or at least not the way you're thinking," Alex admits. "Cassidy and I were best friends for a long time, and that hasn't really changed. I just think it got to a point where that was all we were, and she needs more than that. She deserves more."

"And you don't?"

Alex raises an eyebrow. "Don't what?"

"Deserve more," Elijah answers. "I mean, I'm sure marrying your best friend is incredible, but there *should* be more than friendship, right? You don't think you deserve that as much as she does?"

It's not ideal—or maybe it's perfect timing, actually—but there's a man who wants all the shoes and coats still available, so Elijah jumps up to get a couple of bags for him, while Alex thinks about how best to answer him without unloading his entire life story. He looks down at Poe, who is steadfastly ignoring him, and he flattens his palm against the cover of the book, like there is any real help to be had there.

If there is, Alex hasn't absorbed it by the time Elijah falls back into the chair next to him.

"I think I was comfortable with her, or I guess I *know* I was, and it might have been enough for me to stay that way forever. What I want or need or deserve aren't really things I've considered one way or the other, but being with her didn't hurt and being alone does, so that's kind of where I'm at."

That's more than Alex has ever said about the divorce, and he's tempted to ask Elijah to pour him an early morning shot as a way to excuse his honesty, so unfamiliar with sharing his shit with anyone, much less this guy he's barely met. He doesn't feel as terrible about it as he thinks he should, though, and after another second or two, Alex presses his lips together instead, and he watches as Elijah opens and closes his mouth at least twice before any words make it out.

They're an interesting pair.

"Your daughter's doing okay?" Elijah asks eventually.

"Elena. Yeah, she's—we've tried to be as honest with her as possible. And I hope it's been good for her that there hasn't been a lot of fighting. Just her dad being too stunned to do anything but surrender."

"Surrender isn't always a bad thing, Alex."

"No?"

"Or maybe I'm too good at it—at letting go. Giving up. Walking away." Elijah shakes his head, rising again to go help someone else. "Maybe I need to learn how to hold on to something."

He's only gone for a minute, and Alex is talking before he gets all the way back.

"Okay, so you're a bartender with wonderful memories of this house, but you won't stay here because you're a relationship disaster and it's too big for you, the dog, and whatever your grandpa left behind."

"And you're the newly single father who hangs out at garage sales, probably mostly to spend quality time with the aforementioned dog, though carting an old book back and forth suggests there may be at least one other reason," Elijah retorts, an already familiar grin on his face. "You ready to tell me what's up?"

"Did the books belong to your grandpa?"

"As far as I know, yeah. I mean, he was a huge reader and I remember those bookshelves being full my whole life. My brother and his family brought some of this other stuff with them when they moved in, but I don't think any of the books were theirs."

"Okay, I—I'm probably just caught up because of whatever other shit's going on in my head, but—" Alex pulls the book toward him and takes a deep breath before he opens it. "There are some handwritten messages in here, and I thought they were interesting. Like a secret love kind of thing."

To his credit, Elijah already looks more interested than Alex thought he would be. "Secret love notes? And you think they were written by my grandparents?"

"Maybe," Alex says. "Did either of their names start with E?"

"No, but let me see the handwriting." Alex ignores the bookmark still tucked where he'd left off last night and flips to the first message, then helps Elijah move on to the second and third. Elijah just shakes his head. "No, it doesn't look familiar. Are there responses from E?"

"Nope, that was the weird thing. I was wondering if maybe they used it as more of a diary. You know, just a way for this person to confess their feelings somewhere."

There's a pause as Elijah considers that, but then he frowns and points to the page. "But then this wouldn't really make sense: *because it's one more reason to see you, and these books are the only thing we can give each other.* If they gave each other books, E would have had to see the messages, right?"

"Yeah, okay, that does sound more like the books were a way to pass the messages back and forth, but then where's the other half?"

"Well, it says 'books,' not 'book,' so there's probably at least one more. Maybe E has it."

"And reading through all these notes will only give half of the story, if that."

"Unless you can find something in the other books you

bought," Elijah points out. "Did you look through them yet?"

"No. Hell, I didn't even read all the messages in this one. I started to think I was being kind of weird or creepy about it."

"You're very weird, but not all that creepy. And I think you should definitely check the other books."

Alex snorts. "Wow, thanks for the reassurance."

"Hey, no, it's good," Elijah promises, the tip of his tongue there to tease Alex when it pokes out from between his lips. "I love books and I love history and I don't mind a good love story despite my own inability to live one, so maybe I'm weird too. You gonna read through the rest of this one now?"

"Mmmm, no, I think I want to see if I can find the other half first. Then I can read them back and forth, the way they were written."

Somebody calls out with a quick question, and after Elijah answers, he pulls out his phone. "What's your number?"

"My number?"

"Um, or not. I just—" he starts. "To the neighborhood's certain dismay, I'm not gonna be doing garage sales here every morning, so if you find something else and feel like sharing some of your weirdness—you know, with me or Poe—"

"Yeah, no, sorry, I—of course. Sure," Alex stammers, giving him his phone number just seconds before he hears the chirp of an incoming text.

"Now you've got mine. Fingers crossed you find something good."

"Because then I'll have a reason to text you back?"

"Eh, I don't know. I'm sure you could find a reason either way," Elijah says. "I think you've got enough of your own story to tell."

Chapter Three

A quick stop at home lasts only long enough for Alex to grab his wallet and head back out, taking care of errands he might have done during the week, except that they seem like a good enough excuse to get out of the house now, when there would be too much to think about in the silence. He doesn't want to miss Cassidy and Elena, and he doesn't want to get lost in a love story that doesn't belong to him, and he doesn't want to think about why the last two mornings are the best he's had in a while.

Alex has had constant comfort for so long, a good life with nothing particularly wrong, and he doesn't understand how to want anything different now. Where would he even go from good? Because it seems like maybe better and worse are the only options, and he doesn't know those words outside of the vows he and Cassidy have carefully disassembled over the past several months.

What's better than everything he's had since high school?

What would this adult version of him want now, if he never thought he could have it before?

Even those two questions make him dizzy, so he keeps busy

as long as he can and grabs something to eat while he's out, and he only looks at his phone long enough to make sure there's nothing that needs his attention. He has so little of it to give these days, though almost nothing demands it.

Alex continues to waste as much of the afternoon as he can, stalling until there are only a couple of hours left before Cass brings Elena home, and when the sun threatens to descend, he gives up and stacks his new books on the coffee table, going through them one by one in search of more messages. The first few have nothing out of the ordinary for him, but the fourth one he looks at catches his eye quickly, the same handwriting there.

E, it feels rather perfect to start a new book today, with the ghost of your lips still on mine. I don't believe I have all the words to express the hunger I felt after indulging in that first taste, but I dream of the impossible world in which I could be truly satisfied.

A kiss, their first even, and another message that reads like it could be a diary entry if it weren't for the earlier reference to giving each other books. It also sounds like the author and E still can't be together publicly, which has Alex's chest clenching no matter how long ago this relationship may have been resolved. He doesn't know much, but the phrasing in all the messages seems rather formal, or at least old-fashioned, which would make it possible that these are from a generation before Elijah's grandpa, and while Alex isn't sure it's fair to make many guesses about the handwriting itself, penmanship a different art form decades ago, he doesn't think the person is notably young or old. It's also probably an instinctual vibe more than anything else, but he leans toward it being a man, or maybe he's just imagining himself in this person's place, and the words as the same things he'd write to someone he loves.

Alex turns the pages, the novel itself of no importance right now, and he reads the next passage.

E, I have so many sleepless nights now, most of them when I haven't been able to see you and cannot know how safe you are, but every one of them is worth it when we're together again and I can steal enough time to make myself believe you're still mine. I can't stop worrying about what could happen if we're ever caught, and how violently people could react to this love they don't understand, but I will continue to be there with you because it's the only place I can rest while wide awake.

So, the relationship has grown, some sort of meeting place established now, though it's dangerous to be there together, and Alex doesn't know why it hadn't struck him before, but he wonders if maybe one of them is black, kept apart before the civil rights movement had the chance to bring them together.

He picks up his phone to text Elijah and ignores the slight shake of his hand.

Found another book

The response comes far more quickly than Alex expects.

Yeah awesome. Still to e?

Yep. Questions. Any e somewhere older than grandpa? Great grandparents? Any interracial couples?

Shit yeah my gg was evelyn. Never knew her. Died a long time ago. No interracial I know of why?

Still sounds like they're hiding. Kissed but all secret and worried about being caught

It takes a few minutes before his phone sounds again, and Alex tries not to hold his breath as he continues to flip through the book in search of anything else. He needs to get up and make something for dinner, Elena set to arrive shortly after that, but then he finds the next message just as a new text appears.

Wow ok. Hey about to head to work but you can send questions whenever

You sure

Very. Have a good night

Ok you too

He sets the phone aside and reads from the page in his lap.

E, I am so sorry, darling. I've been ill and at home and so far from you, and I can only hope you will be back to take this book from me when I've finally returned to my office again. And perhaps I can dream of seeing relief in your eyes rather than the reluctance our relationship might deserve. If there is anything certain, it's that I would give anything to have you here with me, the chill unbearable without your love to keep me warm.

Alex finds himself more overwhelmed by his concern for an illness that has long passed than he is amused by the absolute corniness of that last line. It's romantic enough, but sticky sweet, and he just wishes he had any of E's notes to confirm how each of these was received. And he certainly hopes there are more messages to come—that whatever kept them apart didn't do so forever.

He really, really needs to get up now, but he also needs to read at least one more message, and he sighs with relief when he finds it in another margin.

Oh, E, seeing you tonight was the very greatest pleasure, the breath passed between us enough to keep me alive until the day I can give it all back again. It almost felt like we kissed so long that the night could have led us straight into the next. I only wish we could be together elsewhere, my gratitude for our shadows waning when I know there are empty rooms here at my home. When there is so much time we're still not allowed to claim as ours. Touches that remain forbidden.

And with that, knowing that their journey goes on, Alex tells himself it's okay to close the book for a while. He can't talk to Elijah about anything right now anyway, and Elena will arrive soon, so he makes a couple of trips upstairs, the stacks of books in his arms, and he piles them next to his bed for later.

He returns to the kitchen and heats up a frozen burrito that would make half his family weep, then grabs some chips and salsa too, and he's just cleaning up afterward when he hears the doorbell. Cassidy still has a key, as does his daughter, but there are new boundaries in place even when he hasn't requested them, and none of these custodial trade-offs come with opening doors without permission, no matter how easily it will be granted.

"Hey, guys, come on in," he says.

Elena rolls her mini suitcase into the house, her backpack loaded too, and she pauses only long enough for a quick *thumbs up, high five, hi dad, bye dad,* before she's off to her bedroom without a need for an entire conversation, Alex confident that she'll have plenty to tell him later. Cassidy, though, stays on the front porch, the light leaving her halfway lost to the shadows.

"Thanks, but I'm just gonna get going." She takes a step backward, but tilts her head, only the smallest smile on her lips. "You look—rested. Calm, maybe. Did you do anything special this weekend?"

And Alex is so close to telling her the whole story—about the garage sales and the books and the messages and Elijah—and he knows he would have at literally any other time over the past two decades of his life, but something makes him swallow it now, for the privacy of two people he's never met, and maybe just a tiny bit of his own.

"Went for a couple of early morning walks, and I think they were good for me."

She nods. "Looks like. Guess maybe that should become a new habit, huh?"

"That or something like it," he agrees.

"Okay, well, I'll see you next Sunday at my place, then."

Cassidy turns and walks away without waiting for him to reply, always willing to rip bandages off where he might take forever to let them fall on their own. Back inside the house,

Elena has changed into her pajamas and wrapped herself in her hooded wolf blanket, and she's ready to join him on the couch for their newly formed custom of watching TV together before she goes to bed. Alex thinks it's as good a time as any to mention the new things he's bought her, but as was true a few minutes ago, he can't quite bring himself to do it, all the parts of the story blurring into one. Instead, he and his daughter sit with their sides pressed together, Elena almost certainly about to pick out one scary show or another—*I'm just getting us ready for spooky season, dad*—and Alex wonders whether there's something better about already knowing this time with her is something he'll only have for a while, until she gets older or simply adjusts to living in two places at once. Whether there's a comfort in understanding there aren't promises to him she can break, because every vow has only come from him as her father.

Then he thinks back to whether he's ever taken the time to promise himself anything at all.

He doesn't have an answer, but he isn't sure he can work on that many new habits at once anyway.

When they're done downstairs, he and Elena head up to bed at the same time, and he tucks her in as soon as she's finished brushing her teeth and she's snuggled beneath her covers, ready for another week of school. He's ready for another week too, maybe for the first time in a while, but when he looks down at the books he'd set on his bedroom floor earlier, he doesn't bend to pick any of them up, content to work on a crossword puzzle and then turn off his light early, daydreams an indulgence his entire life and gentle when they carry him off to sleep now.

Alex doesn't worry about where they lead, and maybe he should.

The next morning, it doesn't seem to matter that Alex is an early riser, and that Elena isn't exactly terrible about waking either. It's a Monday through and through, and everything feels rushed when it shouldn't, and hectic when there is no reason for them to mess up something they've done so many times before. Even with his precious coffee in his hand, Alex feels rocked by chaos until they run out the door and he drives Elena to school, and he thinks he's only barely settled by the time he gets back home, finishing the rest of his own morning routine and another half a mug before he's back in the car and on his way to his office.

His work schedule has been flexible for a while and he's eternally grateful for it, able to get Elena to school the weeks he has her before he heads into the office for a few hours, usually through lunch meetings, then back home to be far more productive there, working remotely while his only break is when he picks Elena up again. She's always been good about allowing him to work in relative peace, hurrying to finish her homework at the new desk he bought her so she could feel like a little professional herself, and they can both breathe easy again by the time he's almost done making dinner.

"Hey, I forgot to tell you last night," Alex starts, his white lie worth it when he can speak without tripping over anything that might have slowed him down the night before. "I found a garage sale over the weekend and bought some books and games for you. I think most of the books are duplicates, but—"

"But that way I can have copies here and at mom's?"

"Exactly," he says. "And I think all the games are new, so we can keep them here."

"Can I go see what you got?"

Alex shakes his head. "I just took the lasagna out of the oven, and we're ready for you to set the table. You can check everything out after dinner."

They sit down to eat about five minutes later and Elena tells him all about her day at school, including her devastating loss in a new quiz game about fractions and the two songs her class will learn for a fall assembly, plus she catches him up on all the recess drama he missed hearing about last week while she was with Cass. He has a question every now and then, but she's never been shy about sharing and isn't all that interested in waiting for him to keep up his side of anything. At some point, he hears his phone chime with a handful of alerts—emails or texts or whatever breaking news the world wants him to know—but Alex isn't in a hurry to walk away from the best kid he knows, and they continue to talk until Elena eventually drops her fork onto her plate with a satisfied grin.

She doesn't have the same need to cling to time, and she's out of her seat and clearing the table the second he lets her go.

With a sigh, Alex follows her into the kitchen with his own dishes, then wanders over to his phone and swipes away a couple of notifications before he sees a text from Elijah.

Found books here. 2 so far. Think it's my great grandparents. Confused though

Shit, okay. Alex hasn't looked through any of the books since yesterday, caught up in everything else that's kept him busy since Elena returned, but what Elijah's saying is enough to get his heart pounding again.

Confused how? Are the messages written to E or by E?

By. The immediate answer leaves Alex's eyes wide, wondering whether Elijah had kept his phone close waiting for Alex this whole time, but he doesn't have a chance to respond before Elijah goes on. **Kind of a long story. Can you meet up tonight or tomorrow? I'm off work**

Sorry can't. It's my week with my daughter. Could call you later if that's ok. Or you could call me.

There's no answer right away, and Alex can't tell whether he's messed something up without knowing how, turning down the invitation to hang out with Elijah and offering to talk and wanting all of it even while the silence suggests Elijah's no longer as close to his phone as he was a minute ago. Alex looks up at the sound of familiar footsteps then, Elena running into the room with a game in her hand.

"Can we play? Pretty, pretty please?"

"All your homework's done?" he asks, the glance at his phone automatic when it makes a sound.

Don't want to bother you

"Yeah, it was done before dinner."

"Okay, go ahead and get it set up at the table," he tells her. "I'll be in there in a minute or two."

When she scampers off, Alex taps out another text.

Not a bother at all I promise. Want to talk just can't meet up this week.

Sure you're ok with calling me later?

Yeah of course

Nothing else happens after that, so Alex joins Elena at the dining room table for a few rounds of a game that had been only vaguely familiar to him when he'd bought it from Elijah, the two of them fiercely competitive, even as he teaches her how to be a good sport whether she wins or loses. There's a bit of an argument when he tells her it's time for bed, but he thinks she's too tired to fight it for long, and she trudges upstairs with nothing else to say, and he gets the game put away with the others.

About a half hour later, after his daughter is on her way to sweet dreams, Alex is in sweatpants and a t-shirt, sitting on his bed with several books around him, some of which he still hasn't opened. Then he takes a deep breath and taps on the name in his most recent messages.

"Hey," Elijah says. "Sorry if I—sometimes I forget what normal schedules are like."

"No, it's fine. I think mine's only half normal anyway. I don't keep bartender hours, but I only have Elena here every other week, so—I don't know."

"So maybe—never mind, I—"

"No, it's okay, you can—" Alex promises.

"No," Elijah interrupts back. "It's just—I'm not so great over the phone. That whole charm thing you gave me shit about kinda works better in person."

Alex chuckles, relatively sure that Elijah can out-charm him anywhere, but grateful he's not the only one convinced he's bad at this. "I'll keep that in mind then. And how about you just tell me what you found in your books?"

"Yeah, okay. So, I remembered I kept a few books for myself, ones that my grandpa used to read to me when I was younger. They were from the same group as the ones you bought. Or from the same shelves of his, I guess, so I decided to look through them."

"And you found messages written by E?"

"I mean, I'm assuming yes. They're not signed or anything, but it's different handwriting from what you showed me, and they're addressed to P, which would fit with your theory."

"Because P was your great grandfather?" Alex asks.

"Yeah, Peter. And I know he was made partner at some big law firm, and a couple of the notes talk about walking past the firm or something like that, so maybe that lines up. Plus, my great grandparents writing notes back and forth would track with the books being kept in the family. She died not long after my grandpa was born, so I don't know much about her, but my grandpa was always close to his father, and I have some vague memories of my great grandfather. I think he died when I was around 10 or so. Anyway, it would make sense that my grandpa would hold on to his father's books and read to me from them."

Alex nods to absolutely nobody, the walls of his bedroom uninterested in the conversation, though his cheeks are flushed. "Okay, but you said something is confusing?"

"Yeah, I—I just don't get what's up with the implication that their love was forbidden," Elijah explains. "They were both from wealthy families, back when that was important to everyone, and then they married young and started their family, and I never heard any stories about that being a bad thing."

"What did you mean when you said the mention of the law firm *maybe* lines up? It sounds good to me."

"Well, I'd have to ask my mom more about it probably, but my great grandfather wouldn't have been very old when he first got together with my great grandmother—like, at *all*—so while it's possible he worked at the law firm back then, I'm not sure he would've been as important there as these notes from E make it sound."

"Weird," Alex huffs. "Maybe we have to go back another generation?"

"Maybe. I really don't know. Maybe it has nothing to do with me."

"So, we keep reading until we figure it out?"

Elijah hums. "And even if we don't figure it out, at least we get a nice love story out of it."

They're quiet for a few seconds, and somehow it's not as awkward as Alex still thinks it should be, this conversation with someone he only barely knows, but wants to talk to more. He has friends at work, of course, or maybe they're only serendipitous acquaintances of circumstance. He distantly keeps in touch with a group of people from college, except that he was already well into his relationship with Cassidy in those days, so most of those people are her friends too, which isn't bad, but won't do much for him right now. He knows most of his neighbors by sight, and a few by name, but they don't hang out socially, and really, Alex wouldn't know where to begin with that anyway.

But he met Elijah and talking to him has been easy and now they have a reason to talk more, if either of them wants that. If Elijah doesn't already have plenty of friends of his own. If Alex isn't setting himself up for a quick failure chaser after a drink he's nursed too long. But back when they were texting earlier in the night, Elijah had invited him to meet up, so maybe—*maybe* it's not that much of a stretch to think that Alex has met someone who could be a friend, right when he needs one most.

"We should read more of the notes," Alex starts. "But it would probably be good to put them together to see if we can figure out the back and forth. Or not, if you—I wouldn't want that to be uncomfortable for you."

"Which part?"

Which *part*? Alex doesn't know what that means and definitely isn't brave enough to ask.

"I mean, it's your family, right? Or it probably is. I just don't want to be creepy about something they kept so private."

Elijah laughs. "If it was about my parents, I'd probably bail because yeah, no. But this is pretty far back, and I don't think I'm in danger of major trauma."

"Okay, so then if you wanted to meet up next week—are you always off on Mondays and Tuesdays?"

"I am, yeah. Or usually, anyway, and I—" Elijah clears his throat and Alex waits. "Meeting up then would be good. Did you just want to come to my place or—"

He trails off and Alex wants to give him time to say more, but everything is both quiet and loud and he doesn't like it either way, his voice shakier than it should be when it splits the difference.

"Or you can come here. Whatever's easiest for you. Although, you've got—or wait, I guess Poe must be okay hanging out alone every night when you're at work? But I mean, if you don't—I can always—"

"No, it's okay, I—my neighbor. She sort of—" Elijah cuts himself off, though Alex is far from impatient. "It's a long story, but Poe's totally fine when I'm not here."

"So, you'll come here then? That's okay with you?"

It sounds stupid, all of it, but Alex doesn't know how to *do* this, even if he wishes it didn't have to be that way. He sounds like he did when he first asked Cassidy to go see a movie with him and not at all like someone who just wants to comb through old books for notes scribbled in margins.

"More than okay, yeah," Elijah agrees. "And do you think—I mean, should we just wait before we read anything else? How much self-control do you have?"

Alex doesn't know how to tell him his entire life has been self-control, comfortable and careful and not a single risk taken, nor any corners cut. He's waited forever for everything, and while he's intently curious now, maybe about so much more than he should be, a week is really nothing at all.

"I can wait if you can."

"Sure," Elijah says, and Alex swears he can almost hear a smile. "Whenever you're ready."

Chapter Four

The rest of the week passes by like most others, with Alex and Elena heading to work and to school, and catching up over dinner each night, her Wednesday evening art class coming and going and leaving her with a rather large construction paper mosaic to hang on her bedroom wall. They go out to eat at a local pizza parlor every Friday night she's with him, a thing they'd started when Cass first moved out, and he does his best to consider it less of a way to heal everything that's hurt for a while and more as something nice he can do for himself and his daughter now. And between that and everything else, maybe more of his time can start to feel like it belongs to him in a way that doesn't leave him aching to turn it backward.

When Cass had stood on his front porch that past weekend, she'd seemed pleasantly surprised that he was—well, he's not sure *happy* is exactly the word for whatever he is these days, but he's looking forward to the upcoming week, which is something he doesn't think he's ever felt when he knows Elena isn't going to be around.

He loves his daughter, and he misses his wife, but maybe he

can have a good time with Elijah, too.

So, Sunday night, he drives Elena to Cassidy's new place—not all that new anymore, but Alex is still loath to admit how long it's been already—and he goes home to clean up the typical mess left behind by any nine-year-old, glancing at his pile of books once before he reminds himself there's only one more day before he and Elijah will look through them together. They'll read the story of E and P, from beginning to whatever end they might find, and then Alex can figure out what's supposed to happen next in his own life.

Alex doesn't want to have to say goodbye to Elijah quite that fast, but if they're not destined for some kind of friendship, at least he's had practice at watching someone walk away.

Monday he's able to keep busy with work, which is probably good for everyone, and absolutely ideal for his anxiety. He had texted Elijah Sunday afternoon to give him his address and a good time to come over, and now it's only an hour away, the books on the dining room table already, Alex in jeans and a henley that makes him feel like he's not about to crawl out of his own skin.

When there's a knock on the door, Alex tells himself not to worry about why it sounds so timid, hurrying to answer it so they can get past these first few minutes.

"Hey, come on in and make yourself comfortable," Alex offers, mostly because at least one of them should be. "Can I get you something to drink? Beer, soda, juice, coffee, water?"

"Whatever you're having is fine with me," Elijah answers.

He's all the way inside now, the door closed behind him, but Elijah's still unexpectedly cautious about going far, slipping out of his sneakers but moving nowhere else while Alex tries not to study him all that closely. There's no hoodie tonight, just a flannel over a graphic tee and jeans, and Alex stops himself from asking what Elijah wears at work because he can't figure out why it would matter. Elijah's hair is a bit of a mess, and Alex thinks that might always be true, curls destined to remain especially untamed while Elijah traps his smile between his teeth. And there are two books tucked under Elijah's arm, but Alex can't quite catch the titles from where he stands, giving up while Elijah's eyes scan the living room.

Elijah's probably lost in the blank space overwhelming the walls these days, so many family pictures gone while the ghosts of them remain, Alex reluctant to paint over memories that he couldn't hold in his hands if he tried.

"Okay, yeah, I'll grab the drinks. I put my books on the dining room table, but we can move them out here if you'd rather."

"No, no, that's good."

They both move to get settled then, Alex pulling a bottle of beer from the fridge and holding it up for Elijah's approval before he grabs a second one and gives Elijah time to sort the books into whatever order they know so far. They sit across from each other, each taking one novel to start, and Alex works to breathe through any awkwardness the garage sale's fresh air must have swept away.

"Okay, so the first thing I noticed was the word 'perhaps' written next to the first chapter, which obviously didn't have to mean anything until I got to the first full entry where P—presumably—calls E's idea clever," Alex explains.

"Which we can assume means E was the one to suggest they pass messages back and forth in these books," Elijah continues. "And 'perhaps' was an acknowledgment of the beginning of it all."

"Exactly. So, can you tell whether one of your books has those early responses?"

"Yeah, I think so," Elijah says, already looking down at where a folded receipt from the bar has kept his place, a list of what Alex assumes are page numbers scribbled there. It's probably moderately neater, and more sustainable, than Alex's decision to steal an entire handful of bookmarks from his kid. "Okay, here we go: *P, I feel everything too and needed this way to tell you. If you think it's clever, I'll gladly accept that honor, though I'm mostly lonely and eager for the chance to come alive the next time you're near.*"

Alex reads aloud the passage he has about E standing close and touching hands and hoping nobody saw them. "So, other than the fact that they're using these books at all, there's an implication from the very beginning that they don't want anyone to notice them."

"That it's a secret romance," Elijah adds.

"Either because it has to be, or maybe they're just shy

about it at first?"

"Pretty sure it's the former. Here's what's next: *P, maybe we're more wrong than we know, putting ourselves at risk like this, and you in so much more danger than I could ever be. But I want to touch you again. I want more. I want whatever you will give.*"

"Yeah," Alex sighs. "There's definitely a reason they can't be together. And an imbalance of some kind, if P is really risking more than E."

Elijah takes a long drink from his bottle and nods. "Which is why I'm still not convinced it's my great grandparents. Like I said before, they met when they were young, and both came from wealthy families, as unaffected by the world around them as anyone could be back then. I don't get why they'd be sneaking around. I mean, if it was just fun, sure, but—"

"But this sounds more serious than that," Alex finishes.

"Yeah, it does."

They read through a few more, an ease between them returning as they narrate a love story written long before they were born, random theories or reactions shared as they go. P and E continue to pass the books back and forth, apparently the only way they can talk more honestly, seeming to stay quiet even when they see each other to exchange the novels in whatever situation they've created for themselves, and he and Elijah still can't figure why. Then when Alex moves to the kitchen to grab each of them a second beer and some chips, he yells back to where Elijah's sitting.

"Didn't you say there was something about a law firm?"

he asks. "Was that in this first book or the second one you found?"

"It's in this one," Elijah answers. "I think it might be next, actually."

By the time Alex sits back down, he sees Elijah holding the book open, another message there in the margin for Alex to see. "Okay, go ahead."

"This one is a little longer. *P, I walked past your firm tonight and saw a light coming from your office, and only wish I could've been in there with you. And yes, I know I should've stayed away entirely. I know I have no business being nearby late at night when I could be accused of any number of wrongdoings. But sometimes it's easier to dream when the sun goes down and the darkness lets me pretend the world might not hate us both. We have lived like this for nearly a year already. Is there any chance for us to find our way there? To something truly good?*"

"God, it sounds so *sad*," Alex says. "And I already know they kiss later, but I hate how hard it was for them to get there. A *year*? Did you find out any more about whether your great grandfather worked at the law firm back when he first met your great grandmother?"

Elijah nods. "Yeah, I asked my mom about it, and she said my great grandfather did start working there when he was young—I guess his father was already some big deal at the firm—but this sounds like he was more than just a clerk or something, right?"

"It definitely does. He had his own office, which would've

had to mean something," Alex agrees, sitting back in his chair with the beer in his hand. "But there's also the part about E being afraid of being accused of wrongdoing. What's that sound like to you?"

"Prostitution?"

"Hmmm, yeah, maybe. I mean, I guess it wouldn't have even had to be true, because I'm sure it was frowned upon for any woman to be walking the streets alone at nighttime, right?"

"Yeah. But it also could've been true. Maybe he *was* in love with a prostitute and that's why it was forbidden," Elijah muses.

Alex shakes his head. "No, but if he wanted to sneak around with a prostitute, he could do that wherever prostitutes did everything else. He wouldn't have had to wait for some secret book exchange just to touch hands."

"And we *still* might be way off, and this has nothing to do with my family at all."

"Guess that's true, too," Alex sighs. "How about we read a little more and then just call it a night?"

He hates the suggestion, even as it falls off his tongue, not particularly interested in saying goodbye, especially if Elijah decides he's not invested in the story after all. But he has to work in the morning, and he can't expect Elijah to hang out with him and a bunch of old books for that long anyway, free beer or no.

"Yeah, a little more sounds good."

"Okay, this should be next then: *E, I only ever want you close, but please don't risk your own wellbeing for a glimpse at my window. We've both only just become free from the terror of another world war and are so close to terror of our own always. Perhaps it would be better if I could find my way to the warehouses sometime. Perhaps those could be our nights.*"

"World War II," Elijah says, running a hand through his curls. "Fuck."

"Hell of a time to be living, huh? Get through the Depression, go almost straight into a war. I mean, everything is terrible enough now, but—"

"No, it's not—that's not what I was saying," Elijah interrupts as he fumbles for his phone in search of something. "I mean, yes, it was a hell of a time then and it's a hell of a time now, but when I talked to my mom about my great grandparents, I took notes about a few things. The years they were born, where they lived and what they did for a living, when my grandpa was born, when they all died."

"Okay," Alex drawls, something obvious there, even if he can't quite see it yet.

Elijah takes a deep breath. "If these messages were written sometime after the war, E couldn't have been my great grandmother. She died in 1940."

"Oh. Fuck," Alex echoes, draining the last of the beer just before Elijah does the same.

"Yeah."

"So, it sounds like they wrote these shortly after the war

ended, like in 1946 or 1947? Maybe a little later than that? How old would your great grandfather have been then?"

"Um, around 33 or 34?"

"Okay, so he definitely could've been a hotshot attorney by then, with his own office, and it was years after losing his wife, so it's also entirely possible that he could've fallen in love again," Alex says.

"But then he fell in love with someone he shouldn't have. A relationship problematic enough that they were both afraid of being caught."

Alex nods. "And he mentions going to the warehouses sometime, so maybe this is just a massive class conflict. You said your great grandmother had come from money, but what if this new woman didn't? She might have worked at a warehouse of some kind, far beneath someone with a prominent legal career."

Elijah rubs a hand over his forehead before blinking some of his frustration away, and while Alex knows he's not strictly tired, he looks like he's wiped out. "That all makes sense."

"But you—" Alex catches himself, wanting to offer comfort that really isn't his to give to a friend he's only barely made, if he's even done that much. "We can put all this away if you want."

"I'm sorry, I—" Elijah looks across the table at Alex, his lip caught between his teeth again. "This would make a hell of a column, huh? And you've probably got some nice investigative resources at work."

"This has always been off the record, Elijah. I'm not gonna let anything about that change."

Elijah presses a fist to his eye, rubbing away something that might not have been there in the first place. "Sorry, I know I'm being weird about this, but I think I got so wrapped up in the idea of this being my family history, and now I don't know what it is anymore. It might not belong to me at all."

"Hey, no. I understand. And you already agreed that I'm very weird, so I certainly don't have much room to talk."

Alex pushes away from the table then, clearing their bottles and putting the chips away, returning to find Elijah still staring down at the book in his hand when he speaks. "Do you still want to know the rest of their story?"

"I do, yeah," Alex answers honestly, leaning up against the doorway when Elijah slowly looks up at him. "But remember that it was never about my family at all. I was just intrigued by these two people fighting their way together in the margins of some classic novels. It's okay if you don't want it to go any further."

"I have the missing pieces you need, though. The story won't make as much sense if you only have half of it."

"Mmmm, no, maybe not," Alex agrees. "But if there's one lesson I've learned in the past several months, it's that half is sometimes all I get to keep."

"You miss her."

Alex looks around, his gaze safe anywhere as long as it's not pointed toward the same seat Cassidy had sat in every night. "I miss my best friend, yeah. And I miss what we were supposed to be. What I thought we were."

Elijah doesn't say anything else right away, marking his place with the bar receipt, then closing the book and picking it up with the other one he'd brought with him, as reverent as Alex always has been when he holds his own. When Elijah starts walking toward the front door. Alex follows silently, as unsure as he usually is these days, stepping in front of Elijah to open it for him, Elijah turning around as soon as he's safely outside.

"I still want to know what happens next," Elijah admits softly.

"Okay," Alex tells him, but even as he says it, he thinks maybe tomorrow night would be too soon, for reasons he doesn't fully understand. "Do you maybe want to meet up on Saturday, like for lunch or something, before you have to work?"

A sigh of relief rattles Elijah's next breath, and Alex doesn't understand that either. "Yeah, that would be great."

The text from Elijah comes on Thursday afternoon.

You busy tonight?

Alex calls him and doesn't bother with a hello. "Thought you had to work."

"I do," Elijah laughs. "I'm headed out soon, actually. But

listen, you can't get mad at me."

"Well, that sounds suspiciously like something my nine-year-old would say right before confessing to something she knew she wasn't supposed to do, even as she did it."

"Yeah, okay, I—I know I was kinda bummed about what we read on Monday night, and then I spent the next couple of days forcing myself to forget about it."

"But?" Alex prompts.

"But then today I got curious again and I peeked ahead and obviously I don't know what's in your book and please don't look in yours yet which I know is a really unfair thing to ask of you since I totally looked but also if you don't already have other plans then maybe you could come by the bar tonight and bring just the one book with you and we can talk about it," Elijah rambles, breathless by the time he finally pauses. "Please? Come to the bar?"

"Do I even get a hint? I mean, it's raining, but instead of sitting comfortably at home, you want me to just sit by myself in a bar while I watch you work," Alex teases with a smile he pretends he can't feel. "And that's after you went behind my back, so really, I should feel incredibly betrayed and maybe even hang up on you now."

"You are far too nice to hang up on me, especially because I will buy your dinner and drinks."

"So, no hint then?"

"Nope," Elijah says, but then he takes a shaky breath. "But you'll really come? Like, without peeking at the book first?"

Alex pauses for a moment, trying to figure out what just shifted, and he's serious when he answers. "Yeah, of course, if that's what you want."

"I think I—I'm probably just being an idiot. And maybe I'll realize it too late, but yeah—I'll see you when you get here."

Alex is still staring down at his phone when it chimes with a text and the name of the bar, and he can barely wrap his head around the conversation he just had with Elijah, a whirlwind of a thing leaving him unsure of which one of them was really teasing the other. It takes another couple of minutes before he can focus on finishing up his work, but he gets everything done in the next hour or so and then goes upstairs to get ready. He's pretty sure he puts too much thought into all of it but ends up more or less business casual—a thin forest green sweater and dark jeans with a suede jacket to top it off—like he's just going out after work and definitely isn't trying too hard. It was easier when he used to be in the office full-time and would just head out to happy hour with coworkers, or of course, all the times he went out with Cassidy, someone else there to ground him, a contrast to how obviously he'll be alone tonight.

Or not exactly alone, but really only there while Elijah is almost certainly going to be busy, talking to Alex long enough to share whatever got him worked up, then turning back to paying customers and what Alex assumes must be a whole lot of tips.

He splashes some water on his face and scrapes his hands

through his surprisingly neat brown hair and sighs.

What did Elijah find? Why did he go from rambling about it to being so unsure that Alex would show up? And why was he worried that he might have been making some kind of mistake?

The drive to the bar is easy enough, the traffic typical with this many stupid people caught in the Southern California rain, but it's nothing Alex hasn't lived in for his whole life. He parks a couple of blocks away and jogs toward the bar, a small messenger bag slung across his torso keeping the book dry, and he holds the door open for a couple of women before he steps inside and out of the way. The place is near the beach, and it probably brings in a good mix of regulars and tourists, but while Alex would guess it's generally pretty popular, it's a rainy weeknight, and he has his choice of plenty of tables when he goes to sit.

Elijah is in the middle of the bar, a second bartender busy a few feet away, and he leans forward to greet the two women who'd just passed Alex, his smile a mile wide. The sleeves of his deep blue button up are rolled to his elbows and Alex already knows the color of it must make his eyes that much more noticeable, the two women seemingly lost there while Elijah offers to get them their drinks. Alex takes a few steps forward, the movement enough to have Elijah glancing up at him, his smile becoming something strangely shy until he turns away to make two cocktails.

Alex finds a small table against the darkest wall, opposite

the glass doors that open to a patio and are probably only closed tonight to keep them dry, and he sets the bag down on another stool before lifting a small, laminated food menu from where it's tucked between the condiments and an announcement about upcoming live music dates.

"Did the two women scare you into the shadows or did I?" Elijah asks, sliding a coaster across the table, a name tag introducing him as Eli enough to give Alex an uncomfortable itch on his behalf. It doesn't last, though. *Can't* last when Alex catches sight of the tattoo on Elijah's forearm and has to drag his gaze back upward before it becomes impossible.

"No, I—I just thought I should stay out of the way."

"You're not in anyone's way, Alex," Elijah says. "Except maybe your own."

Alex thinks he should probably be offended by that, but he can't quite manage to get there when he's busy wondering what Elijah means by the observation, doing whatever it takes to spin his confusion into some kind of joke.

"Sounds dangerously close to being fortune cookie wisdom."

"Nah, just bartender wisdom. And I don't really have room to talk, so—" He winks and nods down at the menu in Alex's hand. "Most of that's pretty good for bar food. Anything look appealing?"

After no more than a glance, Alex picks out a cheeseburger and fries because it's easy, and a lager because it's even easier than that, and then for the next couple of minutes, he can catch his breath, watching as Elijah taps out the order on a small computer screen and then pours the beer. A few different people talk to him as he moves behind the bar, and Elijah easily responds to all of them, a natural people pleaser where Alex barely knows how to have a conversation without tripping over half the words that flow more naturally inside his head. He's done a pretty decent job of talking to Elijah, he supposes, but maybe every now and then the world makes one simple thing as easy as it should be.

Elijah laughs at something one of the ladies says, then brings the beer to Alex, who nods his thanks and tries not to look back at the bar where everyone waits. His eyes land on Elijah's arm instead, and he surprises himself when his fingertip follows, tracing the black ink he's only just found.

"A swan."

"Once an ugly duckling."

Alex stumbles over a few different responses, Elijah so far from ugly, except that that's not the point of the story anyway, and thinking about the messy layers of that particular fairy tale hurts before Alex can understand why. One fingertip becomes two, and Alex wants to press his entire palm to Elijah's skin, but nothing about a wish like that makes sense when he's never touched another man like this and he doesn't want the tattoo covered anyway.

"This is new. Or it's—I guess, it's probably not new for you, but I—I didn't know it was there." Alex stops, frustrated with himself until he can pull his hand away and smile up at Elijah, eager to change the subject. "Thank you for the beer. And as much as I want to hear why you dragged me out in the rain, you can go back to work if they need you."

"They have everything they need right now," Elijah assures him, quiet and almost too still before he goes on. "And what if I said that I only dragged you here to help you relax a little? To get you out of your house for a night?"

"You mean you didn't want—I mean, it's—I thought this was about the books?"

"Don't worry. It is about the books," Elijah shrugs. "But what if?"

Alex takes a sip of the beer to keep from reaching for the tattoo again, and while he's pretty sure Elijah already plans to wait for an actual answer, he also knows he can't help but want to give him one, like a puppet on a string that he doesn't want to cut. Sure enough, he sets the glass back down and takes a deep breath, Elijah far more patient than he should be with money waiting to be earned elsewhere.

"Okay, well, I'd say thank you—and that I probably needed it. And then I'd stay a while."

"Good."

"Does that mean you're going to tell me about the book and then get me drunk off my ass?" Alex asks.

"Definitely not getting you drunk, no," Elijah promises. "Not now anyway. And give me just a few minutes and I'll be back with your food and what I found in the next message from E."

Alex's first thought as Elijah walks away is "*If not now, when?*" and that's followed quickly by the realization that he'll have to stop reaching for his beer just to have something to do. He pulls his book out instead, resting it carefully on top of the bag and out of the way while he waits, Elijah back with a plate in his hand not long after. It's barely down on the table before Elijah steals a french fry.

"Help yourself," Alex grins.

Elijah smiles back but says nothing as he reaches into his pocket for his phone. "Okay, so I didn't bring the book with me because, duh, work, but I took pictures for you. And again, I really am sorry about being in a dumb mood on Monday night and for looking at the book without you there."

"It's okay, I get it, and you don't owe me any more apologies for it," Alex says. "But I'm not gonna let you take any more fries if you don't show me the damn pictures soon."

So Elijah hands him the phone and Alex turns it sideways to read the message captured there, as steady as he can be while Elijah's watching him so closely.

P, we should find a way to make that happen, meeting by the warehouses. It could happen late at night, in the shadows I know so well. After I've worked too hard for too little, my scarred and calloused hands will be desperate for something beautiful and tender beneath them. Please let me see you there. Please come take what's already yours.

"Any reaction to that?" Elijah asks.

"I—maybe. 'Scarred and calloused hands' sounds kind

of—"

"Yeah," Elijah interrupts, his fingers tap-tap-tapping on the table until Alex can almost feel them, too. "Go to the next one."

P, I haven't stopped thinking about tonight, about the feeling of your strong body crowding mine, and even though we weren't brave enough for more, even if it lasted no more than a minute or two, I will never forget the sensation of your perfectly shaven face brushing against the hint of stubble on mine. I can only hope it didn't hurt you, as it healed everything in me.

"Oh. Shit. It's—they *are*—" Alex starts. "That's—we didn't even—"

"Nope."

"We just assumed."

"Yep."

"But they're both men."

"Pretty sure, yeah," Elijah sighs. "And I think the class difference would've been some kind of obstacle on its own—a wealthy attorney falling for some kind of warehouse worker, I guess—but to be gay on top of that would've been absolutely disastrous for them."

Alex can't even say anything else right then, stuck staring at the phone instead, and he feels Elijah studying him until he must have to go back to work, leaving Alex alone with a chest so tight he doesn't think it will be possible to take more than a single breath. He lifts his glass for another drink and pretends his hand isn't shaking, and while he hates that he's so trapped inside this story, everything hurts now, and he can't imagine that there's a way back out. He looks toward the bar and finds Elijah busy with several people at once, then he starts on his dinner because he can't freak out over a tragic love story that must have ended years ago, swallowing bite after bite while he tries not to wish for a happy ending he doesn't think would've been possible.

He's just finishing the last of his beer when a new one lands on the table, Elijah's finger dragging through the condensation, and any eye contact fleeting.

"Saved a few fries for you," Alex offers.

"Didn't have to."

"Didn't have to be here at all," Alex points out.

"So, why are you?"

"Because you asked me to be, and I—I guess I wanted to be. There's still a lot more of the story, isn't there?"

Elijah finally looks up and nods. "If you want to keep going."

There's something melancholy between them now, and Alex doesn't know whether it's only about the books, or whether he's missed something more, but he gently knocks Elijah's hand away from the beer, and wonders how many more times he'll touch him tonight.

"You okay? I mean with this and—I don't know. Everything?"

"Everything?" Elijah laughs, and it's the heaviest sound Alex has heard in a while. "That's a loaded question better left for another time."

"Like when you get me drunk some other night?"

"What?"

Alex shrugs. "Earlier you said you wouldn't get me drunk now. Just wondering when else you think that might happen, or whether it's something that's supposed to take us both by surprise."

Elijah doesn't answer, rapping his fist against the table a couple of times before he picks up his phone and gestures back to the bar, spending long enough over there that Alex thinks maybe he's supposed to grab his bag and duck quietly back into the rain. In the end, he closes his eyes for a few seconds, strains to hear Elijah's voice among the crowd of people who know how to have fun, and then he opens them as he reaches for the book he'd brought, finding where they'd left off there.

E, yes. Yes, I will meet you there. I'll let you hold me if I can do the same. If you trust the shadows, I'll learn to trust them, too. The next time you deliver to our office, give me a signal. Tell me when and where. And until then...

Alex re-reads it, committing it to memory as much as he's tried to do with all of them. It's the transition from only seeing each other in passing, E delivering the books, alone or with something else, to P at the law firm, and finally agreeing to meet somewhere they can be alone, however briefly. And then there's the message he read on Elijah's phone about P meeting E late at night, no kiss happening yet, but some kind of embrace enough to keep them going.

Bittersweet, always.

And maybe it makes sense that that's when Elijah finally returns.

"You asked if I was okay, and I don't have a good answer for you right now. I just—I don't."

"Not sure you really owe me one," Alex says.

"Maybe not. Still want to try sometime, if you're willing to wait a while."

"Of course. Yeah," Alex agrees. "But I—can I ask you something?"

Elijah looks back at the bar and then at Alex again. "Sure."

"Do you still think this is Peter, or did we just end up with a random story on our hands?"

"I think it's him," Elijah says, his voice somehow both unsteady and firm. "The first initial, the time frame, the law firm, and the fact that my grandpa had these books all kept together on his shelf, like they mattered. I could be wrong, but I don't think I am."

Alex nods. "And you said the books you have are ones your grandpa read to you when you were younger, so he would've seen the notes. You think he knew?"

"I think he must have, yeah." Elijah picks up the mostly empty plate and waits for Alex to down the last of the beer before he reaches for the glass, too, clearing his throat and going nowhere. "You know, those two women at the bar have been asking me about you."

"Okay," Alex says, strangely careful about not looking at

them. He's not sure he's ever known how to do it right anyway. "And what did you say?"

"That you're a friend of mine."

"Okay," he says again, relieved somehow. Settled at the sound of a word that seems so incredibly safe. He wants a friend. Needs one even. Glancing past Elijah for more than that already feels like it would be a mistake, and as he stares at the swan again, Alex tries not to want something new.

"Did you want me to tell them anything else?" Elijah asks.

Still distracted, Alex feels his mouth twist into something that wants to be a smile and hasn't quite made it there. "Why? So, you can be a margin of my very own?"

Elijah laughs at that, though, incrementally lighter than he was earlier. "I've been called worse."

There are so many things Alex wants to say, but he can't imagine how any of them would be okay here, tonight, with the fragility of the love story still on the table, the book closed for now but unlikely to stay that way. Everything feels pulled taut in a way that he doesn't understand, and he's almost certain most of his thoughts would only cause him to fall apart and come dangerously close to bringing Elijah down, too. What he does say is the only thing he thinks he can.

"I um—I should go. I have to work in the morning."

"Yeah, of course," Elijah agrees.

He takes the dishes away while Alex slides the book back into his bag and stands, turning toward the door just as Elijah returns. Looking at him gives Alex such an easy view of the bar just over his shoulder, and the chance to smile at the two women he'd opened the door for a while ago.

He still doesn't take it, blinking up at Elijah instead.

"We still on for Saturday?"

"Looking forward to it."

Chapter Five

In the next day and a half, they only text long enough to agree on where to meet for lunch—a café near Alex's office that he knows has plenty of room for them and the books, and that won't mind if they hang out there for a while. The time they spend apart isn't much though, and as Alex showers and gets dressed on Saturday, he's still trying to make sense out of Elijah's reactions to everything that happened at the bar. Elijah had been so excited to invite Alex there, then surprised and relieved when Alex said yes, teasing when he arrived, certain when he first showed him the pictures on his phone, entirely unbalanced afterward, and then just plain strange when he brought up the two women asking about Alex while he was there.

For his part, Alex tries to convince himself he was only lost in the fact that he and Elijah had fully missed that they'd been reading the tentative beginning of a gay romance, and he's as eager to see where it goes as he is scared of how terribly it might end.

He quiets that part of him that's eager and scared to find out how Elijah's doing, or what this love story might mean to either of them now.

They pull into the parking lot seconds apart, and when Elijah climbs out of his truck, shoves his hands into his hoodie pocket, and tilts his head just so, Alex thinks maybe Elijah feels the same way. It's a terrifying thing to believe in—the idea that they might be on the same page—but Elijah's still standing with the car door open, watching and waiting, so Alex grabs his messenger bag and goes to him, trying not to crowd him there, even if there's an instinct to keep moving closer.

"Everything okay?"

"Yeah," Elijah says, glancing toward the building. "There's a patio, too?"

"Mmmhmm. I've spent many an afternoon there, working on various columns."

Elijah turns around to pull two books from the passenger seat, then he closes the door and nods to Alex, who leads them inside. They order at the counter—Alex paying for lunch after Elijah had taken care of his dinner and drinks Thursday night—and then they take everything out back, the weather just cool enough that most people have opted to stay in. He sets his bag down on the chair between them and Elijah's books get piled on top of that, and then they relax with their sandwiches and just talk for a while.

A very long while, as it turns out.

Alex learns Elijah is the youngest of three, his sister, Vanessa, and her family living in Connecticut, his brother, Austin, and his family in the Bay Area, which Alex remembers from the garage sale. His parents divorced years ago, and neither one lives far away, but Elijah's never been all that close to either of them, his mom and dad somehow always part of his life and also not, and Alex can almost see the bruises left behind by wounds Elijah doesn't even recall.

"Honestly, I was always closest to my grandpa. My grandma too, I guess, but she died when I was in high school," Elijah says. "The rest of my family has never been *bad* to me. It just never felt all that good to be around them, either."

"All the good memories were the ones you said you had at the house."

Elijah smiles, a sad little thing wrapped around his straw as he drinks. "Yeah, lots of them. Again, mostly just hanging out there all the time when I was an awkward kid. Sleepovers whenever I wanted—"

"And a Hans Christian Andersen story before bed?"

"Exactly. And the poetry when I was a little older," Elijah tells him, running a finger along the spines of both books. "After my grandma died, my mom stepped in for a while to help—and I mean, she was grieving too obviously—but then it seemed like it was just my grandpa and me, at least when I wasn't being a typical idiot in my teens and 20s."

"All your relationship attempts and failures," Alex says.

"Basically, yeah. College was a good way to get into that kind of trouble, and then I started bartending, which comes with plenty more. I'd like to think I've been better about it the past couple of years, but I don't know."

"Never married though?"

"Nope. Want to get married. Want kids, too," Elijah tells him. "But sometimes it feels like a crazy fantasy to have when most of my time is spent alone at my place or at work behind a crowded bar."

"Hey, don't knock the crowded bar. Those two women from the other night might've asked about me, but let's not pretend like they weren't happy to be looking at you. And you could always look back, right? When someone you think you might like smiles at you—you can always smile back."

Elijah stares at Alex like there might be a right or wrong answer to his question, and Alex doesn't want his stomach to turn the way it does while he waits, everything made better enough when Elijah's response is hardly more than a whisper.

"Is it that easy to start falling for someone? Or to get them to fall for you? Is smiling back all it takes?"

"I'm not sure I'm the best person to ask," Alex argues. "But you'll let me know if you find out?"

"I can try."

Alex swallows that and pretends nothing gets caught in his throat, then they both take another bite and Alex pushes his chips toward the middle of the table for them to share. "So, do you think reading the messages between P and E has made the wanting better or worse?"

"Worse," Elijah answers immediately, though he looks like he wants to take it back, too honest, too quickly. "Or maybe that's not the right word. I don't know."

"Is that why you weren't sure whether you were okay the other night?" Alex asks.

"I don't—it's not—" Elijah sighs and lifts his hood over his curls, and he looks so damn small for someone who is very much not, the brief description of Peter's strong body—Elijah's great grandfather's body—becoming a tangible thing in front of Alex today. "I still don't know how to answer that—not right now. But I'll say that their story makes me ache and I still want more, and I'm not totally sure how to balance those two things. Not when you're sitting across from me, probably feeling the same way."

A couple walks past them, food in hand, and gets settled on the other side of the patio, and it should give Alex enough time to take a deep breath and think about where to take the conversation from here—for him to back up or turn around or maybe even run away—but then he's asking a question he only halfway understands, and he knows he's less ready for Elijah's next answer than any that have come before.

He knows the answer matters in ways he can barely admit.

"Do you think me sitting across from you makes the wanting better or worse?"

Elijah's eyes fall closed for only a second, but by the time he opens them again, it seems like he has all the self-control Alex lacks, and maybe he lies, if only by avoiding Alex's question altogether. "How long were you married?"

"Twelve years," Alex says, taking the out that Elijah has offered, if it's an out at all. "We were together almost 20, though. Since high school."

"You guys have cute little prom pictures and all that shit?" Elijah teases.

"All that shit," Alex huffs. "Yeah, definitely. And most of it's probably in boxes in my garage now, leaving even more empty space inside."

"You think there's any chance you'll get back together?"

"No."

He waits for Elijah to push for more than that, but he gets nothing but a foot nudged against his, a touch that should probably be there and gone, but one that lingers instead. "You close to your family?"

"Mostly," he admits. "My little sister is awesome. Gabriela. She's just incredibly busy, which means I don't get to see her as much as I'd like. And she's married with two kids, so my daughter loves to hang out with her cousins when we can make it work. My parents are still married and very, very Catholic, so they're not happy about the divorce. Ditto the aunts and uncles and my grandmother. My grandfather, God rest his soul, probably would've just yelled for a minute and then split a bottle of tequila with me. But yeah, they all love Cass and love to look at me like I screwed up, which I guess maybe I did, so that's where things are at these days."

Elijah's eyes narrow. "Why do you think you screwed up?"

"She left me, Elijah. That wouldn't have happened if I'd done everything right."

"It seems so quiet, though—the end of your marriage."

"You're not wrong," Alex admits, a small frown thrown onto the table between them. "But what makes you think that?"

"I mean, you're not screaming about her, which makes me think you're probably not screaming *at* her either. And if you're not screaming at her, there's a decent chance she's not screaming at you," Elijah says. "Not that I don't think you *ever* fought, but you're heartbroken and you're taking the blame, and you've already told me you miss your best friend and what you were supposed to be. So, it's none of my business at all, but I am curious about whether anything else was said out loud."

"By her?"

"Probably, yeah. Because maybe your only mistake—" Elijah trails off and looks over at the couple engaged in a conversation of their own. "No, never mind. Like I said, it's none of my business. You can ignore me."

"Don't want to ignore you. Maybe my only mistake was what?"

But Alex watches as Elijah shakes his head and bites his lip, not intentionally toying with him, though it's a little maddening all the same. Elijah seems like he's a half step ahead of Alex, and maybe has been since they first met in his grandpa's driveway, but Alex doesn't even know where they're going. When he can't keep staring into the blue of Elijah's eyes, Alex drops his gaze to where Elijah's fingers are tangled with his hoodie strings, and it's not the first time Alex has noticed how much Elijah always needs to be touching things. His hoodie.

His hair. His face. It's strangely mesmerizing, and Alex tries not to wonder what Elijah's like in any of those failed relationships, and how badly he might want to touch other people, too. And as though Elijah can read his mind, there's a little more pressure against Alex's foot—just a reminder that Elijah is right there.

"What would you say if I told you I didn't want to look at the books today?" Elijah asks.

Alex takes a deep breath and sits back in his chair, a napkin crumpled in his hand. "I'd ask what you want to do instead."

"More of this."

"So, today the ache wins out?"

"I guess that's one way to put it, sure," Elijah says.

"Are you giving up on the story?"

"Not even a little bit."

"Okay."

And with that, Alex lets Peter and E go for a while, enjoying the chance to get to know Elijah better, and offering up plenty of the same while they talk more about their families and their pasts and their hobbies and their travels and their likes and their dislikes. There's a conversation about favorite carnival rides—the Zipper for Elijah and the Scrambler for Alex—and at least a dozen different movies they were obsessed with as kids. Elijah admits he loves bartending for the way it connects him to so many different human moments at once, and Alex tells him he went into journalism for the same reason, even though those moments come at him more quietly than anything Elijah experiences on a rowdy weekend night.

And then Alex gets to hear about Nora, the 73-year-old widowed neighbor who is all too happy to visit Poe on the nights when Elijah works, in part because Elijah runs errands for her, and maybe mostly because she and Poe are often the same kind of lonely. The fear of his own loneliness is difficult to remember while Alex has spent an afternoon like this, and somehow it doesn't return, even after they've been sitting for too long, and Elijah tells Alex that he has to go home and get ready for work.

"You've got Elena this week?" Elijah asks as he stands to stretch, his hoodie pulled high when he takes the time to raise his arms over his head.

"I do, yeah. Cassidy's dropping her off tomorrow night."

They both grab their things and start to make their way back through the café and toward the parking lot, the two of them saying their goodbyes from several feet apart.

"Is it okay if I text you sometime during the week, just to see if we can figure out another time to sit down with the books?"

Alex swallows something light and warm and pretends he feels neither. "You can text me about anything. If I'm busy doing something with her, it might take me longer to respond, but I will. And I guess you'll be working most nights anyway, but yeah. Whenever."

"Anything, whenever," Elijah nods. "Got it."

After Elena has run inside with her suitcase and backpack and a routine greeting that still feels newer than that, Cassidy slips her hands into her back pockets and fidgets on the front porch. She has something to say, clearly, but she's already turned down Alex's offer to come inside for a few minutes, so he waits her out. Wonders if she has something more to say about how he looks and what good habits he's picked up since the last time she saw him.

But that's not it at all.

"We've been navigating things pretty well, I think. You and me. The uncertainty of how this is all supposed to go. What it's supposed to look like," she starts.

"Yeah, it's—I think we're doing okay," Alex agrees.

"It's hard sometimes, though—knowing where we've drawn lines, or what we're supposed to share."

"Okay," he says. "I mean, whatever we are to each other now, we've been best friends for a long time. We can probably share a lot."

Even as he says it, Alex can't quite tell if that's true. Maybe he's never understood where friendship ends and something more begins, willing to share so much of himself with the woman standing in front of him now, even if it seems like that was never enough. An entire marriage rooted in friendship but really never growing any further off the ground. He trusts Cassidy, and still loves her, but he isn't sure how much that's true the other way around. Can't figure out how long they've been living with such different feelings entirely.

"You can tell me anything," Alex promises, the simplest way he can offer everything he's always wanted to give.

But she looks up the street, uncomfortable in a way that makes his breath sticky in his chest, finally swinging her head back to him. "I've started seeing someone."

"Someone."

"Yeah, sort of an acquaintance of an acquaintance. Met him at a work thing and we've gone out a few times. It's not—I have no idea what's going to happen. It hasn't been that long. I just thought you should know."

Alex clears his throat and tries so hard to keep looking at her. "What's his name?"

"Michael," she says, her head tilted like she wants to ask why it matters. It doesn't, of course.

"Okay, well, thank you for telling me," Alex rasps. "Enjoy your week and I guess I'll see you next Sunday."

"Alex—"

"No, seriously, thank you. It's—I'm okay."

He's pretty sure he's told some version of that lie for the past 20 years even if the words taste unfamiliar now, but she nods and leaves and he stays there at his front door for another minute before he stops shaking long enough to find Elena and settle down on the couch.

The rest of their night is fine. Most of Monday, too. It's mundane and Alex knows how to work with that, lists and rules and patterns and boundaries. It's not until dinner on Monday night, when Elena casually mentions Michael while Alex's fork is halfway to his mouth, that everything catches back up to him and he knows he needs some help to keep from falling down.

Or maybe help getting back up from there.

Because after Elena is asleep, Alex is sitting on his bedroom floor, his back pressed to the closed door and his head staring down at nothing. He picks up his phone to text Elijah because he doesn't know what else to do, three texts fired off in rapid succession.

Cassidy is seeing someone

Sorry

you can ignore this sorry

The call notification is immediate, and when Alex answers, he doesn't even have a chance to say hello before Elijah is talking.

"You don't need to apologize at all, and you definitely don't need to do it twice."

"This is stupid," Alex huffs.

"Which part?" Elijah asks softly.

"Take your pick. Being bothered by something that was inevitable. Not knowing how to do the same thing myself. Sitting on my bedroom floor whining to you about it."

Elijah is quiet for several seconds, though Alex can hear him moving and he wonders whether he's somehow said both too much and too little, but then there's a small sigh on the other end.

"Inevitable things can still suck, you're better at that than you think you are, and I wouldn't have called you if I didn't want to hear whatever you have to say, whiny or not," Elijah says. "Do you want me to hang up so we can do this over text instead?"

And no, that's not what Alex wants at all, actually. "Come over for dinner tomorrow night."

"Tomorrow—wait, what? Isn't Elena there?"

"She—yeah, sorry, if you don't want—forget I said any-thing."

"Not what I meant," Elijah growls. "Of course I want to, but I also know your time with her is limited and I don't mind waiting until next week if you honestly want me to forget about it. I just—don't assume I don't want to see you."

"Because you do?"

"Because I do."

"Then come over for dinner with us," Alex says. "And let me know if chili is okay with you."

It is, of course.

Alex's only problem is that, while chili is easy to make, and the first thought he'd had when he'd extended an accidental invitation, he doesn't have all the ingredients on hand, and beyond that, he'd love to be able to make some cornbread too. So, after he picks Elena up from school the next day, he tells her they have to make a quick stop at the store before they head home. She's fine with it—loves going shopping with him, actually—but she brings a nearly insatiable curiosity with her, and he finds himself shaking his head at the apple that didn't fall very far from his tree.

"I haven't heard of Elijah before. Do you work with him?" she asks as they grab a basket just inside the door.

"No, I met him at the garage sale where I bought your books and games."

"Oh. So, he's a brand new friend?"

"Um, brand new, yeah," Alex agrees. "Just a couple of weeks, I guess. Does it bother you that I have a new friend?"

He can't figure out why it would, but there's a lot he can't figure out these days, and it feels like the right thing to ask. Or maybe not. Elena scrunches up her face like it's the weirdest idea she's heard, her curly hair a mess in a ponytail that had looked much better that morning.

"Why would it bother me? I have new friends all the time."

"Ah, yes, that's true, isn't it? And probably why we get emails about you being a bit of a chatterbox in class?"

Elena rolls her eyes as Alex puts a can of crushed tomatoes into the basket she insists on carrying. "Yeah, but you and Elijah would probably talk during class, too. It's what friends do."

"Maybe you're right. He and I do like to talk a lot."

"What do you talk about?"

Alex warms, everything about it more noticeable in the cool grocery store, and tries to focus on finding the beans he needs. "Well, we talk about our jobs and our families—"

"Including me?" Elena interrupts.

"Including you, yes. And we're—we've been reading together, so we talk a lot about that too."

"Ooooh, what're you reading?"

He stops short of wherever else he needs to go, all too aware that he walked right into that one. "It's kinda hard to explain, bug."

"You can try," Elena argues. "That's what you and mommy make *me* do."

"Mmmm, we do, but what Elijah and I are reading is sort of a complicated and private adult love story."

"Is there *sex* in it?" she whispers loudly, somewhere between intrigued and scandalized.

Alex chuckles when he probably shouldn't, Elena's expression hilarious even when nothing about a decades-old gay romance is funny to him, and he nudges his daughter out of one aisle and toward another.

"No sex, and it's a little bit sad, but Elijah and I are hoping there's a very happy ending."

They finish their shopping—sour cream, a couple of avocados, and a boxed cornbread mix added to the basket before they check out—and they hurry home from there so Alex can get the chili started before he catches up on the work he missed while he was out. Elena, while more interested in dinner than usual, takes her backpack upstairs without a word, and it gives Alex space he hadn't asked for but probably needs. And then it's not much longer before Elijah is at the front door with a six-pack of the same IPA Alex had offered a week ago, his other hand clutching a bottle of fruit punch.

"Wasn't really sure what Elena might like, but my niece and nephew lose their minds over this stuff," he says, handing everything over.

"It's perfect, but you really didn't have to bring anything."

Elijah shrugs and they make small talk on their way to the kitchen to put most of the drinks away, two beers open for them to drink while Alex finishes cooking dinner, Elena still upstairs with her homework. The conversation is good, but Alex is pretty sure he holds his breath until his daughter makes her way back down, the introductions easy when there's really not much to say.

Friend, daughter. Daughter, friend.

Done.

The chili turns out great, but the laughter is even better, the typical dinnertime conversation improved by having another person there. And maybe it's only because Alex and Elena are both still used to that dynamic and haven't totally adjusted to being a pair, or maybe it's because Elijah fits well here, but all three of them are engrossed in conversation without seeming to work hard at it at all, any friendly interrogation by Elena countered by all the questions Elijah fires right back.

They all move to the living room after they're done eating and play a couple of games of Clue, Alex and Elijah next to each other on the couch while Elena kneels on the other side of the coffee table. And when it's time for her to go to bed, Alex asks him to stay where he is while he follows his daughter upstairs and tucks her in, returning to fall at Elijah's side a few minutes later, the two of them sipping at their second beers as they lean back against the cushions.

"She's awesome, but I assume you already know that," Elijah says.

"I do, yeah. I love that kid. And she thought you were pretty awesome, too."

"Really?"

"Oh, shut up," Alex laughs, bumping his knee against Elijah's without bothering to pull it back again. "Pretty sure you're the same guy who was bragging about his charm when we'd barely met. That *was* you, right? I'm not confused?"

Elijah's bottle rests against his thigh and his head rolls sideways to look at Alex. "Didn't know you were out there meeting so many different guys."

And Alex blushes—completely fucking blushes—but when he meets Elijah's eyes, there's something there, beyond the obvious teasing and all the dull edges that come from a couple of drinks and a big meal. He's searching for a reassurance Alex didn't think he'd need and doesn't really know how to give.

"Never really had to make friends on my own before," he admits. "I'm not sure I know what I'm doing."

Elijah nods, then finishes the last of his beer. "Well, like I told you last night, you're better at it than you think you are."

He leans forward to slide the empty bottle onto the table, and only glances back at Alex for a second before he pushes up from the couch to leave, Alex's hand closing around Elijah's wrist before he can take more than a step. Alex thinks he blushes again, and it's getting harder to mind.

"I forgot to tell you, I—we have this work retreat thing in Big Bear next week. Enlightenment or empowerment or enrichment or something."

"Okay," Elijah breathes, staring down at Alex's hand.

Alex slowly pulls it away and hurries to stand, picking up Elijah's bottle so he has something to hold on to when he walks Elijah to the door. "It's Monday to Wednesday, so I know it's been a while and we're supposed to get back to the books, but we might have to wait until the weekend after that. Maybe another lunch?"

It feels far away, the week and a half they'll have to wait after seeing each other three times in the past six days, but Elijah nods. "Yeah, that would be good. Just text me after you get back."

Chapter Six

The enlightenment/empowerment/enrichment retreat is not the first one Alex has been on and it's probably not the last, something everlasting about the newspaper wanting a bunch of strangely competitive introverts to bond over trust exercises and health food. Alex will be among the first to admit that it *is* incredibly relaxing breathing in the cold mountain air, and he makes a mental note to bring Elena up for a day or two once there's snow on the ground, but he's hardly disappointed by the time they're all packing up to head back home. He's had so much time to sit with so many things, three quiet days to reflect on his relationship with Cassidy and on her new relationship with Michael and how his relationship with Elena changes a little more each week, a natural shift encouraged by time and circumstance. And all of that has left him with a closer look at himself, a striking awareness of the man he's always been, and the question of what he might want after twenty years of not knowing how to want anything that he didn't already have.

When they're gathering up their things in the afternoon, duffel bags stuffed and notebooks closed, his colleagues all confirm plans to meet up that night at a bar a few blocks from their office building. It's a curious tradition established long ago, when someone decided their general desire for solitude had been overcome long enough to allow for one good night of drinking not permitted at the retreat itself. And as everyone else buzzes about the fun they've had in years past, Alex tries not to think too much about how easy it is to tell them he has somewhere else to be, or how badly he wants to be in that other place, away from all of them.

If his goal is really to make more friends, there's no denying he's doing a terrible job of it now.

And maybe it's not all that much of a surprise when Alex's editor, Steven Liao, pulls him aside to call him out as gently as possible. At the newspaper's sporadic charity events or holiday parties, Steven's been the one by Alex's side most often, their wives hitting it off a few years back, and while he and Steven have never really had a reason to spend time together anywhere else, Alex assumes it would go well. Just like he assumes he would've sat near Steven for a beer or two tonight, chatting easily about a dozen different things.

Instead, Steven raises an eyebrow. "Usually when we get blown off with a vague 'somewhere else to be' excuse, I figure it's a way for you to spend the rest of the night at home alone. Tonight? Maybe not so much."

"Do I bail on you guys that often?"

"Since you and Cassidy separated, mostly," Steven says. "Everyone still doin' okay with that?"

Alex kicks at the side of their firepit. "Yes, but that isn't—I mean, we're not—I'm not blowing you off to see her tonight."

"Nah, wasn't really thinking you were."

"But you don't think I'm gonna be alone either."

"If you're worried that I'm gonna ask you to write about it, you can relax," Steven promises, careful even as he teases Alex. It's why Alex hasn't tried to run away, and why he doesn't look elsewhere when Steven goes on. "I don't need your story at all. But if it has anything to do with why you've been walking around lighter than I've ever seen you, like maybe you found something you didn't know you were missing, ditching us tonight is the right call."

Steven walks away then, like perhaps he wants to prove that Alex doesn't owe him an explanation, and Alex uses the next minute or two to will his heartbeat into something normal. He'd already made the decision about *where* to go tonight, but now Alex is wrapped in the *why* he's been trying to ignore for a few weeks, and it's only a car full of people waiting to drive back down the mountain that gets him moving again, daydreams and fears left to wait until he's closer to the beach.

After they've all carpooled back, Alex goes home just long enough to drop off his bag, folders full of scribbled notes, and a book gifted to him by a colleague he barely knows, and then he checks his phone one last time for anything important, everything else swiped away until they're tomorrow's problem. His reflection in the hallway mirror catches his eye, and he wonders if he should change his clothes first, his button up left untucked from his jeans, everything just a little rumpled, but he doesn't want to look like he's trying too hard, no matter how long that's been uncomfortably true. He runs his hands through his hair, for whatever good that does, then he locks up behind himself and makes the drive toward the beach, no rain slowing him down this time.

There are no women thanking him for holding the door this time either, and that can't possibly be a sign of anything, but Alex is relieved anyway, and happy to be alone when he looks up at the bar and then makes his way toward the same table he'd sat at before. Another bartender is working the far side of the room, and Elijah is in the middle of making a drink, but he's good at his job and quick to notice when someone new walks in and his eyes catch up when Alex is only halfway across the floor, his surprise obvious and his smile immediate.

Alex settles onto the stool and plays around with the menu even if he already knows what he wants, careful not to look up again until a beer slides onto the table, a familiar hand slow to leave the glass behind.

"Welcome back," Elijah says. "You smell like a campfire."

"Oh, god, I didn't even think about that. I mean, I swear I'm *clean*, but it was cold up there and we had lunch outside today and—shit, I should've—"

"Wasn't a complaint, Alex," Elijah interrupts.

"Okay, I—you're sure? I just dropped off my stuff and then came here and I wasn't—"

He trails off and sighs because it feels like small pieces of himself are falling everywhere only for him to trip over them, and maybe he should blame the mountain air for leaving him lightheaded, but he thinks it might have more to do with the man fully amused by him now.

"I'm very sure," Elijah insists, his eyes bright whether or not Alex is imagining the exact shade of blue. "What would you like for dinner?"

Alex takes a deep breath and orders, then lets Elijah get back to work while he distracts himself with aimless people-watching, his shoulder pressed against the dark wall while he drinks his beer and waits. He's left alone there too long, or maybe it hasn't been much time at all, but when Elijah returns with a plate in his hand, he studies Alex for a moment and cocks his head.

"Too much enlightenment this week?" he asks. "Or do you think you might find more answers at the bottom of that pint glass?"

Alex hums when he looks down to find half the beer gone already. "Sort of an accidental tradition when we get back. Three days of forced oversharing ends with a bunch of us getting drunk together and dragging ourselves into the office a few hours late the next morning."

He sets the glass down for the first time since picking it up, and he takes a bite of his burger, knowing all too well that Elijah's still a step ahead, two plus two solved before Alex had the equation fully out of his mouth.

"But you didn't go out with them tonight."

Alex swallows and takes another drink instead of making eye contact. "I did not."

"I'm glad," Elijah says, not waiting for a reaction to that before he turns and heads back to the bar.

It's like that for a while, Alex enjoying his dinner while Elijah works, the buzz at the bar steady but not all that busy on a chilly Wednesday night. They're able to talk plenty in between, and though they'd texted a few times over the past week, there's more they can catch up on now. When Alex is all done, everything left empty in front of him, Elijah brings him a second beer, an unspoken invitation to stay, and Alex nods and whispers his thanks before his voice gets a little stronger.

"Have you peeked at the books at all?"

Elijah's eyes narrow a touch, a smirk on his face. "No, why? Have you?"

"No, but I'm not the one who did it last time," Alex says, knocking into Elijah's shin with the toe of his shoe as he takes a sip. "I've been perfectly patient."

"Okay, yes, fine. I was kinda restless at the beginning, when we were trying to figure out what we were even looking at. But now, we—I think I know enough that I'm willing to wait and see."

"You're not curious?"

"I'm incredibly curious," Elijah huffs. "But not in a rush anymore."

"It's not gonna be easy for them—for Peter and E," Alex sighs. "And there's no way to know where it goes from here.

I'm curious too, but it's scary—having no control over what happens next. I'm nervous about how much the story might hurt and how abruptly it might end."

"Had enough of that for a while?"

Alex scrapes something bittersweet from his tongue. "I have."

"But you still don't want to walk away from this."

It's not a question, but Alex answers anyway. "I wouldn't begin to know how."

Elijah's quiet for a while, and Alex thinks he'll probably have to go back and check on everyone at the bar soon, but a quick glance shows them both that there's not much to do, and Elijah doesn't seem to be in a hurry to worry about it. His finger draws an invisible line back and forth across the table and Alex gets mesmerized by the predictability of it, silently drinking and unprepared for Elijah to change the subject.

"It's still none of my business, and I know I told you to ignore me, but if you—" Elijah stops his drawing and reaches for Alex's coaster instead, tracing the edge until the continuous motion threatens to leave Alex under another spell. "What did Cassidy say to you when she first wanted to leave? You told me you were best friends all along, and maybe it had started to feel like that's all you were, and that she needed more or deserved more, but was there—" Elijah's gaze flickers higher just in time to meet Alex's there. "I really want to know what she said out loud."

Alex takes a much longer drink, and he's about to respond—he really, really is—but then three people walk in from outside and grab seats at the bar, and Elijah frowns.

"Go," Alex whispers.

It's as much for himself as it is for Elijah, encouraging someone to leave and knowing that this one will come back when he can. Still, Alex's throat is tight with everything he's screwed up so far and everything he might be about to screw up again. He's so fucking confused and the beer isn't helping, the things he wants coming into focus just as the rest of the world begins to blur, but Alex knows he was wrong about his feelings for Cassidy for years and he doesn't want to make that same mistake now.

He's terrified to get this all wrong, too.

Still, Elijah keeps leading him here, into conversations about Alex's past that only help make him sure he wants something different in the future. Simple words that lead to complicated thoughts, any actions wholly unfamiliar to Alex, and breathtaking if he doesn't fight the very idea of them away.

Elijah, whose forearms are pressed to the bar right now as he leans forward with a brilliant smile, one Alex has seen often, even though it's so much wider than the ones usually aimed at him. Less honest, too.

Elijah, who is gone for a while, maybe because of the three people who arrived or the two who are getting ready to leave or the food he runs from the kitchen or the drinks he's still serving, or maybe just because he needs this break too, no matter how willing he's been to bring them this far along.

Elijah, who finally, *finally* returns to Alex's table to find an empty glass and a silent, dark-eyed plea.

"I'm sorry," Elijah says, and Alex assumes he's referring to the fact that he has to wander off to work every now and then, but he doesn't ask that, unwilling to take too many chances at once.

"Will you pour me a shot?"

"You driving home tonight?"

"I don't have to," Alex tells him, and he pretends neither of them blinks. "Tequila?"

"Cheap shit with salt and a lime, or the good stuff without?"

"Without. The salt and lime are better when someone else is drinking with you."

Elijah chews on his lip, picks up the empty pint glass, and backs away, only turning his back on Alex when he has to. When he returns, he's holding three shots of clear tequila and another beer, the beer landing in the middle of the table, two of the shots set next to it, and the first one held in the air for Alex to pull from Elijah's grip.

"Brought a few just in case. You know, as long as you're not driving," Elijah says, stupidly slow when he licks at whatever must've spilled over the side of his hand.

Doing his best to ignore him, Alex downs the first shot of tequila without flinching and reaches for the next one. "Cheers."

"Careful," Elijah smiles.

Alex throws the second one down just as smoothly and

presses the glass back into Elijah's waiting hand. "She told me she loved me, and that she knew I loved her, but that we'd both been lying to ourselves for too long, even if we hadn't meant for it to be that way."

"Lying how?"

"I asked her that," Alex says, pulling the beer closer and taking the longest possible sip while Elijah clings to the two empty shot glasses in his hand. The temptation of the third remains on the table between them. "She said she'd spent the past several years trying to convince herself that having a family with her best friend was enough."

"Mmmm," Elijah hums. "So, what was your lie?"

The question stings even when Alex knew it was coming, and he thinks back to that day Cass had stood in the middle of their bedroom, tears streaming down her face, and so gently accused him of something he hadn't been able to deny and has tried so hard to ignore ever since. And now he could easily keep it going by telling Elijah he'd only convinced himself of the same thing she had, but the look on Elijah's face suggests he already knows better, and Alex doesn't want to keep lying anyway.

"That I had ever loved her as anything more than a friend," he says, his voice threatening to break. "Or that it was possible I ever could have."

Elijah gives Alex time to distract himself with the beer, and he steps back just enough to give Alex some space too, but Alex doesn't want it, not with alcohol and honesty coursing through his veins, so thick and slow. He finishes the last shot instead, then uses his free hand to reach forward and curl a finger through one of Elijah's belt loops, tugging him closer, Elijah perfectly sober and moving easily in response, comfortable where he lands between Alex's legs.

"Careful," Elijah says again.

"Because people might see us?"

"Don't care about them," Elijah murmurs. "And I'm not the one who's still sitting in the dark."

"Just like they did."

"Maybe."

Alex nods, then feels the crease between his brows come and go. "That day at the café, when I said maybe I screwed up with Cassidy, you started to tell me something."

"I remember."

Even from where he's sitting on the high stool, Alex has to look up at Elijah, a flash of dizziness leaving him with a smile. It's funny because Alex has never considered himself to be all that small, at least as broad and tall as most people he knows, but Elijah has him beat and he's grateful for it without understanding why.

"Tell me about it now?"

Elijah's eyes fall closed, like maybe he's trying to heed his own warnings, and Alex thinks he might close his too if he weren't afraid the room could start to spin. Instead, he holds on to the belt loop, nowhere near brave enough to move his hand anywhere else, and he waits to see if Elijah will find somewhere better to be.

He doesn't.

"You said she left you, and that it wouldn't have happened if you'd done everything right."

"I remember," Alex echoes.

"And I guess I was just going to agree with what she had already said to you. The lie you just shared," Elijah sighs. "That maybe your biggest mistake was the one you made at the very beginning. Thinking you were ever going to love her the way you so desperately wanted to."

"Or that I was ever going to want her the way I so desperately would have loved to."

Elijah smiles, impressed. "That was rather poetic for someone a few drinks in."

"I've built my entire career around my ability to put words together," Alex says. "Every now and then, I can do it off the clock."

"Duly noted." He's gentle when he pries Alex's finger away and nods toward the beer that had found its way back to the table when neither of them was paying attention. "Finish your beer. I'm gonna go make sure everyone else is still good over there."

"Okay, can you bring me my check when you come back? I'll take care of that and get a ride home."

"No and no," Elijah says. "Dinner's on me, and I don't live far from here. We can come back and pick up your car in the morning before you go to work."

"What about the beer and tequila?"

"Dinner *and* drinks are on me, and I don't live far from here," he amends. "We can come back and pick up your car in the morning before you go to work."

"Elijah."

"Alex," Elijah bites back, nothing sharp about it. "I'm obviously not going to force you to come home with me, but I have a very comfortable couch and an old dog who will probably keep you company there."

"Oh, well, if Poe will be there—"

"Mmmm, works every time," Elijah quips.

They both grin, the easy happiness almost out of place as Elijah heads back to the bar and Alex picks up the glass again. He has no idea what the hell he's doing, and right now he's finding it very hard to care, watching as the crowd dwindles and a few stragglers laugh. Elijah starts cleaning and restocking while the other bartender takes care of a drink or two, and then he looks to be closing up his register before ducking into the back, Alex's third beer gone by the time Elijah reappears with keys and a hoodie in his hand.

"You can leave already?"

Elijah shrugs and picks up the empty glass. "We close soon anyway, and Tyler said he's got it. I'll probably just stay later tomorrow night."

"Because of me."

He shrugs again and gestures for Alex to head toward the door while he drops the pint glass at the bar and waves goodbye. They have a few blocks to walk, Elijah's truck in a nearby parking garage, but the cold air feels good when Alex is this unsteady, and he watches his breath get lost in the dark as Elijah untucks his shirt and pulls the hoodie over his head. The streets aren't totally empty, but it's late enough on a weeknight that the silence feels right, and neither one of them seems to be in a hurry to change that. The ride to Elijah's condo is as quick as he promised, and Alex follows him inside, Poe there to greet them both, as calmly friendly as he has been since the morning they met.

While Alex shuffles toward the sectional that takes up plenty of the cozy living room, the dog close behind, Elijah goes into the kitchen and brings back a bottle of water, pushing it into Alex's hand.

"Drink that. I'll be back with clothes and blankets and stuff."

Alex does as he's told, and when Elijah comes back with sweatpants, a t-shirt, a pillow, and a couple of blankets, the water gets set aside and his makeshift bed gets made. Poe is comfortably settled on the opposite end of the sofa, already fully adjusted to the new sleeping arrangements, and Alex goes to change in the bathroom, a splash of water on his face and his reflection in the mirror suggesting nothing is all that different—red eyes aside—even when he's afraid everything is.

He's wrestling with his past and Alex doesn't want to have to fight it at all, doing what he can to make peace with everything when he opens the door just as Elijah comes out from his bedroom, his hoodie gone, and his hands shoved into the pockets of his pants instead. Elijah's untucked shirt is only partially unbuttoned, like maybe he changed his mind about it somewhere along the way, and because the hallway is too small or because they're standing too close, Alex doesn't think before he reaches for the hem, as though there's a chance that one point of contact can make the present important enough that memories of the past won't have to hurt.

"It was never bad—being with her. I didn't hate it or anything," Alex rasps, his eyes trained on where his fingers are curled around soft blue cotton. "I mean, being married to her was good and easy, but the rest—the physical intimacy—I never thought it was bad."

"It probably wasn't. But I think you're being a little unfair to yourself by trying to define any of it in those terms. Sex can be more than one thing at a time."

"It still wasn't enough for her."

"Among other things, no, it probably wasn't. But Alex, you—" Elijah trails off and takes a deep breath. "At some point, you're gonna have to be more honest and ask yourself if it was really enough for *you*. Whether good and easy and content and comfortable were ever going to be enough when you could let yourself have those things and so much more."

Elijah already has his back to the wall, but while there's nowhere for him to go when Alex slips that much closer, he doesn't push him away either. Alex lets go of Elijah's shirt only to play with one of the buttons instead. He feels a little like

Elijah now, so eager to touch.

"Tell me what you think I could have. Tell me about more."

"Probably not a good time for that," Elijah says, his voice devastatingly low, and his mouth a hiccup away from Alex's ear.

"M'not that drunk," Alex argues.

"You're not that sober either."

"Maybe not."

"We can't do more than talk right now."

"I wouldn't know how anyway," he admits, and he finally looks up to meet darkness he didn't expect to find in Elijah's eyes. It's so new, this chance to see his own desire reflected in another man's gaze, and Alex isn't ready to walk away. "So, tell me everything. All the things I don't know."

It only takes a single step for Elijah to press Alex into the opposite wall, his hands out of his pockets now and nearly bruising against Alex's skin, just above where the waistband of Elijah's own sweatpants ride low on Alex's hips, their bodies kept carefully apart while their foreheads fall together.

"You can want to be with someone, not because it's soothing or feels *nice*, but because it sparks something blazing hot beneath your skin and makes you claw at the other person for relief. You can want to reach for them, not because it's part of a routine you memorized a while ago, but because every goosebump on their skin, every whimper or moan or gasp you pull from the back of their throat, will leave you aching with need."

Alex chokes on at least two of those sounds now, his fingers curling around Elijah's forearms. "Isn't that selfish?"

"You can be selfish sometimes," Elijah whispers. "I'm not worried about you knowing how to give, but I want you to know you're allowed to take, too. You need to learn how to *take*, Alex."

"From you?"

Elijah's breath is so fucking warm where it ghosts over Alex's mouth. "From me."

"Just not tonight."

"No, not tonight."

"But you—if you know how to do all of that—if you know how to feel all of those things and tell everyone they're allowed to feel them too—" Alex pauses, Elijah's hands searing where they hold him still. "Why have so many of your past relationships failed?"

It takes a long time for Elijah to answer, and for a while, Alex thinks maybe he's not going to. They both stay quiet while he lets go of Alex and backs away, gesturing for Alex to move into the living room and watching with his lip caught between his teeth while Alex gives into the pull of exhaustion, finally settling under the blankets. Elijah glances to where Poe is already asleep at the far end of the sectional, then back to Alex, and he sighs as he turns off the light.

"Because I've never had good and easy and content and comfortable before."

Chapter Seven

Alex wakes earlier than he should, his body clinging to habit in spite of the alcohol and a later night than usual, and he's not about to wake Elijah just for the short ride back to the bar. He's as close to silent as he can be while he greets Poe and uses the bathroom and changes back into his clothes, already looking forward to tonight when he'll finish with work and dinner and be able to go to bed early. And though he's not a huge fan of poking around anyone's house, Alex easily finds a pad of paper and a pen attached to the side of the refrigerator when he steals an extra bottle of water, and he scribbles a quick note to leave on his pillow, blankets already folded and stacked next to it.

Didn't want to wake you, so I got a ride back to my car. Still on for lunch on Saturday?

And thank you. For everything.

A car picks him up minutes later, and he's home after battling morning traffic and a headache he probably deserves. His house is still too big and too quiet when he gets there, but it feels less like a penance of some kind and more like a basic fact of life, so he pushes past the empty walls and treats himself to a long shower to finally wash the campfire and Elijah away.

Once he's dressed, coffee in hand, he starts working his way through three days of emails, his phone chirping as soon as Alex has forced himself to stop staring at it. Something about a watched pot, he supposes.

Yes and you're welcome. Sorry I didn't say goodbye

You said goodnight. Didn't need more than that

It's too much, he thinks, suddenly too sober and unable to breathe, but Alex sends the text anyway and tries not to worry when he doesn't hear anything back. He throws himself back into work, heading into the office for the rest of the day because it's louder there, and staying a little late because he can. Elijah is already at the bar by the time Alex is making dinner at home, and he'll be there after Tyler leaves as repayment for last night, but that's good too, no temptation to check in with him when Alex gets tired again and his defenses wear down.

Friday is more complicated for him, even with both of their jobs pulling them in opposite directions again, and Alex pretends not to notice the timing of Elijah's next text, and how easily he's able to avoid a longer conversation.

Headed to work in a min. lunch at my place tomorrow? Pizza?

Yep I'll see you then

That has to be enough for Alex to believe that things are okay between them, even with however stupid he'd definitely been Wednesday night and how cowardly he might have been

Thursday morning. After an expectedly restless sleep, he drives to Elijah's on Saturday, books resting on the seat next to him, convinced he'll keep his mouth mostly shut while they read about Peter and E for the first time in two weeks. But when he knocks on the door and it swings open seconds later, Elijah's smile is shy in a way it doesn't have to be, and Alex offering one back might be the thing that nudges both of them closer to something brave.

"Damn, I thought you were the pizza guy," Elijah quips.

"I can get out of the way if you'd rather spend the afternoon with him," Alex teases back.

"Nah, I mean, if you're already here, I guess you might as well stay," Elijah says, moving to the side to let Alex in and closing the door behind him. "You can set the books down on the coffee table, and then we can eat on the patio if you want."

Alex looks over Elijah's shoulder at a small area he hadn't noticed the other night, not really big enough to be called a backyard, but kind of cute all the same. There's a little table and two chairs and a small stretch of grass for Poe, who probably doesn't run around as much these days, and Alex nods, dropping the books off while he looks around at everything else he'd missed the first time he was here.

To his right is the hallway leading to Elijah's bedroom, the bathroom, and a second room Alex hasn't seen yet, maybe a little office or gym or something. To his far left is a cute kitchen with a dining area just on the other side of a high countertop, nothing fancy but good enough for the handful of people ever likely to be hanging out in a two-room condo. And here in the living room is the sectional and coffee table, a decently big TV, a couple of bookshelves—

And a record player.

"You bought one," he breathes.

"I—what?" Elijah asks from the kitchen.

"You kept the vinyls and bought a record player."

Elijah ducks his head, his cheeks pink, shy when he looks back up at Alex and shrugs. "Someone suggested I should."

"You work at a bar. I'm guessing a lot of someones suggest a lot of things," Alex points out.

"Maybe, but none of them have made me want to listen."

There are a couple beats before either of them moves, but eventually their food gets delivered and they take it outside, where lunch is relaxed, and everything Alex needs to finish settling his nerves. They enjoy soda and pizza and cheesy bread on the sunny but cold afternoon, and they have hours to themselves before Elijah has to go to work, taking their time to exchange stories and laugh plenty, and though they don't touch, everything about that feels okay. There's only the shadow of tension between them, not like there had been in the hallway when they'd shared a breath for a moment or two, and maybe Alex wants to look for it again, or maybe it's going to have to look for him.

Eventually, Elijah pops the last piece of crust into his mouth and grins around it. Alex reaches down to pet Poe when he walks by.

"*We loved with a love that was more than love,*" Alex recites, pulling a memory from a high school English class where he'd sat with Cassidy by his side.

The turn of Elijah's head is strangely slow, his eyes wide. "Alex."

"Oh, no. Wait, no, I—" Alex shakes his head, his cheeks warm. "It was just because of Poe. I was quoting—"

"'Annabel Lee.' Yeah, no, it's not—I—it's Uncle Edgar."

"Edgar Allan Poe was your *uncle*?" Alex asks, the furrow of his brows almost painful.

"No, god, I—" Elijah stands and scrubs a hand over his face, somehow lost and still very much right there in front of Alex. "I can't believe I didn't figure it out sooner. How could I not—oh my *god*. Poe belonged to my grandpa, and like you said, the name fit because of the whole 'Raven' thing, but it was also a nod to his Uncle Edgar, who wasn't his *literal* uncle, but was—"

"A very close friend of his father's," Alex finishes. "E."

"Peter and Edgar."

"So, that means your grandpa definitely knew, and he kept their secret his entire life."

"Seems like it, yeah," Elijah agrees. "Which is really fucking sad because he's probably also a lot of why it was so much harder for them to find ways to be together back then."

Alex nods. "Because he would've been a kid, still at home with Peter, and likely with some other live-in childcare after Evelyn died. Sneaking Edgar into his house might have been risky no matter what, but Peter definitely couldn't have tried it with his son there."

"And Uncle Edgar would've lived somewhere crowded and loud, if he had somewhere official to live at all, so my great grandfather would never have been able to go there."

"So, then, Edgar was some kind of what—errand boy between the dockside warehouses and the fancy office buildings in town?"

"Probably, yeah," Elijah says. "I know he was younger than my great grandfather, so that tracks. Then they met at the law firm somehow, and everything grew from there."

"Wait, did you ever meet Edgar?" Alex asks, pushing up from his chair to help clean up their lunch and move back inside.

"I—yeah, I—it's so vague," Elijah sighs, still stunned as they stack everything on the kitchen counter. "I feel like there was a birthday party for my grandpa in San Diego one year when I was little—I remember my parents taking us to the zoo one day we were down there—but yeah, I—I'm almost positive my great grandfather lived down there, and I think Uncle Edgar might've been with him."

Something loosens in Alex's chest at the thought of them staying together all those years, but tightens again when he realizes that the relationship doesn't seem to have ever been a public one, and it both sharpens and dulls every one of his own fears. He falls onto the couch and waits for Elijah to join him there.

"You don't remember the rest of your family ever talking

about Peter being gay?"

"Nope," Elijah says, the line of his jaw tight when he sits next to Alex. "But so much makes more sense now."

"Like your relationship with them?"

"Yeah. Peter was my mom's grandfather, but it never seemed like she knew that much about him, and maybe she didn't. And there's no way my grandpa would've judged them, but maybe he was so intent on protecting his father's relationship that he didn't let his own kids see Peter all that often."

"What about that trip to San Diego, though? Seeing Peter and Edgar together there? Did something happen before or after that?"

"Like, did my parents figure something out about them being gay?" Elijah shrugs. "Maybe. I honestly don't remember them saying anything at all, but they both seemed very 'don't ask, don't tell' my whole life. Loudly approving when I liked girls and then remaining remarkably silent when I—did not. It got to the point where I tried to mix it up enough that they were satisfied half the time."

Alex pulls one of the books from the table so he doesn't wrap his arms around Elijah instead. "Okay, and you said you were really close to your grandpa. Were your brother and sister close to him, too?"

"Not like I was, no," he admits. "They were always close to my parents."

"So, maybe your grandpa saw something in you that needed to be protected, too."

Elijah's head falls and Alex isn't surprised when a teardrop lands in his lap. "Fuck, I miss him."

"Would you rather talk to me about him instead? We don't have to read anything in the books today."

"No, I—" Elijah takes a deep breath, but doesn't look up, his fingers caught in his hair again, something belonging to Alex in danger of becoming trapped there too. "I want to know their story."

"Okay, but please tell me if we need to stop. This is—it's your story too, and I—"

"Alex, I'm not going to want to stop. It's—I can't imagine wanting to stop."

It's impossible not to hear everything Elijah isn't saying, and Alex squeezes his eyes shut before he swallows too many questions at once, then carefully opens the book he's been holding.

"We left off when they had finally met by the warehouses, pressed close to each other, but not going any further than that, so then the next note is this: *E, I'm sorry I remain so afraid, even cradled in your arms. There are so many reasons for the world to refuse us this, so many things the world could take from us both. You know I don't care about myself, but you and my son are everything to me, and I fear what might be torn from my arms if I hold you for too long. And as much as you insist that this is good—that I am good—please forgive me the nights I leave before either of us is ready.*"

Elijah leans forward to pick up his own book, clears his

throat, and reads Edgar's response.

P, my love, you need none of the forgiveness we should demand of those who have denied us this. Furthermore, please don't fear what could happen to me when your dear son will always be the one we need to keep safe from harm. I'll continue to hold you each night you come to me, however rare they might be, and delight in the times you're brave enough to embrace me in return.

"Uncle Edgar was prioritizing the family, long before he even would've met my grandpa," Elijah says. "And this sounds like they didn't even see each other often, but Uncle Edgar didn't ask for more."

"He didn't push, even when Peter was terrified."

"No, he didn't," Elijah agrees, his head rolling against the back of the couch until he can look at Alex. "What good would that have done?"

Alex doesn't answer, glancing back down at the book instead. "So, it's already been over a year for them."

"Sounds like it, yeah. We read about it being 'nearly a year' a while ago, and I think the messages went back and forth a lot more slowly than it seems when we're reading them. I assume they would've had to rely on the times when Uncle Edgar could have a reason to deliver to the law firm *and* actually have the chance to interact with my great grandfather. They wouldn't have let their story be passed through anyone else."

"Why have two different books at all?" Alex asks. "Wouldn't that have made an exchange more cumbersome? Couldn't they have written back and forth in the same one?"

Elijah considers it for a moment, but answers with the same guess Alex might have made on his own. "Some kind of plausible deniability if only one book landed in the wrong hands? Keeping the two halves of their love story separate, just for the pretense of safety they couldn't find anywhere else?"

"Until your grandpa could hold on to both."

"And we could give them a voice."

It takes them another several seconds, but they duck back into the books then, Alex with Peter's words and Elijah with Edgar's, written memories of small moments on dark nights with careful touches shared between them. Fingertips light against the other's face, pinkies linked together when the press of their entire palms together felt like too much. And the chance for them to talk, or whisper really, entire conversations they couldn't have anywhere else but in the shadows of warehouses while they should be asleep. There are several of those messages, remembering what they said to each other while they shook with each courageous new thing, and it leaves both Alex and Elijah nearly breathless.

But however emotional it is to follow Peter and Edgar's journey, everything gets a little worse when Alex reads on.

E, it's been so long since I've seen you, and today I'm gripped by unimaginable fear. There was a rumor after our latest delivery, talk of a late-night attack near the docks, a "sissy" beaten and left for dead. It was said that he's alive and being cared for, but my darling, please return and tell me it wasn't you.

"No," Alex chokes, quick to look at Elijah, who is already

turning the pages in his book.

He's too close to the end, though, and meets Alex's eyes, barely able to speak. "There's nothing left in this one."

So, Alex hurries to find what he can, and it doesn't take long.

E, every part of my body aches, but I know it must be nothing compared to the way you've been hurt, and I don't know what to do from here, when I know you have to be hidden away as you recover, and I have no way to reach you now. I can only write here, all too aware I may never have a way to give you this book again. We've heard nothing more about you, nor can I ask, but there would be no other reason for you to stay away. No other reason my heart would be so broken.

Alex keeps looking after that. "There's one more here."

E, I won't keep writing to you here, my entire heart tucked into the margins of pages you may never touch, my body left to the same fate. It would be too much to ask you to be with me again after all these weeks apart. But though we have never kissed, though I've only barely stopped being a coward long enough to hold your hand in mine while we talk, or brush your cheek with my own while we breathe, please know I will never stop loving you.

"Christ, I—" Elijah's voice breaks.

Alex doesn't notice whether any tears fall this time, his own vision blurry as he closes the book and puts it back onto the coffee table, adding Elijah's atop it a moment later. Then he sits back and reminds himself to take one breath after another, trembling with grief resolved years ago and the anticipation of something brand new. He feels caught between the two right now, and lost without another margin to cling to, but after giving them a few more minutes to sit with Peter and Edgar's uncertain ever after, Alex chases something sure.

And maybe he should worry about how much his hand shakes when it moves toward Elijah's lap, but Alex is so much more worried about keeping it to himself.

He curls his pinkie around Elijah's. "They came so close to losing each other, and all they'd had was this."

"Mmmm, they had a little more," Elijah says, threading their fingers together. "When they were brave enough, they could do this too."

Scarred and calloused hands. Something beautiful.

"And there was the very first night they met by the ware-houses—"

"The message that made us realize—"

"That they were two men," Alex mumbles, another several heartbeats spent staring down at where they've joined their hands against Elijah's thigh before he slowly pulls his away, turning his entire body toward Elijah's instead. He's cautious, maybe unnecessarily so, and Elijah makes no move to hurry him, his eyes only fluttering shut when Alex finally reaches up to comb his fingers through Elijah's curls, Alex leaning far enough forward to bring his mouth to Elijah's ear. "The scrape of stubble, for only a second or two."

"What happens when our two seconds have passed?" Elijah asks.

"I don't know. I have no idea what I'm doing, but I don't want to let go," Alex admits, too easily turning it into a plea as he drags his lips along the line of Elijah's jaw, stopping when he reaches the corner of his mouth. "No tequila today. Tell me about more."

"I already told you, if you want it, you're allowed to take it. You're allowed to be selfish."

"Elijah."

"Take it."

He does, just barely, his hand still tangled in Elijah's hair when they first kiss, a tiny and tentative thing that can't do more than promise the chance for another. Elijah continues to wait for him there, Alex trapped between the past and present in so many ways, too aware that he hasn't kissed anyone but his wife for the past twenty years just as he realizes the same might have been true for Peter way back when. But Alex aches for himself now and does what he can to soothe it, a little steadier when he kisses Elijah a second time, then a third, teasing him open with the tip of his tongue once he's lost count, and whimpering when Elijah eventually responds with more than small, silent answers to each of Alex's questions.

It's different, every sensation delivered by their kiss, the taste of Elijah's lips so new, the sounds he makes unfamiliar, and the relief humming through Alex's body something he didn't know he'd been seeking. Elijah's hand comes up to rest against Alex's hip, but it's not enough, and Alex keeps trying to move closer, nearly whining into Elijah's mouth, the warmth of it something he wants surrounding him. And then the grip at his side becomes more confident, reminding Alex of Elijah's size and his strength and making it so incredibly natural to do something Alex has never done before, his entire body shifting until he can straddle Elijah's lap.

"M'selfish," he mumbles in between kisses that have no real beginning or end.

Elijah doesn't hesitate to adjust to the new position, his hands slipping beneath Alex's shirt, warm and ready where he brackets his waist. And Alex still has one hand at the back of Elijah's head, the other landing at his shoulder and trying so hard to be gentle while he lets himself want and want and want.

"You're learning," Elijah says, his smile pressed against Alex's jaw before he kisses him there, moving to his neck in the next breath. Alex is curled over him and it's so easy to drop his head to the side when Elijah sucks at every sensitive spot there, too slow to demand what's already being given.

He understands it—already, even this soon—the difference between comfortable and *this*, moment after moment leaving him desperate for the next. His body is begging him for things he thinks he should be embarrassed to consider at all, his imagination too good to make him anything but pathetic with need now, but when his hips begin to roll forward, driven by instinct and little more, Elijah's hold on him tightens quickly, his mouth back to Alex's for a long kiss.

Still, it's enough to have Alex pull away, licking at his lips like Elijah's still there. "No?"

"I—you—" Elijah doesn't bother to catch his breath, dragging Alex back to him instead and distracting both of them with another kiss until Alex is nearly dizzy with it. "You said you have no idea what you're doing, but I—*Alex*."

"I *don't* know. I don't know anything."

Elijah reaches up with one hand to cradle the side of Alex's face, his thumb brushing over Alex's lower lip before he chases it away with his own. "But you're okay?"

"Yeah, but I don't—you said I could take it, but then you—are *you* okay?"

The laugh is soft and so quietly intense against Alex's mouth, felt at least as much as it's heard. "I'm far better than that, and yeah, you can take it all, anything you want, but not—I want you to go slow."

Alex blushes. "I wasn't going to—I wouldn't—not all of it."

"No, but even this. I want you to go slow."

"Because you think I'm not ready?"

The hand still under Alex's shirt coasts over his back, Elijah's eyes blazing a beautiful black-blue. "Because *we're* not ready. Even with everything I've—this isn't the same for me. I already know this isn't the same."

And Alex doesn't have a response for that, doesn't think he could speak if he tried, so he moves to take Elijah's face in both of his hands and pours everything he has into their kiss, every second of it devastating, but somehow made a little more perfect when they both know it won't become anything else. Elijah's arms are fully around him now, holding Alex tight against his own body, everything tender in a way Alex wouldn't have thought it could be, and they don't break apart again until Elijah has to get ready for work.

While he changes, Alex goes into the bathroom, unable to keep from smiling when he sees how fully wrecked he looks, already having admired how perfectly kiss-swollen Elijah's lips had been just a minute ago. And he waits near the front door until Elijah comes back out, nodding toward the books in his arms.

"We already know their first kiss comes next," Alex says. "Wonder what happens after that."

"You wanna come back tomorrow and find out?" Elijah asks.

"I don't know. That slow enough for you?"

Elijah takes a step closer, then another and another, pressing Alex back against the door and nipping at his bottom lip before he soothes it with a kiss. "It's perfect."

Chapter Eight

If anyone were to ask Alex what he did the rest of that night, there's no way he'd be able to tell them, those hours passing in such a blissful haze. He makes dinner and eats in front of the TV, a movie on even if he's paying no attention to it at all, and he stalls for as long as he can before he heads upstairs. There's no real need for it, but he takes a shower anyway, just to waste a little more time, then Alex turns to his crossword puzzles in lieu of any book that might have him staring at empty margins.

Elijah texts him to say goodnight.

Alex's sleep is mostly dreamless, and he doesn't know how that's possible.

The first thing he notices when he looks outside the next morning is the fog, such a normal thing here, but reminiscent of the day he met Elijah all the same. Alex goes for a run—his first in a while—and it feels so good, his body hungry and begging to be satiated.

He's ready to feed it at least a little more when he picks up lunch on the way to Elijah's a few hours later, his heartbeat far from under control when he knocks at the door.

"So much better than yesterday's pizza guy," Elijah teases as he lets Alex in.

He smiles. He exhales. He walks through the door and keeps moving. But the thing is, Alex doesn't know how to do this any more than he knows how to want, or how to slow down the wanting once he's started, or whatever other step comes next in a dance he never properly learned. He took a pretty girl to the movies when he was a dumb teenager, tripped over himself for a while after that to make himself fit into a role that maybe never really belonged to him, and now he's here, with no idea what to do when his second forever might have started last night.

"You sure? There's probably still time for me to get out of your way."

Elijah snags the hem of Alex's shirt and pulls him closer. "Don't want anyone else."

Their kiss is careful, intent enough to mean something but just light enough that they can let go, Alex easily getting settled on the patio again while Elijah grabs a couple of drinks. They talk just as they had the day before, so much to still find out about each other, both of them more eager now and holding nothing back while Poe looks up at them every now and then, like maybe he's absorbing some of it too. And when they're done eating, they trace yesterday's footsteps and land on the couch, ready to move on to the second pair of books.

"The first books covered what—a year and a half or so?" Alex asks.

"Yeah, something like that. So, we're probably in the late 1940s."

"And you think you saw Peter and Edgar together in the mid-90s?"

"On our trip to San Diego," Elijah says. "Yeah."

"Then even if these books somehow carry us through a few years—"

"There will still be about four decades of the story we won't know," Elijah finishes. "How they end up together all those years later, and why they never let anyone know how much they loved each other."

Something knocks at the back of Alex's head, a question or answer he can't quite hear, but he only fights with it for a moment before he offers something of a counterargument.

"I'm not sure there's that much mystery to be solved about why they never let anyone know," he says. "Two gay men, from entirely separate classes, only able to communicate through messages scribbled into the margins of books passed back and forth between them, and only able to touch in the middle of the night while they hid in the shadows of some shabby warehouses? And then Edgar being attacked, plus whatever other hell we don't even know about? Even as times changed, that's a lot of very quiet trauma to overcome."

"So, you think at a certain point they kept the secret because it's all they'd known?"

"I can't be sure, obviously, but it makes sense. Feral animals don't just become tame the moment you let them into a home."

Elijah nods, thoughtful. "And my grandpa knew at some point, so they weren't totally alone, but yeah, I—it just hurts knowing how much it hurt them. We look back and celebrate all the brave people in the communities that fought for a better life—for their chance to love out loud—but maybe we forget that the quiet ones weren't cowards."

"Nah, just victims who were already sacrificing their safety to have any moment of honesty at all."

"Okay," Elijah sighs, taking a deep breath to regroup. "Then we read on to see if we can learn more about how they get away from the late-night visits. And depending on how much is still unknown when we're done, I could always try talking to my mom again."

"You think that would go over okay?" Alex asks. "I don't want this to be any harder for you than it already is."

"She didn't seem all that bothered when I asked questions at the beginning of all this. She just kinda paused and then answered. Not sure she cares enough to worry about why I'm asking, and I wouldn't tell her about the books anyway."

"Didn't figure you would." Alex smiles, though it feels sad. "Okay, here was Peter's message about their first kiss, the one I read when I found the book that first weekend: *E, it feels rather perfect to start a new book today, with the ghost of your lips still on mine. I don't believe I have all the words to express the hunger I felt after indulging in that first taste, but I dream of the impossible world in which I could be truly satisfied.*"

"Definitely no way to know how long Uncle Edgar's recovery took, other than the 'weeks' mentioned at the end of the last book. We don't even know exactly what happened in the first place."

"Nope," Alex agrees. "But Peter took it as some kind of sign to stop being so afraid, all the restraint from before apparently gone once they were able to meet up again. How did Edgar respond?"

P, waiting for that first kiss was torture for my body and soul, but waiting now for all the others we might share is so much worse. I have nothing else to give but everything you already know is yours, but I'll be ready to try whenever you come to me, tonight or for the rest of our lives.

Alex glances up at Elijah as he finishes, then turns to the next entry in his book, another one he's already read, but not one he's shared yet.

E, I have so many sleepless nights now, most of them when I haven't been able to see you and cannot know how safe you are, but every one of them is worth it when we're together again and I can steal enough time to make myself believe you're still mine. I can't stop worrying about what could happen if we're ever caught, and how violently people could react to this love they don't understand, but I will continue to be there with you because it's the only place I can rest while wide awake.

"Yeah, maybe the restraint was gone, but I can't imagine that ongoing fear for my great grandfather," Elijah says. "Being apart for what we're assuming are long stretches in between, and not having any way to know if something happens. Just waiting any time there's a delivery and hoping Uncle Edgar would be there."

"Edgar would've been able to relax a little more, if relaxing were a thing anybody could do under these circumstances. I mean, Peter technically had more to lose, but he had a lot more to protect him, too."

"A wealthy widower with broad shoulders and a solid build was definitely less of a target. Not the kind of guy most people would've targeted for being gay the same way they had done to Edgar."

"But I'm guessing Edgar's about to reassure him that he's fine," Alex says.

"And you're right. Here it is: *P, I know I'll never be able to stop you from worrying after what happened to me, and maybe it would have been impossible long before that, but please know every day of my life is worth the fight if it means tomorrow could bring you back to me. And while it may feel like the shadow of the warehouse is the only place I can be yours, I ask you to remember that I am always yours, everywhere you go.*"

"Edgar was smoother in hidden messages than I've ever been a day in my life," Alex mutters.

"Eh, I don't know. Showing up at my garage sale two days in a row was pretty hot."

He laughs and elbows Elijah. "Hey, I just went out for some fresh air. Didn't know you were gonna sell me a love story."

"Is that what I did?"

"Certainly seems like it," Alex answers, but then he remembers something else and tilts his head. "That night you invited me to the bar, when you'd already figured out that they were gay, what happened right after I read those messages on your phone? Why did it seem like you were suddenly sorry I was there?"

For a second, Alex thinks maybe Elijah will deny there was anything wrong then, but after another moment or two, Elijah nods. "You want to know why I went from being so eager to share what I'd found to walking away from you."

"You walked away a couple of times, yeah. And you wouldn't tell me if you were okay, but you said you might have an answer if I was willing to wait a while."

"We're probably past a while by now."

"I think so," Alex agrees.

"I don't want to take anything away from their story. It's about them, it's—none of what we're reading is actually about me," Elijah says, scratching at an invisible spot on his jeans until Alex slides his hand under Elijah's and gives him something to hold. "But when I read those, I felt like it loosened something in my chest. Made it easier to breathe, just knowing maybe it wasn't just me. That I wasn't the only one in my family."

"I don't think it's ever wrong to connect with the things other people write—I mean, my entire career sort of relies upon it—and it's especially not wrong when those words were written by a great grandfather you actually met."

"Yeah, maybe. But I also already knew I liked you—a *lot*—and I didn't know if I was imagining that you might feel the same way. I couldn't tell whether I was just caught up in the story. So, I wanted you there, and I wanted to show you what I found, and I wanted it to make it easier for you to breathe, too."

Alex thinks back to that night, sitting next to the wall, the hard stool and the crispy fries and the cold beer and the sudden awareness of what they'd been reading, all of it colliding with what he'd already started to feel. He'd frozen there, he *knows* he had, and Elijah had left him to figure out the rest alone.

"I couldn't breathe at all."

"I noticed," Elijah says, an admission more than an accusation. "And then neither could I. I got worried that you were disappointed in what we'd read, like maybe a story about two gay men wasn't one you still wanted to follow."

"And you thought that if I was disappointed in what we'd read, then that might mean I'd also be disappointed in you. And uninterested in us."

"Which wasn't fair. I knew that even then," Elijah sighs. "But I think I'd built up a moment in my head where you'd read those messages and then look up at me and we'd just *know*, and instead you went cold, and I thought maybe I was so, so wrong."

"You kept coming back to me, though."

"I did, yeah. You didn't leave and I couldn't stay away."

Alex cocks his head. "The other night, when I stopped by after my retreat, I pulled you close to me, and you said something about me being the one still in the dark—that you didn't care who saw us. Does that mean you're out at work?"

"Mmmm, I wouldn't say I'm *out* out, but I don't really hide, and anyone paying attention probably made assumptions a while ago. Tyler knows for sure. He's stood too close to me too many nights to think I have any sort of preference about who I might want to take home."

"Have you taken *him* home?"

"Tyler?" Elijah asks, his eyebrows high. "No, I—no. He's straight and I haven't screwed up that badly in a while."

"Did those women at the bar really ask about me? That first night, when things got weird."

Elijah chuckles. "Oh, absolutely. And that definitely didn't help while I was having a whole crisis about my feelings for you. But you didn't seem to care when I told you about them, so I relaxed a little."

"You told them we're friends."

"Aren't we?"

It's what Alex has told himself from the beginning, and he won't begrudge Elijah the question now, even if he won't answer it either. He takes a deep breath and leans close enough to kiss Elijah instead, squeezing his hand before letting it go and turning back to the book in his lap, his fingers light against the page as he reads another one familiar to him from those first couple of days.

E, I am so sorry, darling. I've been ill and at home and so far from you, and I can only hope you will be back to take this book from me when I've finally returned to my office again. And perhaps I can dream of seeing relief in your eyes rather than the reluctance our relationship might deserve. If there is anything certain, it's that I would give anything to have you here with me, the chill unbearable without your love to keep me warm.

"So much for Uncle Edgar being able to relax about my great grandfather's wellbeing. Guess he disappeared for a while, too."

"And however much time has passed since Edgar was hurt, another lengthy separation had to bring them right back to that fear that it could be over for them," Alex says. "There were plenty of other ways to communicate, but none they would have considered safe, so what would've happened if Edgar had just stopped delivering to the firm? Would Peter have had to risk multiple trips to the docks to find him there? Would he have prepared himself to let Edgar go?"

Elijah nods down at the page. "It sort of sounds like he already had. 'The reluctance our relationship might deserve' was a pretty carefully constructed wall."

"He was giving Edgar an out, or at least steeling himself for the possibility Edgar would want one."

Something about that stings, and Elijah only hums before he goes on.

P, please don't apologize any further for making me wait for tonight, and the chance to hold you again. Though we did nothing more, having you in my arms for longer than we usually dare was enough, my relief there for you to claim as yours. I think I could've stood there until dawn. Someday, maybe we can have that, too.

Elijah frowns for a moment, and Alex has the fleeting thought that he might be able to kiss it away, but then Elijah corrects it himself and looks at Alex. "Every one of these messages is so damn romantic. Poetic, really. And on the one hand it feels like it's kind of over the top, like maybe they should be so much more casual than this after what might be close to two years together, but then I get chills when I think about how little time they really had."

"Yeah, their two years together wouldn't have been anything like that," Alex says. "And these messages are literally half of their entire relationship. They feel intense to us because they had written them that way, so many emotions condensed into the only moments they got."

"And knowing that is really kind of beautiful, right up until it hurts again."

Oh, E, seeing you tonight was the very greatest pleasure, the breath passed between us enough to keep me alive until the day I can give it all back again. It almost felt like we kissed so long that the night could have led us straight into the next. I only wish we could be together elsewhere, my gratitude for our shadows waning when I know there are empty rooms here at my home. When there is so much time we're still not allowed to claim as ours. Touches that remain forbidden.

"How old would your grandpa have been around this

time?" Alex asks.

"Mmmm, about 14, I think?"

"So, there was still no way to bring Edgar home," he sighs. "Go ahead."

"Looks like the same thing was on Uncle Edgar's mind. *P, my love, I would never ask you to put J at risk, but he won't be at home with you forever, and whatever remains forbidden now may not always be. You just told me about an organization only whispered about, rumors of men like us who are no longer content to hide. To be clear, I will hide with you for as long as you need. But I'll also dream of a time when others no longer make that decision for us.*"

Alex rolls his head toward him. "Your grandpa was J?"

"James, yeah. Or I guess I heard most people call him Jimmy by the time I was old enough to notice, but he always introduced himself as James, so maybe it's what he preferred."

"Sounds like a familiar story," Alex says. "Was he the one who called you Elijah?"

Elijah smiles. "Protecting me *and* my name."

"Seeing you. Honoring the person you are instead of the person everyone else assumed you should be."

"And I have no way to thank him for it now."

"No, you don't," Alex agrees. "So, maybe you just honor him back by living the way he knew you could."

"The way they couldn't," Elijah says, his touch reverent when he drags his fingertips over the faded ink in front of him. "Even when the decisions became theirs."

"You understand why they stayed quiet, but it hurts you, too."

"I think it ended up hurting everyone."

Alex swallows against all the layers of that, the knowledge that Peter and Edgar's decision to keep their relationship a secret, even a while after they really would've had to, affected Elijah's grandpa and his mother and then him, an accidental domino tipped over decades ago. He closes his eyes, opens them again, and reads.

E, we meet more often now and exchange these books far less, eager to be with each other more than we need to document the same. And I truly cannot write about tonight, with no words to describe a touch I've never known and the respect to avoid trying to describe it at all. I'll only thank you for letting every sound I made land gently on your tongue, and for letting me taste more moments later.

"Well," Alex starts, clearing his throat. "That was—something."

"You don't think they—"

"No, not there. Not like that. But still, they—"

"Yeah," Elijah says. "But it wasn't sudden. I mean, even taking into account the broader timeline, this message makes it sound like they've been able to signal meetings without having to rely on the books. Probably could've for a while, but just hadn't broken the habit."

"Now the books are just for the occasional thoughts they want to share," Alex notes. "And the physical relationship is growing."

"Which means these two books might carry us further than we'd guessed."

So, they continue to read, and while it had taken them nearly a month to stumble through the beautiful beginning of another couple's love story, Alex and Elijah continue to race through the middle of it in a single afternoon, their pace reckless when they should be terrified of where it all ends. The tone of Peter and Edgar's messages certainly tips toward risqué for a while, far from explicit, but just enough for it to be clear that they wanted more than they could have, even as they started to have far more than they were allowed. And as months went by, maybe another year or two passing in the pages they turn, Alex and Elijah begin to sense that Peter and Edgar's lingering reluctance had become stirred with newfound hope. James would be moving away in the next few years, even if they suspected he already knew more than he'd ever said, and there was still danger everywhere, even if there were the first hints of fights to be won. There were the early rumblings of places to go and communities to join and precautions to take, but Peter and Edgar kept a tight hold on the sliver of safety they already knew, pushing the boundaries of it until it seemed like they were finally ready to leave it behind, a new chapter beckoning them forward.

By the time Alex closes his book, Elijah taking another several seconds to do the same, he aches with the realization that Peter and Edgar were so close to something that might have become everything, but that there's nothing more of their story left to read. They both set their books down, Alex giving his back to Elijah now that they're done.

"The end?" Alex whispers.

"I don't want it to be."

"You have to go to work soon," Alex says, standing and holding out his hand for Elijah to take.

He does exactly that, and then lets go once he can cradle Alex's face instead, his kiss devastating. "Don't want to go anywhere. Don't know *how* to go anywhere. And I want you to stay."

Alex's fingers catch in the material of Elijah's shirt. "I want to stay, too. But Elena will be back tonight."

They stumble toward the front door, an entire afternoon spent in the past leaving them only with a few minutes of the present, and Elijah wraps his arms around Alex there.

"Are you gonna tell them?"

Alex's first instinct is to ask Elijah what he means, except that they both already know *exactly* what he means, and pretending otherwise might be one of the worst things Alex could do. Unfortunately, what he says instead isn't any better.

"I don't know."

It's a lie, bitter on his tongue and left to dissolve there when Elijah stopped kissing him before the words were fully formed. The answer is no—it was the answer before Elijah asked and still is now—because Alex spent the last two decades failing his best friend and he's terrified of screwing up again, and for as long as he can feel all of Peter and Edgar's mistakes living in between his own heartbeats, he thinks mimicking their silence might be the only thing keeping him from denying himself entirely. Alex has only just learned what it's like to want, and it twists him up to imagine anyone else watching closely enough to catch the moment that goes wrong too, and whatever dishonesty Alex can taste inside his own mouth, Elijah eventually leans back in to steal a little bit of it for himself, as if he really needs confirmation that it exists at all.

"Okay," Elijah says when he pulls away.

Alex doesn't think it is.

Chapter Nine

Cassidy doesn't go any further than the curb while she watches Elena roll her little suitcase through the front door, and while there's nothing wrong with her staying behind, the decision leaves Alex without his breath for an extra heartbeat or two. It's representative of too many things at once—Cassidy's new relationship with Michael and the boundaries she's drawn, the achingly empty house Alex lives in now when he wants to be anywhere with Elijah instead, Elena's ability to transition between them with no need for anything more than a smile and a hug on either side. So many things have changed these past several months, but Alex has become someone different just in the last four weeks, and he's not sure he fits here in his doorway or anywhere else.

Elena helps just by being there, of course, because Alex refuses to let any of this rain down on her little world any more than it already has. They have a good night and a good week and however much he is still trapped by the tendrils of a love story he's barely finished, and another he's barely started, his daughter never fails to make him smile. And Alex doesn't think too hard about what it means that he's bitten his tongue a hundred times, or that Elena might have noticed how close he came to bleeding when she asked how Elijah was doing, but one way or another, he's able to keep his worlds separate until Friday night. He and Elijah have texted a handful of times, almost distantly flirty about it, but that's been enough until Elena is in the restroom at the pizza parlor, and Alex's beer has tipped him toward needy, and he doesn't have to worry about an immediate reaction to that because Elijah's already at work anyway.

Come over tonight after work? Just for a little while

There's no response, which is fine. It's good. Elena comes back and they finish up dessert and they go home to blankets and stuffies and a movie. And then his phone makes a noise and his heart thumps in his chest, a reaction wholly disproportionate to the two words Alex reads.

You sure?

Yeah. Please

He hears nothing else until after Elena's been asleep for hours, and he thinks he must have drifted off too, because it's so late when his phone startles him, and he knocks it to the floor in his attempt to pull it from the coffee table. Alex blinks at whatever is still playing on the TV, then looks down at the message.

Leaving work now if you still want me to stop by

Alex fumbles through an answer, his vision still blurry.

Yeah I'll unlock the door for you. just come in

As soon as that's done, Alex turns off the TV and hurries

upstairs to brush his teeth, pretending it matters what he looks like when he still has creases from the couch pillow on his cheek. He'd changed into pajamas a while ago, but it won't surprise Elijah to find him like this in the middle of the night, and he only splashes water on his face before he returns to the living room to lie back down. He keeps his eyes closed until he hears the soft click of the door and tries to smile, even if he's too tired to do much of anything.

Elijah kicks off his shoes, his work shirt already untucked when he steps toward the couch, blond curls everywhere, and his hand squeezing the back of his neck as he looks down.

"Why am I here?" he asks, the question soft, even if it feels like it cracks something open in the silent room.

"C'mere," Alex mumbles. "I can rub your neck for you."

"Pretty sure that wasn't your plan when you texted me at dinnertime," Elijah says, though he sits down as soon as Alex makes room for him, the blanket carelessly draped across the back of the couch now. "You okay?"

"Yeah, just missed you all week and didn't want to have to wait 'til Monday. Take off your shirt."

"Alex."

"No?"

"Not no, but—" He sighs and unbuttons quickly, shrugging out of the shirt and setting it on the coffee table with his phone, keys, and wallet.

And he's—his body is—it's not like Alex couldn't have imagined. Not even like he *hasn't* imagined it, having already been wrapped up in Elijah a time or two. But even more than a little drowsy, seeing Elijah half undressed on his couch is enough to have Alex reaching for him in a way he doesn't think he's ever reached for anyone before, a shame all on its own. Elijah shifts until he can turn his back on Alex and let him stare, and Alex manages nothing more until he curves his hands over Elijah's shoulders and catches him shivering beneath his touch.

Alex tries to remember that he's not as alone as he sometimes feels.

There's another tattoo, gentle ocean waves wrapped around Elijah's bicep, and it's only because there's so much more bare skin in front of him that Alex saves his admiration of it for another time. For now, his thumbs press into tight muscles, and he works up Elijah's neck and all the way down his spine, any of the chill Elijah might have carried in from the cold outside gone under the warmth of Alex's hands. Neither one of them speaks, though they don't bother to stop the small sounds they haven't tamed, and Alex thinks maybe he could do this until morning if he wasn't so scared of each minute as it comes. But then his touch slows, and he sees the goosebumps on Elijah's skin, and he leans close enough to kiss them, far too tired to tell his body it can't have what's right there.

"God, you're so—"

He doesn't know how to finish the sentence, so many possibilities on the tip of a tongue licking at the back of Elijah's neck now, his hands flat against Elijah's back and then his ribs and then his chest. His mouth lands at Elijah's ear and he could probably say anything, but he bites down on his lip instead—a move copied from the man in front of him now—and the sting of it only lasts until Elijah turns in his arms and opens his mouth for a kiss, the next several seconds closer to filthy than anything they've done so far.

"Why am I here?" Elijah asks again.

But Alex doesn't have a better answer now than he did the first time around because saying that he missed Elijah and didn't want to wait until Monday is true, but it's not nearly all of it, and he just needs this certainty for as long as he can have it, something too close to slipping through his fingers altogether. He gives and he takes until it becomes a beautifully mutual thing, and as their tongues drag together, Alex feels Elijah begin to push him backward, Elijah's weight pressing him into the cushions and Alex left to gasp into his mouth. There's not really room for them here, not for long, but Alex doesn't know what he expects them to do anyway, his body screaming for something it's never been given before. And Elijah is so sturdy and solid and strong on top of Alex, everything about that heady enough to promise him he'll be safe when he finally puts a fantasy or two into words.

For now, he claws at Elijah's back, and it leaves Elijah rocking against him, Alex burning when he realizes his pajama pants won't hide any of his secrets.

Maybe he's only trying to keep them because lifelong habits are hard to break.

But he has to bury a moan in Elijah's skin when he's sure he can feel Elijah's cock responding too, Alex arching off the couch in search of more, even when he already knows he can't have it yet.

"I can't—not here—I just want—" Alex stammers, stealing another kiss before he chases Elijah's body again and tries to go on. "I can't stop."

There's not much there, but it's enough to make Elijah go mostly still, his body heavy against Alex's, but his mouth light at his jaw. "We can always stop. Always."

Alex blinks up at him, slow and stupid. "You drove all the way over here. You live so much closer to the bar, and you drove all the way over here."

"Missed you, too," Elijah admits, his hair even messier from where Alex must have touched him without thinking, and Elijah's fingers comb through his curls once he's finally pushed himself away from where Alex still lies, his eyes flickering toward a jacket Elena left draped over an armchair. "Have you told them?"

He's grateful Elijah isn't close enough to feel the way his entire body tightens, but Alex must give something away because Elijah backs up even more, falling against the couch and tipping his head backward until he can stare at the ceiling, discomfort in every breath he takes.

"It's not—it has nothing to do with you," Alex tries, though his *it's not you, it's me* defense sounds terrible even as he offers it up. And maybe he could argue that he doesn't know what there is to tell when so little has happened between them, except that it would've sounded weak enough last Sunday and would be laughable now. Alex is already upside down and in danger of falling somewhere from there, and he could handwrite a hundred messages of his own about exactly that.

Elijah just sighs. "I should head home. We both need some sleep."

Alex wants to sigh too, because while he's sure he's doing something wrong by holding on to those hundred unwritten messages, he's still at least a little confused about why Elijah seems *this* bothered by Alex keeping them to himself for now. They haven't even talked about what *them* entails, and Alex sure as hell hasn't figured out who he is apart from Elijah or whether he's supposed to have a name for it or how he's supposed to explain it to anyone else. He trusts Cassidy, maybe more than anyone other than his sister, but there's something scary about thinking she's known too many things about him for too long and still left him to put those pieces together alone—very few of them the result of something she broke, but so many of his feelings too sharp to pick up with his bare hands. And Elena's been forced to adapt to a few new realities lately, so no matter how much she and Elijah had hit it off over bowls of chili, it would be careless to do anything but pause and consider how this might affect her.

Plus, Elijah shouldn't want to push Alex out of whatever proverbial closet he's in, right? It doesn't make sense when it's unlikely he would've demanded that Peter and Edgar do anything at all.

But it's the middle of the night, and Elijah *should* head home, and they both *do* need sleep, so Alex follows him to the door and kisses him goodbye, the click of the lock behind Elijah quiet and somehow still loud enough to echo until dawn.

Until the morning fog clears and reveals nothing.

And maybe he can still hear it all day Saturday and then Sunday, too, Alex glad he'd already planned to take Cassidy's cue and stay at the curb when he drops Elena off, because he's fairly certain he hasn't stopped flinching at the sound and doesn't feel like answering questions about his own telltale heart.

Alex doesn't hear from Elijah again until Monday afternoon, while he's at the office.

In the neighborhood today. can I take you out to dinner?

And that's—it's a date. He's being asked out on an official date. Alex knows it instinctively, and his entire body responds in conflicting ways, his stomach turning while his skin warms, and his breath catching while his fingers ache, and he wants and fears all of it at once. It's a date and a test of some kind, and while Alex is certain it wouldn't include plans to make out over their plates—while there would be no grand announcement sung like an all too happy birthday song—he feels so damn transparent already, and he doesn't know if he's ready for an audience of strangers any more than he's prepared for a conversation with the people he loves.

There's no major risk of being hurt by anyone around them, at most a single disapproving glance among dozens of other diners who won't care at all, but Alex thinks it would leave him bleeding anyway.

Maybe they'd get a smile of support, but Alex thinks that could cut him even deeper.

So, after frustrating Elijah on his own damn couch, Alex still can't pretend to be ready for anything more, but he's too far gone on Elijah to settle for nothing at all.

Can you come here instead? A quiet dinner at home would be nice

Sure

That single word carries the same tone as when Elijah had said goodbye Friday night—or early Saturday morning—and Alex knows it's his fault. That he's the one who could make it better. But he shakes his head and taps out a response.

Great see you then

He finishes up with everything that needs to be done at work before he can go home, then he ducks out and stops at the store on his way to pick up a bottle of wine and some fresh bread. He'll make pasta and a salad and turn on some music and make this as romantic as it can be when Elijah will probably be disappointed when he first arrives, dating a coward who hasn't learned how to do anything but apologize with food and a kiss.

Dating? Is that even what they're doing here? Can they be *dating* if Alex won't let them go on a *date*? Is he just supposed to tell Cass and Elena that he's found someone he keeps hidden at home?

Again, is he really supposed to tell them anything when he's only known Elijah for a little over a month?

When there's a knock at the door, Alex rinses his hands, throws a dish towel over his shoulder, and hurries to let Elijah in.

"Hey," he says, steadier than he feels when he pulls Elijah close enough to kiss.

"Hey to you, too," Elijah smiles against him. "It smells incredible in here."

The truth is, Elijah smells incredible too, probably having just showered, his curls still damp and his skin warm and reminding Alex of the fall. He looks casual and not, a button up left open over a tight shirt and snug jeans, probably toning down his appearance once he knew they'd be staying in, though Alex can't dodge the thought that he'd brought something with him to change into that afternoon, or whenever he was "in the neighborhood."

"You were at your grandpa's house?" Alex asks as they make their way into the kitchen, Elijah snooping at everything Alex has been preparing.

"Yeah, I kinda took a break after the garage sales, but I've gotta finish clearing everything out of there and get a few things fixed up before we're ready to put it on the market after the holidays."

"Who actually got the title to the house after he died?"

"The three grandkids—my sister, my brother, and me," Elijah answers, watching as Alex tastes the sauce before he moves over to slice the bread. "My mom was an only child, so it's just us."

"And you said your brother lived there with his family?"

"Just for a while, yeah. It was good timing because he was looking for a new job and they didn't really want to renew the lease on the place they had. Probably helped with some of the cleaning out, actually, because he and his wife boxed a lot of stuff and moved it to the garage and den just to get it out of their way. Gave me a head start, at least."

"But that's it? You're really not gonna try to keep it?" Alex pushes, handing over the bottle of wine and nodding toward the glasses so Elijah can pour.

Elijah takes the bottle and shrugs. "Seems kinda crazy, doesn't it? To buy them out of their share just to sit in a big house full of memories?"

"Guess you kinda got your fill of memories handwritten into some classic novels, huh?"

"Kinda did, yeah," Elijah huffs.

They carry everything to the dining room table and get settled there, lifting their glasses of wine to toast something left unsaid before they take a sip and then begin to eat. There's nothing but small talk for a while—gossip from the bar about people Alex doesn't know and a quick retelling of the movie Alex and Elena watched on Saturday and a few things in be-tween—but then Alex lets the wine bring him back to the topic that gave them a reason to have a real conversation on that foggy Sunday morning.

"It's been a week now, since we finished the books," Alex says. "Any more thoughts about it all?"

Elijah takes a bite, and Alex assumes he's buying himself more time to answer, though he doesn't give up much when he does. "Too many, probably."

"Care to share?"

"This food is incredible," Elijah tells him. "The wine, too."

"Sounds like that's a no."

"I don't know what else to say, Alex," Elijah sighs, putting his fork down with an unnecessary clatter. "I really don't. What we read was a beautiful and painful story, but there is still so much of it missing, which means I have no goddamn idea how I'm really supposed to feel about it now. I love that they loved each other, but I hate that it made it hard for the rest of my family to do the same. I hate that I didn't know any of this while my grandpa was alive, and I love that I was able to learn it all with you. I love that so many things inside me finally feel right, and I hate that every time I look at you, it seems like maybe you're still afraid that nothing ever will."

"Elijah," Alex croaks. "It's not—"

"About me," he interrupts. "Yeah, that's what you said after you had my entire body grinding against yours in the middle of the night. And I'm not *mad* at you. I need you to know that. This isn't me issuing an ultimatum that you publish an announcement in one of your columns, or else. I'm just sad, and

I don't know how much of it is because of my great grandfather and Uncle Edgar's story, or how much of it is because we seem to be on our way to repeating it now."

"It's only been a month for us."

"All years start that way," Elijah notes.

"But you said you didn't think they were cowards for staying quiet all that time."

"I don't. I think they looked at the world around them, and at everything they had with each other, and then made what they thought was the best possible decision for them at the time," Elijah says. "You're not them, though. *We're* not them. And I can't figure out who you think you're making decisions for right now, but I'm not convinced it's you."

Alex looks up at the ceiling, like there's any help to be found there, and then lets his head roll until he's staring at a closed window. "I got everything wrong for twenty fucking *years*, Elijah. I hurt the people I love, and now I—maybe it's not about making a decision. Maybe I'm scared shitless that I'll hurt *you* and end up being the bad guy all over again."

"You've gotta stop pretending that's how any of this works," Elijah hisses. "There didn't have to be a bad guy or good guy in your separation from Cassidy. It just was. And there doesn't have to be a bad guy or good guy with us either. We just are."

Alex chews on his lip. "And Peter and Edgar just were."

"They just were."

"Except that we don't know that for sure," Alex tells him, tilting his head as he toys with his glass. "We got as far as we could with their story, but we don't know what happened after that or whether they even stayed together. You have a fuzzy memory of seeing your great grandfather with another old man, way back when the zoo was a much higher priority for you. But that could've been anyone—a neighbor or a friend or, hell, maybe Peter fell in love again. I don't know, but I'm not convinced Elena could tell you much about the adults at get-togethers we had a few years ago, so we're putting an awful lot of faith in a memory from over 25 years ago now. Maybe we want to believe in a happy ending that never came close."

Alex can tell Elijah wants to argue that point, but there's not much he can say. "Fine. But however many times they might have loved and lost, neither one of them ever had to be a villain in those stories. And you can't keep worrying about being a villain now. It will get *you* nowhere, and I have no idea where it leaves *me*."

In the months since Cassidy moved out, the house has been painfully quiet for more nights than Alex could count, but the silence is so much harder to take when all he wants to do is scream and can't find any of the strength it would take to be that loud.

"You're really not mad that I haven't told Cass and Elena about us? You're really not mad that I wouldn't go out on a date with you tonight?" Alex mumbles, the strongest thing he can choke out when he isn't sure whether he's hopeful or skeptical.

Elijah finishes his wine and then shakes his head. "No, I'm

really, really not."

"So, what happens now?"

"I don't know," Elijah sighs. "Is there any dessert?"

Alex finds it in him to chuckle and forces himself to get up from the table despite all the weight on his shoulders and how difficult it is to shake any of it off. He ducks back into the kitchen and comes back a minute later with the bottle of wine and a handful of fun-size chocolate from the stash Elena gathered on a stupidly successful night of trick-or-treating.

"'Tis the season," he says as he drops the candy bars between them and refills their glasses. "I'll apologize to her later, though I'm not convinced she'll notice anything is missing."

It's all just enough for them to let the rest of their conversation slide, and somehow their hands find each other against the table while they drink in mostly silence, though Alex isn't actually sure which one of them made the first move. They don't let go, though, not until the bottle is empty, and they take a while longer to move from there, unsure of where to go.

"I'm gonna head back over to my grandpa's house for the night," Elijah says, answering a question Alex is almost positive he didn't ask.

"You don't have to. I mean, you could stay here," Alex offers.

The look Elijah gives him makes him want to take it back, Alex certain that he's screwed up again, when he really just doesn't want Elijah to go. He wants this mess, whatever it is, and he thinks maybe if they say goodbye tonight, it will hurt in a way that isn't guaranteed to heal. And then Elijah pushes himself away from the table and stands just to shuffle across the house, his fingers still threaded through Alex's as he wriggles back into his shoes and then falls back against the front door.

"I definitely cannot stay here," he finally says.

He doesn't do anything else either, though. He doesn't turn to leave, and he doesn't drop Alex's hand, and he doesn't look away, and when Alex closes the space between them and tilts his head for a kiss, Elijah doesn't stop him. Alex needs this, and maybe so does Elijah, this one thing that might be familiar to them already. Every other step Alex takes seems to be set in the middle of a carnival funhouse, uneven ground and mirrors that lie, and no obvious way to make it to the other side, but kissing Elijah is something quick to warm his body and leave it believing it could have so much more.

It's not even tentative now, the first touch enough to have Elijah's mouth open, Alex's tongue there to taste wine and chocolate and a sound he gives right back. They must not be holding hands anymore because Elijah's touch is gentle at Alex's back, first over his shirt and then under it, where he skates up and down Alex's spine with his fingertips. Alex's fingers are buried in Elijah's hair again because he can't help himself, and he doesn't know how he's able to press himself any more tightly against Elijah's body, but he needs something firm when everything else is so incredibly soft. It's the wine, he thinks. It's what makes each second syrupy sweet. But Alex can't actually care about it for long, Elijah's tongue sliding against his while they hold each other at his front door for a very long time.

Elijah leaves eventually, but neither of them says goodbye, and Alex doesn't know if that's how any story is supposed to end, except that he can't help but remember Elijah's confession from the day they learned each other's names.

Maybe I'm too good at it—at letting go. Giving up. Walking away.

Chapter Ten

You wanna come over for dinner again?

Alex sends the text around lunchtime and tries to push the phone away so he doesn't keep staring at it, but Elijah's response is too quick.

Thanks but I've gotta take care of some stuff around here.

It's not a surprise somehow, how easily Elijah blows him off, and Alex has a hard time knowing why he's upset by something he should have expected all along. He vaguely remembers Elijah telling him that inevitable things can still suck, and this definitely does, the disappointment on his face apparently enough to have Steven stop by Alex's desk to make sure he's okay.

He's not. Or maybe he's always been fine. But Alex wants to be so much better than that now.

He refocuses on work the rest of that afternoon and runs too many errands on his way home. On Wednesday, Alex goes to the office early and jogs around the track at the neighborhood park when he gets home, and he avoids the detours that could take him to Elijah's grandpa's house. Thursday brings Steven by his desk again, with a happy hour invitation

Alex accepts, and he's careful to avoid getting drunk enough or sad enough or stupid enough to leave a voicemail he'd regret. Friday is weirdly fine, and the kind of busy he doesn't mind when his job is mostly predictable, and his mind needs somewhere safe to wander.

Through the entire week, all his texts to Elijah are answered within a reasonable amount of time, but nothing either of them has to say is more meaningful than something Alex could send to Elena's fourth grade teacher, and he can't help but wonder whether an actual fight would feel any better, a blatantly bleeding wound maybe better than the ache of a phantom limb.

As if it's gone in search of an answer, it's Alex's body that wakes him in the middle of Friday night, his hips grinding downward into his mattress while a moaned name gets mostly smothered by his pillow, and he wants to cry because he can't do this now. He can't be desperate for Elijah's touch when they aren't even talking the way they should, but Alex is only caged by bars he's very carefully placed one by one, and he finally gives in to the need to kick at a couple of them, rolling onto his back and stroking himself over his boxer briefs until it's not enough. Alex shoves his boxers out of the way and thrusts into his own hand, already so fucking close and hating that everything could be exactly this easy if he would only allow it to be. He imagines Elijah on top of him again, and he thinks about Elijah's fingers and Elijah's tongue and Elijah's cock, and that's all it takes before he's coming all over his hand and onto his bare stomach, his body shaking with something too close to a sob until Alex is on his feet just to force himself out of a moment that must be unfair to at least one of them.

By late Saturday afternoon, Alex is just frustrated enough to keep rattling the bars of his cage, and maybe to keep being a little unfair too, stuck on the idea of seeing Elijah after five days apart. It's not the same as a date out in public, but Alex decides that making another appearance at the bar has the chance to scare the hell out of him almost as much, and perhaps Elijah will see it for the small step it is.

Alex's shower lasts too long, and getting dressed afterward seems to take even longer, everything about the process making him feel increasingly bare even when the exact opposite is happening. It's not all that late when he leaves home, and the traffic treats him well enough, giving him hope that maybe the bar isn't all that much more crowded than the streets, Saturday night or not. That maybe he and Elijah can talk, however selfish that might be.

There's music coming from inside as he walks up the sidewalk toward it, and Alex realizes he'd forgotten about the live band there once a week. He considers turning around, but then someone coming out of the bar holds the door open for him, and there's no real option but to thank them and take what's been offered. Dodging a handful of people hanging out near the makeshift stage, Alex notices two bartenders he hasn't seen before, then Tyler, and then Elijah, just returning from the back and finding Alex immediately, like there was any way he could've known.

There's some kind of smile there, but it takes Alex a moment to find it.

The table he's sat at the first two times is taken now, but he's impressed enough to find another one open next to it, most of the crowd in the room seeming to gravitate toward the patio and the music and the bar itself, Alex's dark wall there only for the people like him who don't have anywhere else to go.

He slides onto the stool only a few seconds before a coaster and beer land in front of him.

"I'm not really working anywhere but behind the bar tonight," Elijah says.

Alex assumes it's the truth, but he's not sure what to do with it. He looks around, blinking at the new view of everything, so much the same while it's also just different enough to make him a little dizzy.

"Okay. Does that mean I should stay or go?"

Elijah shakes his head, the weight of something else slowing him down. "It doesn't mean anything, Alex. Just letting you know where I'll be."

He's gone again, as smoothly as he'd appeared, back to work as Eli, with his wide smile and bright eyes and the ability to charm every person in front of him at once. Alex watches, as much to see whether a seat might open up there as for any other reason, but nobody moves away from Elijah, and Alex can't imagine why they would. It's a convenient excuse, of course, a bullshit explanation for why he remains exactly where he is when he could be anywhere he really wants to be. Tyler stops by eventually—whether to check on him professionally or otherwise, Alex doesn't know—but he waves off a second beer and thanks him for the trouble and finishes what he's got while nobody bothers to watch him all that closely.

Then Alex slips some cash under his empty glass, nods one more thank you to Tyler, and leaves the bar.

The drive home is all loud music and rolled down windows on a crisp, windy night, and he doesn't hear the text he wouldn't have seen until later anyway. But when he picks up his phone after he's parked in his driveway, he couldn't look away from Elijah's name if he tried.

Please let me know when you're home safe

So he does, and then he goes inside to do just about anything but sleep.

He's a zombie the next morning, but there are no more messages from Elijah, and Alex forces himself out of the house for a run on legs that spend the entire time screaming at him. He eats and tastes nothing and showers and feels little, but Cassidy will drop Elena off that night, and while it's not even a little bit fair for him to rely on his kid to cheer him up, Alex is grateful for the easy reason to smile for a week, fully unsure what he'll do with his free time after that. Thanksgiving is coming up, and he's not sure he's dreaded a day like this in a very, very long time, his entire family poised to push and pull and observe and condemn, all in the name of love.

But that will be then, and this is now, and when he hears

Cassidy and Elena pull up outside, he moves to the front door and opens it for his daughter.

And Cass is there, too.

"Hey, I didn't think we were walking her to the door anymore," he mumbles stupidly, Elena already running past him and upstairs to put her stuff away.

Cassidy smiles. "No, we're not. Not really. But I wanted to talk to you about something and now—now I'm kinda wondering if what I was going to talk to you about is the same reason you look like—"

She trails off and sort of waves her hand toward his face, but it's unnecessary when he can assume just how terrible he looks, though he's avoided mirrors all day just for the sake of sparing himself some of the probably well-earned pain.

"I'm flattered," he says as he backs up and holds the door wide open. "You want to come in?"

"Sure."

"You want a drink?"

"Sure."

Alex nods and moves into the kitchen, grateful when he finds an unopened bottle of Jameson he thinks Cassidy probably should've taken with her when she moved out, and he returns to her side with two glasses in hand just as Elena skips back down the stairs.

"Hey, bug, how about you grab our blankets and get started with the TV while mommy and I go out back to talk for a little bit?" he says, turning toward his daughter even as he presses the drink into Cassidy's waiting hand.

Elena looks back and forth between them, and Cassidy is quick to reassure her. "We're just talking, babe."

"And I'll make us some popcorn as soon as we come back inside, okay?" Alex offers.

His daughter still looks a little skeptical, the last several talks between her parents resulting in their impending divorce, but she's been bought off by a bribe or ten before and it works again for now.

"Yeah, okay," she agrees.

He and Cass make their way outside and close the sliding door most of the way behind them, the night cold, but the patio heater quick to change that for them as they sit down, everything about this so painfully familiar when it's nothing like it was before. Alex looks out over what used to be their backyard and takes a long sip from his glass.

"So," she starts, and somehow he already knows what the next word will be, even while he isn't prepared for it at all, the sound foreign on his ex's tongue. "Elijah."

"Elijah," he echoes.

"He was your early morning walk."

"My new habit," he confirms. "Elena told you."

It's not exactly a question, but she shrugs and answers. "Not in so many words, but she's used the phrase 'Daddy's friend, Elijah' enough times for me to wonder. Mentioned that he came over for dinner, too."

"Yeah, I guess I've heard plenty about Michael."

"Ah, but she and Michael have never met," she says. "Which is what I originally wanted to talk to you about. Introducing our kid to significant others without a heads up about it."

Alex looks over at her, startled by at least a couple of things she said and doing his best to stay calm while the thump of his heart underscores his attempt at a response. "I—I'll admit I hadn't thought about it one way or another, and that's—I didn't realize she and Michael hadn't met yet, but also I swear I didn't—I really had no idea what Elijah and I were going to become when I invited him over that night. And for what it's worth, I'm not sure we're significant anything now."

"Yeah, the fact that you look like shit kinda gave that much away."

"Thanks."

"Of course," she murmurs. "Wanna tell me about it?"

His head is still turned in her direction, so he catches all the sincerity in her offer, and it threatens to take his breath away. She hasn't looked away either, this person who has known him better than anyone else for more than half his life, and she just waits for him to decide what he's going to do.

She's not the only one who might be waiting, and Alex sighs at that before he chases the realization with a sip of whiskey.

"His grandpa lived a few streets over from here, died a couple of years ago, and Elijah has been cleaning out his house. I went for a walk when he was having a garage sale, and I stopped to buy a few things."

"And got one hell of a deal, huh?"

He starts to chuckle at that, but then remembers his goal that morning and laughs a little more. "Funny thing about it was that I actually bought books I was going to give to you for Christmas. Some leather-bound classics."

Cassidy frowns a little, and it's still adorable, even now. "But I'm not getting them anymore?"

"No, we, um—" He pauses for a second because as much as he loves her, he won't give her the whole story. Their story. "Elijah and I found out they were actually really important to his family—his family's history, really—and then we got to talking about them—his family and who they were and how they loved, and I—I really didn't know."

"Didn't know what?"

"I didn't know any of it," he admits. "Who *I* am and how *I've* loved. And I know that just sounds like denial, but Cass—you were my *everything*."

"Mmmm, no, Alex. I really wasn't, though," she argues, so gentle about it. "I was enough, and you thought that was the same thing."

"And I'm allowed to want more."

"He told you that?" she asks.

"Yeah."

"Smart man."

"Among other things, yeah," he says.

"So, what the hell happened?"

"I don't really know if anything did. Maybe we weren't

enough of a thing for it to matter yet," he huffs, knowing full well it's a lie. They were barely together before they went back to being apart, but *something* happened in between. Could still be happening, if Alex lets a story from the past teach him anything about the present. "I just—I was wrong for so long. I was wrong and I hurt you and I hurt Elena and I—I don't want to be wrong like that again. I'm terrified of it."

She looks like there are a few things she wants to say in response, but she keeps it simple. "And what does Elijah have to say about that?"

"That he doesn't think I'm a coward, but he's still sad that I'm afraid. That he's not mad at me for not telling you guys about him, but that maybe I didn't make that decision for me. That I should stop thinking of myself as the bad guy when relationships don't have to have any villains at all."

"Smart man," she says again. "And you said you're terrified of being wrong again, but I don't think you were wrong the first time. I just don't think you asked any of the right questions. But then I asked them, and it sounds like Elijah has too, so maybe it's finally your turn. For what it's worth, I really, really hope it is."

Alex rolls the glass in his hand, watching as the ice cubes and liquid collide softly over and over again because it's easier than looking at Cassidy right now.

"I loved you, you know. Still do."

"Love you, too, Alex. But don't stop yourself from falling *in* love with him just because you're scared you'll have to have this same conversation in another 20 years."

It's not the longest he and Elijah have gone without seeing each other, but even with Elena at home with him and work still a little busier than usual, Alex has to claw through another week, struggling to keep from looking at the clock and the calendar and the rest of the books he'd bought from Elijah—ones without Peter and Edgar's story, but maybe ones he should return to Elijah all the same. He supposes it would give him an excuse to stop by Elijah's sometime, and who knows, maybe Cassidy wasn't wrong.

Maybe there's still a chance for more than that.

Cassidy hadn't left right after their conversation Sunday night, deciding to spend some time with Alex and Elena right there on the couch, a bowl of popcorn shared among them. They'd been careful not to touch—careful not to mislead Elena about anything—but it might not matter for long anyway, Cassidy having told Alex that she'd like to invite Michael to have Thanksgiving dinner with her and Elena. Alex had agreed easily, though he can't stop thinking now about the fact that it only gives him one more reason to want to sleep straight through the holiday instead of showing up at his parents' house, even as she'd nudged him again to listen to all her good advice.

But Alex knows he needs to listen to her, and he needs to

listen to Elijah, and he needs to listen to himself, maybe just this once, because he's finally allowed himself to want, and he hasn't figured out how to stop.

In the end, he doesn't have to do much except pick up the package waiting on his doorstep when he returns home from work on Friday afternoon, Elena right behind him with another week of school conquered, small hands wrapped around the straps of her backpack.

"Did you order something?" she asks.

"No, I—it was dropped off here, not mailed," he mumbles, hurrying to unlock the door so he can read the note tied to the top. "How about you go upstairs for a little bit before we head out to dinner? You have those new library books you wouldn't put down this morning before school."

She squeals at the reminder and runs off, and Alex carries the box into the living room, setting it down on the coffee table without looking inside, careful when he pulls the note free. It's folded in half with his name scrawled on the outside, and he opens it to find a print of "Annabel Lee," a message to him written in the margin.

A, I found this book at my grandpa's house, and I thought you should see it too, but I didn't want to show up unannounced while you're with your daughter. I haven't read through it all because I don't know if I'm ready yet, but I've seen enough to know it's the rest of their story. You said you didn't want it to be the end, and it doesn't have to be, but I'm putting everything in your hands now.
~E

Alex swallows hard and blinks away whatever has made it difficult to read Elijah's note the first, second, and third time he does so. He glances at his phone, then toward the stairs, and back to his phone again, picking it up and tapping until he hears the ringing in his ear.

"Alex," Elijah answers. "I didn't—you didn't have to call me. It's not why I—"

"No, I did though. I wanted to make sure I caught you before you left for work. I think we need—"

"M'not going to work tonight," Elijah interrupts with a sigh. "I called out. I just—finding that book took a lot out of me, and I don't think faking a smile for the next several hours is gonna help anything."

The book. Shit, Alex hasn't even opened the box yet. He pulls the lid off and sees a gorgeous collection of Edgar Allan Poe works, thick and bound in leather and inscribed with something delicate. But he can't go any further than that while he still has Elijah on the phone and his mind is whirring with another idea already.

"Okay, hey, listen, can I call you right back?" Alex asks. "I just need to check on something."

"Yeah, I mean—you really didn't have to call at all. You don't—"

"No, I—just give me a few minutes. Please."

Elijah agrees, and Alex takes a deep breath, leaving his phone on the table with the book so he can run upstairs and talk to Elena. Over the past handful of months, these Friday night dinners with her have been so special to him, and he hopes they've been as important to her, so he's not about to mess with their plans if there's any chance she'll mind.

"Wait, Elijah's coming with us on pizza night?" she squeaks a minute later, her eyes wide and her smile even more so.

"Well, I haven't invited him yet," Alex says. "And I don't know if he'll be able to. But I wanted to make sure it would be okay with you if I asked him to go with us."

"Yes, yes, *yes*. He's awesome, and he makes you so silly."

And that is a lot to hear from a kid who's only met Elijah once, but he also needs to manage her expectations tonight.

"Okay, yes, he's very awesome, and he does make me a little silly, but also he might not have quite as much energy for all of that right now."

"Is he sick?" she asks.

"Nope, not sick," he promises. "He just has a lot on his mind, so he might not be very focused on being funny tonight."

Elena shrugs. "Okay. But he'll probably be fine by dessert."

Alex smiles and his eyes fall shut for a moment while he takes it all in. Sure, she might not know as much as Cass, might not be able to see through him quite so easily, but his kid is happy and comfortable and bothered by so little, and he just nods when he looks at her again, careful not to dislodge her ponytail when he caresses the top of her head.

"Thanks, bug. I'm gonna go talk to him about it now."

He settles back onto the couch, takes another several seconds to catch his breath, and then calls Elijah back.

"Hi again," Elijah answers carefully.

"Will you please come to dinner with us tonight?"

"I—dinner? It's Friday night."

Alex chuckles. "Do you not eat on Fridays?"

"Shut up, you know what I mean," Elijah huffs. "You and Elena always go out on Friday nights, just the two of you."

"Which is why I already asked her how she feels about it being just the three of us."

"But I—I called out of work because I think I'd probably make exceptionally shitty company right now. That book—I—Alex—"

"Hey, no, listen, you don't have to entertain us or anything. Just come with us and get out of your head for a while and then—this doesn't have to be anything else. It can just be pizza."

There's a beat of silence. Maybe two. "You know I want it to be more than pizza."

A third, and then a fourth. "I think it already is. I think it has been."

"And you're still okay with me being there with you and Elena?"

"I *want* you with us," Alex says. "And Cassidy knows. We talked on Sunday night when she was here."

"Oh. Okay. And?"

"And she fully took your side on everything."

"Alex, I told you, there don't have to be sides here," Elijah sighs.

"Okay, fine. She fully agreed with you that there don't have to be sides here."

Elijah laughs, maybe in spite of himself. "Smart woman."

"God help me, I am going to have to supervise you two very closely if you're ever in the same room."

"Kinda feels like the same room thing will be inevitable if this is more than pizza."

"Kinda does," Alex agrees. "So, does that mean we're on for dinner?"

"As long as Elena's okay with it, yeah, I'll get changed and head out soon. Should I meet you at your house or the restaurant?"

"Our house. We can drive there together." *And I wish you could stay after.*

They say goodbye and Alex yells up to Elena that they'll be leaving in about half an hour, and then he finally, *finally* takes a closer look at the book still resting inside the box on his coffee table. It's huge, though he supposes a complete collection of Poe's work would be bigger than the other books Elijah's grandpa had kept. Alex makes a note to ask where this one was, if not with all the books Elijah had already sold or kept for himself, but then he runs reverent fingertips over the cover and takes a peek inside to see what had made Elijah so sure he'd found the rest of Peter and Edgar's story.

And oh—

Oh—

Oh.

Alex can't wrap his head around any of it. That all of this exists or that Elijah would trust it in his hands or—

There's just so much there because it's not actually a book at all, only a container made to look like one, and hollow inside until it was filled with more letters and cards and pictures and ticket stubs and *memories* than Alex could have ever imagined. Whatever story had started in the margins of a few classic novels had become this, a collection more precious than whatever Edgar Allan Poe once dreamed of putting together, and Alex only just starts looking through some of it when he feels overwhelmed by it all.

Now Alex understands why Elijah didn't feel like he could fake a smile all night, because while there might still be a happy ending here—while it might be even more likely than before—they'll probably find a lot of heartache too, and maybe some answers to questions they've only barely asked.

And there's no time to ask more now. Alex carefully closes the cover of the book, leaves Elijah's note on top, then puts the lid back on the box just as Elena comes running downstairs.

"Was it a good package?" she asks.

"It was, yeah, bug."

"Is Elijah coming over?"

There's a knock at the door then and they both laugh, Alex moving forward to open it. "Pretty sure that's him, actually."

Elijah is tentative when he steps inside, and Alex hates that he did that to him—made him doubt whether he could be fully comfortable here—but he'll work to change that, starting now. Elena's smile is suddenly timid too, and Alex kinda wants to knock everyone's heads together until they forget that anything was ever awkward.

"It's okay if you're not feeling so great right now," Elena offers to Elijah. "The pizza is *so* good, and I already told dad you might need some dessert."

Elijah's head tips backward when he laughs, and it shouldn't be nearly as attractive as it is. "I think you're probably right, and I will be happy to share dessert if you think you might need some, too."

So, the three of them head out, Alex driving while Elijah and Elena find that they have plenty to talk about, internal turmoil and unexpected shyness gone before Alex has a chance to worry about it for long. Dinner is a whole lot of the same, Elena carrying most of the conversation from where she sits next to Alex in the perfectly worn vinyl booth, Elijah smiling just fine from across the table without having to fake anything for either of them. He and Alex each have a couple of beers, they share a plate of the best cheesy garlic bread, and eat more pizza than they probably should, and then Elena looks at them wide-eyed and Alex gives into the plea for dessert, Elijah insisting that he'll be fine with whatever she picks out.

And Alex is—he's so far gone. His hand inches closer to where Elijah's rests on the table while they wait, but he looks toward his daughter and then up to Elijah, who's watching him carefully and just nods.

"Hey, bug, there's something I want to tell you before we all get a few bites of cheesecake, and if you have any questions about it, you can totally ask, okay?"

"Okay," Elena says, experience leaving her just a bit wary.

"It's not bad, I promise," Alex hurries. "But you know how your mom and Michael are dating now?"

"Yeah."

"Okay, well," he starts, moving his hand the rest of the way until he's holding on to Elijah's. "Elijah and I are dating, too."

Her eyes dart between them, back and forth and back again. "No way. So Elijah's coming to all our Friday dinners now? That's so awesome, I'm gonna scream and I—"

"Whoa, slow down, Laney-bug," Alex laughs. And he's just—he's blown away that it was just that easy, and that her only question has to do with how many times she might get dessert with her new partner in crime. "We appreciate the screaming, but don't actually need to hear it. And Elijah usually works Friday nights, so he won't be here for dinner, but I'm sure we can have him over to the house some other times, okay?"

"I will definitely come over to your house if that's okay with you," Elijah promises. "Maybe you and I can bake cookies or brownies sometime."

Alex sits back with the realization that every dream and nightmare in his future might feature Elijah, Elena, and Cassidy hanging out in his kitchen. With cocktails, sugar, and way too much honesty, probably.

But after their shared slice of cheesecake, they finish up and head back to the house, the three of them piled on the couch for a movie Elena insists she can stay up to watch, even while Alex already knows better. She falls asleep between them, but Alex waits until the movie is over to bother picking her up and taking her upstairs, changing his clothes as long as his room is right there.

Elijah eyes his joggers and hoodie as soon as Alex makes it back to the living room. "Looks cozy."

"Would've brought you something to wear, but I have a feeling you won't stay long enough for that."

"No, I won't," Elijah admits. "It's been a big night, though."

"How are you doing with everything?" Alex asks, folding himself onto the couch next to Elijah, his hand landing on his thigh, still cautious when so many things feel fragile.

Elijah leans in for a kiss, just as careful. "Still sort of stunned, I think. Off balance, maybe."

"Because of what was hidden in the book, or because of me?"

"Isn't it all kind of the same thing by now?" Elijah huffs.

Alex doesn't bother to answer, because they both know Elijah's right. "Obviously it wasn't kept with all the other books. Where did you find it?"

"Under my grandpa's bed, of all places," Elijah tells him. "I guess when my brother and sister-in-law moved in and packed some stuff up, they just never bothered with anything he'd kept there. Wasn't really in their way, so it was easy to ignore,

I guess."

"And when you were going through the house to find stuff for the garage sale, that wouldn't have been a top place to look."

"Nope. And I broke down the bed from the spare bedroom, and sold all the dressers and whatnot, but I'd kept his bed just so I'd have a place to sleep when I crashed there. Figured I could sell that easily enough down the road."

"So, it's a mostly empty house now, but it was able to keep one last secret until today."

Elijah nods. "Probably right when we needed it."

Alex looks down at Elijah's lap, where his hand is now covered by Elijah's, their fingers loosely threaded together. It's such a small thing, but several days ago, he didn't know if he'd ever touch Elijah again. Even after his talk with Cassidy, he didn't know *how* he'd be able to touch Elijah again.

"I'm sorry," Alex whispers.

"Hey, no, look at me," Elijah urges. But when Alex does, whatever Elijah was about to say has to wait, another kiss taking them both by surprise. It's so tender at first, but then maybe they both remember the night Elijah had left Alex by the front door, when they were both walking away from what they wanted because neither could quite find the right way to fight for it. So, they curl around each other now, their mouths open and warm and needy, Elijah breathless when they finally part. "There are no bad guys and we both made some mistakes. And I think it's good to apologize for those—it's not that you can't say you're sorry. But I'm sorry too, because I was trying so hard not to push you, that I convinced myself I could just let go, and I—I don't want to. I never wanted to."

"And how much of that was always Peter and Edgar's story, too?" Alex muses. "Peter scared. Edgar not wanting to push too hard for more. Neither one of them ever wanting to let go. You think they ever got close?"

"To letting go or loving each other out loud?"

"Both, I guess."

Elijah shrugs. "I have a feeling we'll find out—or at least learn enough to make a better guess about how it all happened."

"You don't want to do any of that tonight, though."

"No, not tonight. Tonight, I just want this. Us."

Chapter Eleven

The Poe collection remained untouched that night, Alex and Elijah content to spend another hour or so together on the couch while they talked about nothing particularly important and held each other like it meant everything. Saturday, Elijah was back at his grandpa's, and he stopped by for a quick hello with Poe before going home to get changed for work and ready to smile for anyone and everyone, even if all the best of him was saved for Alex, and maybe Elena too. Then on Sunday, Alex and Elijah decided to have a lazy day with Elena, all movies and music and board games and hot apple cider, hours of laughter keeping them from the box Alex has moved to a shelf in his home office for the time being. It was only when Elijah was getting ready to leave, Elena having gone upstairs to pack for her week at Cassidy's, that they finally mentioned it again, Alex inviting Elijah over for dinner the following night.

The knock at the door that Monday evening is soft, but Alex has been waiting for it, and he tugs Elijah inside as soon as he can, his hand at Elijah's side when he kisses him hello, deep and filthy.

"We're never gonna open that book, are we?" Elijah teases as Alex pulls away.

"We definitely will," Alex tells him. "Just needed that first, and then maybe some dinner."

"It's strange how much quieter this house is when Elena's not here, even though she's not really a noisy kid."

"God, tell me about it. I've been wandering around like this for months."

Elijah follows him into the kitchen, where Alex has a pot of soup on the stove and a loaf of sourdough warming in the oven, and Elijah opens the refrigerator to grab two bottles of beer while Alex slips oven mitts over his hands.

"Was there any argument between you and Cassidy about who would keep the house in the divorce?"

"Nope," Alex says, putting the sourdough on a cutting board before he stirs the soup for another several seconds. "No matter what the actual reasons for the split, she always said that it was her decision to leave, and that she wouldn't kick me out. She's still on title, but there was no fight about me being the one to live here."

"But it's hard, being here alone."

"Yes and no. It's hard being here because there's just so much empty space full of far too many memories, and it all starts to rattle me when I think about it too much. The alone part I don't really mind, but the size of this place bothers me more than I ever thought it would. I'd probably let Cassidy have it if we could go back and do it over, but she's happy where she's at now."

Elijah takes a sip of his beer and nods. "You could always move, right? Find something smaller for you and Elena."

"Sure, but I'm not gonna take her away from the friends she has in the neighborhood, or the park she practically took her first steps in," Alex shrugs. "And of all the things to whine about, I'm not sure having a big house is a fair one."

"I'll just have to come over and make noise a little more often," Elijah says.

"Why do I have a feeling you have very little trouble being loud?" Alex teases, but the moment he hears it, he blushes furiously, comforted only when he catches Elijah ducking his head to hide the same, his knuckles tight around his bottle. "Okay, fuck. Yeah, I'm just gonna take that back."

"No need to take it back. We can definitely—I'm sure we'll—" Elijah shakes his head and offers a resigned sigh. "Just—we should probably have dinner now."

They move into the dining room a minute later and do exactly that, the conversation light until there's a shift they can both feel, an anxiousness about the rest of Peter and Edgar's story, set aside for days and screaming for attention now. The rest of the meal is mostly silent, not uncomfortable but with a goal of finishing quickly so they can move into the living room, Elijah eventually clearing the table while Alex goes to get the box from his office.

They meet on the couch, nervous.

"Why does it feel like everything is so different now?" Alex asks. "Why is this harder than it was at the beginning?"

"Everything *is* different now, which is probably exactly why it's harder, too. A couple of months ago, I didn't even know you, but now we're in the middle of this story and we don't know where it goes from here. It's a little scary."

"But worth it?"

Elijah smiles. "I'd like to think it's always worth it."

They open the box, then the faux book, and it's still just as overwhelming as it had been the first time, but they decide to try to get some kind of control over it now, sorting through everything they find, most of it meticulously dated so they can put the rest of Peter and Edgar's lives in order before they read on. The pictures slow them down though, often breathtaking even without the full context, proof of their relationship without being proof of anything at all, two men so often careful not to touch with the camera there to catch them, but so clearly in love all the same. And one picture, taken in the early 70s, their backs mostly turned to the photographer, one hand at the other's back, leaned in to tell a secret, like that wasn't the way they'd lived forever.

"Someone took all of these," Alex says stupidly.

"Yeah," Elijah agrees. "My grandpa, maybe. Or they—there had to have been someone else in their lives, right?"

"I hope so."

They go back to sorting things for a while—letters appearing more often at the beginning, cards for all sorts of occasions taking over the majority later, random ticket stubs or pictures or scribbled notes everywhere in between—and then they sit back to read what seems to be the first thing tucked away after they'd written in the margins all those years ago.

My dear Peter, it's been nearly five years since the first time I stepped through your front door, since the first time I kissed you in your home, and since the first time I spent the entire night in your arms, only to have to sneak away under that bright, bright sun. It's been so much longer than that since I first knew I loved you. It will be an eternity before I stop. Every moment I have with you has always been so good.

Now we find ourselves in something of a routine, with enough manufactured reasons for me to visit you at home, even if all the rest can't be explained at all. Our relationship remains a secret kept from the outside world, but we are so regularly joyful within the walls of your beautiful house, and that joy means we no longer need to pass books in the quiet of your office. We are louder now, but those early days were something.

The truth is, I miss those books sometimes. I really do. Today we're caught in something in between.

So, I write this letter to you now, even if I'll be able to place it in your hand and follow it with a kiss to your lips, only because I miss being able to write to you when it was half of everything we had. Please accept it with all of my love and keep it close to you tomorrow once I've left again.

Always yours, Edgar

Neither of them moves or speaks for a minute after Elijah's finished reading the letter aloud, still staring down at the page and hearing so much of a voice they don't really know.

Eventually, Alex clears his throat. "So, you think your grandpa went away to college or something, and that gave Peter the chance to have Edgar come over sometimes?"

"Yeah, that sounds about right," Elijah agrees. "And maybe Uncle Edgar couldn't actually live there, but I could imagine enough excuses for why he might be there at any given time."

"You really don't think anyone got suspicious about it?"

Elijah shrugs. "I mean, it's possible. And we have a lot more to read, obviously. But I think my great grandfather's wealth would've allowed for some privacy in the neighborhood, even if they had to take basic precautions."

"What do you think Edgar meant about being caught in between?" Alex wonders.

"I think it was probably a confusing time for him—emotionally, anyway," Elijah says. "It always seemed like he was a little more willing to take chances, even early on, but they were really, really limited by circumstance. As long as my grandpa was still young, when there was something obvious to lose, they sort of had to stick to the book exchanges and middle of the night meetings in a shady part of town."

"But then your grandpa moved out, and Peter and Edgar were able to really *be* together for the first time and had these five years of not having to look over their shoulders while they held each other, even if it was only for a night at a time."

"And that was great, except they still couldn't walk out the front door together and be honest about anything. I mean, I guess they *could* have, but not really. Not back then," Elijah huffs.

"Not safely," Alex agrees. "So, on the one hand, it felt like they'd made major progress in their relationship—and they had, really—but yeah, I could see why it was still only an in-between. There was so much more they wanted."

"Uncle Edgar, especially, maybe."

They set the letter aside and move on to a response from Peter not terribly long after, and it's a lot of what both of them could've predicted. Apologies for how hard it's always been for them, wishes that it could be different, promises that their love will last regardless. A mix of some greeting cards and letters followed, more spread out now that they could spend nights together, but it's not long before they see the first mention of James meeting the woman who would become Elijah's grandma, and Alex catches the wistful smile on Elijah's face as the history he's familiar with crawls closer to them now.

Talk of a wedding is soon after, one that Peter attended alone while surrounded by people who must have thought they knew him well, and Elijah swipes at a tear when they find a picture taken of Peter and James that day. Something else has both Alex and Elijah wide-eyed a minute later, Alex reading the newest letter aloud.

Edgar, my love, there is no reason for me to be writing this at all when you were at my side for one of the most wonderful nights of my life, but I still feel the need to capture every memory here.

Maybe that's a lingering habit from years ago, or maybe it's the hope that this letter will far outlive me so that my family—your family, too—will know that there is always new joy to be had, always happiness to be celebrated. I'll always regret that you couldn't be there for James and Annie's wedding, and I'm certain that is a wound that will never fully heal, but being able to hold your hand tonight as they shared their wonderful news might have been the closest I could get to forgiving myself for any sins of my past.

Throughout dinner, I knew there was something they needed to say, and I was so sure it would be good, but I don't think I could have ever been prepared for this, not so soon.

A grandchild. It takes my breath away.

My love for you has always felt right, but we both know I've always been terribly afraid of all the ways I'm wrong. All the reasons I cannot loudly have what I wish I could shout from every rooftop. But then we sat there, together as we always should be, and my son and his wife told us they are expecting a baby. They were excited to tell us—both of us—because for all the ways this world might not understand what we are, James has never turned away, gentle since the day I first told him about you, and finding a wife who has been tender with us, too. And now, their child, certain to be born into a family full of love, even while our part in it must remain a secret.

Or is that no longer true?

As a new generation is born, is there hope that we might finally have a place outside these walls?

After years of you carefully pushing me to be as brave as you've always been, have I finally arrived there?

Time will tell, as it must do for everyone's story.

All my love, Peter

Elijah pushes up from the couch and walks toward the bathroom without a word, while Alex takes a few deep breaths and refolds the letter. His hand is shaking, which is something of a surprise, but then so much of what he just read was a surprise too, and he needs to give himself the time to come back to the present, Elijah probably working so much harder at doing the same.

It's another five minutes or so before Elijah returns, eyes rimmed red, and his voice rough when he speaks. "Sorry. That was—it was a lot to read in one letter."

"It was, and you definitely don't need to apologize," Alex tells him. "You also don't need to hide from me. Wanting to be alone is one thing, but I don't want you to think you can't stay right here where I can see you cry."

Elijah looks like he fights back the first few things he wants to say, but then he nods. "Okay."

"You want to talk about this one?"

"I just—they both knew," Elijah huffs. "My grandparents both knew, and I—I'm not sure how many of my reactions to that make any sense. I'm kinda feeling it all at once."

"Well, I don't think there are any right or wrong ways to feel about any of this. No good guys or bad guys, right?" Alex says. "But do you want to try to get it all out, however messy it sounds?"

Elijah runs a hand through his hair and Alex watches as the curls end up everywhere at once, longing to help put them back into place and aware that the best he can do is sit back and let Elijah lean on him instead.

"I hated the idea that my great grandfather and Uncle Edgar were all alone, and then when I realized that my grandpa knew, I was—I guess I was relieved that they at least had someone they could be honest with, you know? Just that little relief when they were buried under so many lies." Elijah wraps an arm around Alex's waist, the two of them sort of tangled on the couch. "But now knowing that my grandma was told probably early in her relationship with my grandpa—it's only one more person, but it feels like it changes everything. Like it was only a huge secret in those first years, but then they started letting people in, and I—I don't know."

"You feel like you got left out," Alex concludes.

"Yeah. Doesn't seem like that's very fair to them, though."

"Eh, I'm not sure your feelings have to be fair to anybody. You were close to your grandparents—your grandpa especial-ly—and they knew about Peter and Edgar—"

"And they must have at least guessed about me—"

Alex nods. "So, fair or not fair, you get to be hurt that nobody ever told you. It won't change anything—or it *can't* change anything, I guess—but I think it would be a lot less fair to pretend you're fine about it, even if more of their story can offer you some answers."

"Okay, yeah," Elijah sighs, the smallest mewl caught in his throat before he goes on. "What about my mom?"

"The baby on the way."

"Mmmhmm."

"It certainly seems like they planned to tell her too," Alex says. "I mean, hell, the end of the letter makes it sound like Peter's finally ready for everything to change, after Edgar had been the one more relaxed about it from the beginning."

"And *that* was still incredible after the night of his attack," Elijah points out. "But yeah, it does seem like their relationship was at least going to be something the family knew about, even if the world wasn't ready to see them holding hands anywhere else. So, something happened. And it's gonna suck to find out what it is."

Alex presses a kiss to Elijah's temple. "It probably will, yeah. So, how about if we put all this away for now and go upstairs?"

"To your bedroom?"

"Yeah. I mean, unless you—you don't have to."

"Not sure I'll be very loud for you right now," Elijah mumbles.

"I—Christ, no, that's—" Alex freezes, and then absolutely loses it the second he pulls back to look at Elijah, who's still plenty rocked by everything they've read tonight, but who's also biting his lip to keep from giggling, his cheeks pink. Rolling his eyes, Alex presses a hand to his own chest in mock outrage to play along. "I wasn't suggesting anything of the sort, and I am *appalled* that you would think I'm using any of your vulnerability to my advantage."

"What if I think you'd actually be doing it all for me? For my advantage?"

"Elijah," Alex breathes, everything spinning back to something tender even before their teasing has fully tripped off their tongues. "There's so much I want to do for you, and—"

"And?" Elijah asks, pulling Alex's hand away from his chest so he can thread their fingers together in his lap.

"And once upon a time, you said I could take from you, too."

"You will. Probably very soon."

Alex relaxes into that, content to wait as long as it's still something Elijah wants. Or something Elijah will encourage Alex to want. Or maybe a lot of both. But right now, he moves away to gather everything they've read, and Elijah grabs his phone, presumably to text Nora about Poe, Alex patient until he'll be able to pull Elijah close to him again.

"C'mon, let's go to bed."

"You have to work in the morning," Elijah reminds him as he pockets his phone, Alex putting the lid back on the box before they make their way upstairs.

"It's okay. I'll be quiet so you can sleep in. Just lock up behind you whenever you go."

Elijah hums, quietly pleased. "That sounds incredibly domestic."

"Maybe I just meant to sound lazy," Alex teases, catching him for a kiss. "But seriously, help yourself to whatever in the morning, do whatever you have to do all day, then come back to me tomorrow night."

"A little dinner, a little emotional upheaval?"

"Yeah, something like that." When they step through the door, he nods toward his dresser and pretends it's the most casual thing in the world. That it's not the only time he's ever had anyone in his bedroom like this—or the only time he's literally *slept* with anyone like this—other than his wife. "Need to borrow anything to wear to bed?"

His voice breaks a little on the question, but Elijah is right there to put him back together, seeing right through him and stepping close enough to touch his hands to Alex's waist without holding too tightly. "Hey, I don't have to stay here tonight. Or I can sleep on the couch if you want some kind of compromise."

Maybe the couch makes sense, and Alex considers it for the split second it takes to reason his way right back out of the idea. His bed isn't the problem, no matter how many nights he shared it with Cassidy—not when Elijah has already settled into so many of the blank spaces she left behind—and he swallows around the knowledge that it's only what he wants to *do* in the bed that is leaving him stunned now.

"No, I want this. I've just never—"

Elijah kisses him then, so slowly and so deeply Alex thinks he could drown in it. "There hasn't been anyone else? Even before?"

"Nobody," Alex admits. "And it feels really stupid to say that out loud."

"It's not even a little bit stupid, actually. It's beautiful, and I'm honored to be the one here with you right now, but I promise it's okay if you want me to go," Elijah insists. "I promise I'll come back tomorrow."

And Alex closes his eyes and lets Elijah wrap his arms around him, strong and sure in the middle of a bedroom in which Alex has maybe never been either one. He lets himself nuzzle into Elijah's neck and breathe in all the warmth there before he gives himself permission to taste it too, his lips just barely grazing Elijah's skin. Elijah doesn't move, his embrace neither tightening nor threatening to disappear, though it's impossible to miss the quick hiss when Alex lands just below his ear.

"Don't want you to go," Alex says. "Just need you to be patient with me."

He doesn't wait for an answer—doesn't know if there's one for Elijah to give—too lost in the sensation of his mouth against Elijah's stubble to care about much of anything. Alex drags himself back and forth until he trips back down Elijah's neck, his hands a little clumsy when they curve around the back of Elijah's arms, like he hasn't figured out whether to push or pull.

Eventually, Elijah decides for him when he just barely backs away. "Look at me, sweetheart."

"Sweetheart?"

Elijah leans in to nip at Alex's lip. "No?"

"No," Alex says. "I mean, yes, sweetheart is good. And I'm

looking at you, I'm just—I'm trying."

"I know that. And I know we've talked about so much of this before, but I really need you to believe that everything that happened these past two weeks—the tension between us—none of that was because you weren't running around screaming to the entire state about me or blowing up social media with a bunch of heart eyes or—I don't know—putting it into a column that you and I are a couple, just like I said that night at dinner," Elijah tells him. "It wasn't because we haven't done more than make out on each other's couches or at each other's front doors. It wasn't even because you wouldn't go out to dinner with me or because you were hesitant to talk to Cassidy and Elena. It was just that—you didn't seem sure about you. Not even about you and me together, really. You just didn't seem sure about *you*."

"I wasn't," Alex admits. "How could I be sure when I didn't know who the hell I was all that time? Even now I—how can I be sure I won't make the same mistake all over again?"

Elijah doesn't look away as he lifts his hand to cradle the side of Alex's face, Alex leaning into it instinctually, his mouth falling open when the pad of Elijah's thumb drags across Alex's lower lip.

"Does this feel the same?"

"No," he whispers.

Then Elijah slides his hand further back, his fingers scraping through Alex's hair until he can hold him there, his other hand light at Alex's hip. He tugs on Alex just enough to tip his head up toward him and then he's there when Alex surrenders to him without question, Elijah's tongue so goddamn tender even as it makes demand after demand.

And then he's gone, his lips at Alex's cheek. "Did that feel the same?"

"No," Alex repeats, though it sounds an awful lot like a whimper this time.

Elijah smiles—Alex can feel it more than he can see anything at all—and then the hand at Alex's hip moves to his lower back, holding him there as Elijah steps that much closer, slotting their legs together and teasing Alex with the immediate friction.

"How about this?"

Alex chases another kiss instead of answering and is eager for another one after that. "Please."

But while Elijah keeps them pressed together, he does nothing more, allowing Alex to grind against him however much he'd like. It's probably not all that physically different from the night Elijah had pinned him on the couch, but there's none of the frustration now, and Elijah's patient enough to let Alex absorb the sensation of rubbing up against another man's cock, over and over and over. They're both so hard and Alex aches with a desire he's only just getting to know, and when he starts to moan, Elijah helps him get lost in kiss after kiss before he carefully slips away from it to blink down at Alex again.

"I'm not her, and I—I don't mean that as anything good or

bad," Elijah murmurs, just enough pressure on Alex's hip to slow him down. "But whatever mistakes you think you made before, I need you to know they won't be the same now. You'll make some—we both will—but this isn't the same."

Alex nods, his head heavy and his mouth still half open against Elijah's. "Is it going to be a mistake to sleep together tonight?"

"To sleep together tonight? Or to *sleep* together tonight?" Elijah asks with an amused hum. "Because no, it's not going to be a mistake, and nah, it probably wouldn't do irreparable harm, but I'm not convinced we should test that theory."

Something about his tone warms Alex from the inside out, the subtle mix of humor and something so much more serious. Something that has absolutely lit him on fire. "You didn't answer me about whether you need to borrow clothes."

"No, I'm okay," Elijah says, pulling his hoodie over his head before he lays it over the back of a chair Alex keeps in the corner. He strips off his socks and jeans next, and Alex tries not to stare once Elijah's wearing nothing but his t-shirt and a pair of boxers that don't bother to hide his arousal, Alex turning quickly toward his dresser to grab some sweat shorts and a t-shirt of his own.

The next several minutes are a perfectly dizzy kind of awkward, taking turns in the bathroom and crawling into bed and turning off the lights, neither one saying much as they go through a routine they don't share. But then they're facing each other and kissing again, and whatever need Alex thought could wait for another night begins to coil inside him again, and he wants to be even closer to Elijah, doing what he can to rock into him now while his body responds almost instantly. Elijah's does too, and it has both of them groaning into their kiss, and when Elijah reaches for Alex's leg and hooks it over his own thigh, it's so much easier to feel everything.

Alex wants to feel *everything*.

"Can I touch you?" he pants.

"Jesus, that's—" Elijah just barely manages to laugh as he sucks at Alex's neck. "Did I mix up my answers about which kind of sleeping together we're supposed to do?"

"Is that a no?"

Instead of saying anything out loud, Elijah's hand curves over Alex's ass and their next kiss turns filthy before it slows into something that's anything but. It takes longer than that for Alex to figure out what will happen next, Elijah moving his hand again just so his confident fingers can find their way to where Alex's shake, making enough room between them to lead Alex past the waistband of his boxers. The angle is awkward until Alex can turn his wrist and curl his fingers around Elijah's cock, the sensation of touching another man utterly overwhelming already. And Elijah doesn't leave him alone, guiding his first tentative strokes, their kiss forgotten for a moment while they breathe against each other, and Alex tries to memorize everything Elijah wants him to learn.

There's so much more to absorb when Elijah brings Alex's hand high enough for the pad of his thumb to drag over the head of Elijah's cock, everything so fucking slick there, and easy to spread when they keep moving.

"That's because of you," Elijah says. "You do that to me."

Alex swears under his breath or makes some kind of pitiful noise, and he has so many questions and confessions and pleas, and when he rocks into Elijah again—or rocks against their joined hands as they stroke Elijah's cock—Alex is pretty sure he makes at least one of them heard. Elijah watches him closely when he lets go of Alex's hand and trails a fingertip along the top of his sweat shorts, back and forth until Alex can barely maintain his own rhythm, nodding dumbly at something Elijah has only sort of asked.

"Yes."

Elijah doesn't just slip his hand into Alex's shorts though, working to push them over Alex's ass instead, and careful when he eases his cock free too. And because Alex has all but given up on however he was trying to touch Elijah, he begins to help, sliding his shorts all the way down his legs until he can kick them off entirely, naked from the waist down and nervous and so fucking turned on.

He's probably lucky he doesn't come as soon as Elijah swipes his thumb through the fluid Alex has been leaking for a while, because Elijah does that to *him*. It's another close call when Elijah lifts that thumb to his own mouth and sucks it clean, slowly withdrawing it before he brushes his lips against Alex's.

"You happen to have any lube nearby?" Elijah smiles.

"Might make this a little better for you."

Alex wants to ask what exactly *this* is, but he also can't quite take his eyes off of Elijah's mouth, curious about whether there's anything left of himself on Elijah's tongue, and after a few more seconds, Alex goes in search of the taste just because he thinks he can. He licks into Elijah's mouth and doesn't pretend there's any reason for it other than his own hunger, and Elijah lets Alex take anything he wants for as long as he wants it. But also, there was a question Alex forgot to answer and he halfway nods and mumbles something even as he tries to keep kissing Elijah while their cocks drip side by side.

"Drawer. Behind me."

Elijah rolls them just enough so he can reach for the nightstand, and his weight pressing Alex into the mattress is already becoming a familiar thing, though it's there and gone once Elijah has what he needs. When they're back to facing each other, Alex throws his leg over Elijah's again and kisses him with abandon and grinds against him for another few seconds, Elijah's boxers still mostly in place except for where his cock is thick and hard and pressed alongside Alex. Even with so little room to work, Elijah is able to get his hand between them, lube covering each of their cocks after a couple of individual strokes, and Alex clings to the back of Elijah's shirt while he moans into his mouth.

"Fuck—that's—*fuck*," Alex gasps when Elijah opens his hand wide enough to jerk them off together.

Elijah nips just below Alex's jaw and laughs there, only the slightest puff of air giving him away. "Not completely, but it'll be close enough for tonight."

"It's so good. I—god, I didn't know."

"You wanna help, or you just wanna hold on to me?" Alex pulls his head back to look at Elijah, hoping that even the dark room will allow him to be given a clue about how to respond to that as he aches with need, and can feel himself getting wetter, and so badly wants to know if Elijah is too. But then Elijah is brushing the tips of their noses together and Alex can't comprehend how something so tender and playful can be perfectly paired with the vulgar sound Elijah's hand is making as he works them over. "There's not a wrong answer, sweetheart. You can always tell me what you want."

He can still barely talk though, so Alex only moves to release Elijah's shirt and put his hand somewhere near Elijah's instead, closing his eyes when he can feel so much at once—the play of Elijah's muscles as his fingers slide and twist, the veins on their shafts when he can brush up against them, the almost unnoticeable slits threatening to spill more than they already have. And Elijah's panting now too, which makes Alex think something about this is going right, even if it's going to be over all too soon.

"I'm gonna—too much—"

"S'okay. Let go. I'm close too."

Alex has a feeling that's not always true—that Elijah can hold out for a very long time when it's what he wants, a trick likely to make Alex lose his entire goddamn mind—but at least some part of this is new for Elijah too, and if tonight can be this small and special thing, Alex is grateful for it. Their hands speed up together and each breath is a little more of a struggle than the one before and they kiss when they can, except that Alex is so far gone that Elijah might be the only one doing anything at all. When he comes, it's so unlike anything he remembers feeling before, his entire body involved somehow, and the sounds he makes through each aftershock are almost embarrassingly loud in his own head. Alex doesn't want anything about the moment to pass, and in some ways, it doesn't, Elijah stroking himself obscenely with so much more than lube covering him now, and Alex's hand is still right there when Elijah comes all over both of them with the longest, most beautiful moan Alex thinks he's ever heard.

Elijah's shaking, or maybe Alex is, but they're still face to face and neither one of them is looking away, so Alex takes a chance on a smile and watches when Elijah matches it with one of his own.

"That wasn't the same," Alex says quietly, closing his eyes only when he leans into Elijah for an almost chaste kiss.

"Mmmm, no. Wasn't the same for me either," Elijah agrees. Then he bites back a laugh. "Think I might've been wrong about needing to borrow some clothes, though. I'm kind of a mess."

"But you're my mess."

Elijah doesn't bother biting anything back then, his laugh

warm against Alex's lips. "Are you always this sappy after an orgasm?"

"Only one way to find out," Alex teases, careful when he uses his own shirt to clean up what he can before he rolls out of bed to help get rid of that and Elijah's clothes, too. His sweat shorts are on the floor nearby, so he puts those back on and pulls an extra pair from his drawer to toss toward Elijah, then he crawls back under the covers, soft and sated and seeing so much of the same on Elijah's face too.

They're both still figuring this out, and there's no chance to process what just happened when Alex has to get up early for work to be as productive as anyone is the week of Thanksgiving, so he only combs his fingers through Elijah's hair and sighs happily when Elijah brings the tips of their noses together again.

"Thank you for letting me stay."

"Thank you for coming back."

Chapter Twelve

Just as he'd told Elijah he would be, Alex is careful to stay quiet in the morning, though he's not sure how late Elijah will actually sleep when neither of them is used to whatever the hell they're doing now. He takes a quick shower and gets dressed in the bathroom before he gives Elijah one last glance and slips out of the bedroom. In the kitchen, he considers leaving notes or instructions or something, but realizes Elijah's perfectly capable of making coffee and grabbing whatever else he might want before he goes. After another few minutes, Alex finishes up his own quick breakfast and then packs up for the office, going in earlier than usual with the hope that he can leave early, too.

The sooner he can wrap up his day, the sooner he and Elijah can get back to the Poe collection.

Whether what they find there will make Elijah feel better or worse is anyone's guess.

But the day goes by faster than Alex might have expected after he receives a good morning text from Elijah and they enjoy a flirtatious back and forth from there. He daydreams through a meeting Steven was too optimistic about scheduling, nobody on the team prepared to accomplish anything of substance during a holiday week, and then there's some kind of impromptu potluck in the office break room when everyone orders too much food for lunch. There's a little more work to do at the office in the afternoon, but plenty Alex can finish at home, so he says goodbye to everyone when it seems professionally acceptable to do so, and he hurries to his car.

He didn't figure Elijah would still be hanging out at his house, but somehow Alex is disappointed that the familiar truck isn't parked along the curb.

The disappointment is gone twenty minutes later, when Elijah calls.

"Good timing," Alex says, in lieu of a hello. "Just got back from the office."

"Still have some work to do now?"

"Some, yeah. But you can come over whenever," he tells Elijah, such an easy thing to say even as his cheeks grow warm. "I mean, if we're still on for tonight."

"Yeah, we are, but is it okay if I just grab dinner for us on the way? I think I'd rather have something quick so we can get started a little earlier."

Alex hums. "You want to get through the rest of the stuff tonight."

"I just—" Elijah sighs. "After last night, I'm not sure I'm gonna want to stop reading once we start. Unless you'd rather—"

"No, no," Alex interrupts. "A quick dinner is fine, and reading through everything tonight is fine. I ate a lot at lunch though, so pick whatever you want."

"What if whatever I want isn't something you actually like?"

"I'm pretty confident you can figure out what I like," Alex says, his voice lower than he expects it to be when he quietly ribs Elijah.

In response, he's treated to a few moments of relative silence, and Alex wonders whether Elijah is trying to decide how much he can push, even if Alex thinks the limit is further away than either of them has imagined. In the end, it's easy to hear Elijah's smile, and the sound only settles Alex that much more.

"We're talking about dinner."

"Okay."

"Okay," Elijah echoes, his next breath loud but steady. "Raw onions are a no, grilled onions are fine. Ranch for dipping if there's anything to be dipped. Hold the lettuce on most things, but you'll eat a salad if I go that route. Anything involving a form of bread with some cheese is a safe choice. Add avocado or guac anytime it's offered with anything. Mushrooms are good as long as they're not huge and slimy. If I get fries, I should also get some for you or you'll just steal some to pay me back for when I did that to you at the bar. Pesto or any cream sauce over red. Burritos over tacos. White over wheat, but sourdough is usually better. Pizza is always okay, even though you already have it every other week with Elena. Sushi is a tricky one, and I'm not gonna guess either way, but other than that, how'd I do?"

"Shut up," Alex growls. "You already know."

"Maybe. So, I'll see you later?"

"Yeah. And you can plan to stay again if you want, unless Nora can't—or you'd rather—"

Elijah's abrupt laugh interrupts Alex. "You can shut up, too. I'll definitely plan to stay again."

He arrives a couple of hours later with a duffel bag and dinner, and they allow themselves a minute to kiss each other senseless before they catch their breaths and focus on the rest, Alex grabbing the soda Elijah's requested before joining him at the dining room table. They'd probably eat at the coffee table and get started on the next handful of letters and cards, but Alex thinks they're both a little paranoid about possibly spilling on anything in the book, so they sit down with their burritos, chips, and guacamole, and they relax for however long they take to finish without making their stomachs hurt in the process.

When they settle next to each other on the couch, they open the box and Alex reaches for the batch of things they'd read the night before, setting that pile aside so they can focus on the rest. There's a lot, and he doesn't know whether they'll make it through everything—it will probably depend on whether Elijah needs some breaks in between—but they're absolutely ready to try.

"Hey," Alex says, twisting toward Elijah to kiss him for just a moment. "Whatever we find out, we're okay, but if you need time to be *not* okay, just tell me. You can be alone, or I can be with you, and you can be quiet, or we can talk about it. I—just tell me. I want you to tell me."

There's a crease between Elijah's brows, and Alex reaches up to smooth it as Elijah sighs. "I don't want to be alone. And if I—I don't want you to let me be alone. Not tonight."

"Okay," Alex promises.

They get started then, having left off on such a hopeful note after Annie's pregnancy announcement, but bracing themselves for whatever happened between then and the vague childhood memory Elijah has of San Diego. Everything remains somewhat spread apart, the written communication more of an indulgence than a necessity for them, though there's a flurry of activity when baby Laura Rose Thornton, Elijah's mother, is born. There's a birth announcement and a couple of pictures and a card in which Peter writes to Edgar that Laura is "today and always, your granddaughter, too."

Elijah shakes his head, then picks up another small card.

Oh, Peter, however brave you've always told me I am, I often think I'm a little crazy too, but I've seen the way you've bloomed while surrounded by the love of our family, and I only want more. I always seem to want more. So, when you talk of other men like us, people who understand and might even welcome us to meet with them outside your home, of course I want to know them. I have never pushed you, and I never would, but if you're ready, so am I. ~Edgar

"They wanted friends," Elijah whispers. "They finally felt

like they had family, so they wanted friends."

"Makes sense, doesn't it?"

"After being so isolated in those first several years, yeah. Do you think they were actually living together yet?"

Alex looks down at the letter he's just picked up. "Nope."

Edgar, darling, I'm writing now because we aren't talking the way we should. The way we usually do. We fought last night, and you went back to your house and left me feeling so alone in mine. I would say it's times like these that I wish you had already moved in with me, except that I've felt that way for years and I don't understand why you're still not here with me. At home.

(I do know. It's because I haven't told you how much I need you to stay.)

So, please, before we talk more about meeting with others. Before we talk about the places we might be welcomed, bars at which we might be able to sit close together. Before we talk about finding these small pockets of comfort in a world that feels suffocating more than a place that might allow us to breathe freely. Before we do anything of the sort, please stay and be mine every night and every morning and whatever waking moments we have in between. My neighbors have turned their heads for long enough, careful not to concern themselves with your visits, and I'm certain they'll continue to keep their eyes averted if you're here every day. So again, please. Stay.

Forever.

It would be so good.

Stay.

Elijah rubs his hands against his thighs, shaking. "All of this is 'so good,' really—other than the fact that they fought, obviously—but it feels like it's—I don't know. I can't tell whether it's better or worse that we already know they were never comfortably out."

"I think it's probably better," Alex says. "It hurts, but at least we're braced for it."

There are some birthday and holiday cards from James, Annie, and little Laura, and a couple of pictures, too, Peter and Edgar still standing apart, almost painfully so. Lost in the sight of them for a moment, it takes Alex another breath or two to realize that they're posed in front of a home just a few streets away from where they're sitting now, at least one chapter of this tender family story unfolding in the same place he first met Elijah. He isn't sure why he hadn't considered it before, or asked Elijah where his mom had grown up, but when his heart kicks at his chest and he shakes his head as though it might help, Elijah seems to understand.

Of course he does.

"Yeah, Peter and Edgar visited my grandpa's house."

"They were right there." Alex shakes his head one more time before they move on. Letters and cards suggest Edgar did move in with Peter sometime after the invitation to do so, and there's ongoing mention of meetings with others in the area, Alex torn about whether he wants to know any more about the danger that might have put them in. But then they stumble upon it all, their state's history of arrests and riots and raids and demonstrations, so much hate in response to so much love, and violence an unsurprising consequence of all that hurt.

They look at each other, Elijah clearing his throat first. "They didn't get involved, though. These things were happening around them, but they were still so careful."

"Beginning to risk an occasional dinner at someone else's home, but nothing more. At least not yet."

"Not yet," Elijah echoes, nervous as he catches his breath. "You don't think my grandparents cut them off, do you? If maybe they started to participate more? If they began to take bigger risks?"

Alex reaches over to squeeze Elijah's hand, then gets up to make some hot cocoa for them, continuing the conversation from the kitchen. "Why would they do that, though? Especially after being supportive since way before it was clear there was a larger gay community starting to make some noise."

"Maybe it got to be too much once they had my mom to protect, too."

"Okay, yeah, I guess I see your point, but as of now, they're still including them in family celebrations, and your mom's little scribbled name is on their cards."

"Yeah, but she was still young and just barely reaching an age where she'd remember more details about them—she would've been seven, then turning eight throughout this stretch. And she certainly wouldn't have known enough to clock that they were different before that, especially if the whole family was calling him Uncle Edgar, the same way I heard about him later," Elijah points out. "So maybe my great grandfather and Uncle Edgar started feeling free to get more involved with the community around them, and my grandparents got scared about how it might affect the family as my mom got older."

"What about your grandpa's birthday party in San Diego?" Alex asks, stirring the packets of chocolate powder into the milk he's just heated in the microwave. Nothing about it is fancy, but it'll do for tonight, and he tosses the spoon into the sink when he's done, Elijah still piecing the story together.

"Maybe a late attempt to mend fences before my great grandfather died?"

Alex returns with the two mugs, and they sit far enough away from everything to be confident that they won't spill on anything that matters, but Alex only takes a quick sip before he tips his head toward Elijah.

"I don't think you're necessarily wrong about anything, and I guess we'll find out soon enough, but you knew your grandparents pretty well. Do you really think it's a decision they would have made?"

Elijah eyes him carefully. "You're a father. Would you cut off any of your family to protect your kid?"

And yeah, he absolutely would, though he doesn't bother to say that out loud because he can tell Elijah knew the answer before he asked the question. Alex turns to set his mug down on an end table, Elijah doing the same on his side a minute later, and they look through another half dozen smaller things before they get the beginning of their answer, so close to what Elijah was guessing, and somehow not at all what they expected.

My dear sweet Peter, you are the love of my life and I have never been as sorry for that as I am now. All these years I've sought a way for us to fight for a place in this world, and I stupidly thought we might have found such a small, safe way we could do exactly that. I was wrong.

I will document every error here because I deserve no less.

Helping our community organize and strengthen through passed messages and clandestine meetings brought me back to those days in your office and all the nights we spent pressed up against old warehouse walls. All the years when we'd had nothing but each other felt like they'd led us to a time when we could help others have so much more. Honestly, I think you felt it too, but I'll take all the blame for us both. I should've known one day I'd push too far.

Spending time with your family has meant the world to me, too. The way James has never once hated me when it would've been so easy for him to do just that. Annie, sweeping into his life and then tumbling into ours, her laughter brighter than a thousand suns. And then beautiful Laura. My little rose petal. I've always loved her like she was my own, and then I watched the confusion in her eyes and hurt I couldn't chase away when you were gone, and I will never forgive myself for that.

It was supposed to be so easy, a favor done under the midday sun. Lunch with Laura, and the promise of ice cream after. Maybe even a walk in the park. A little girl out with her grandfather and uncle, just as she had been plenty of times before, but this time, unlike all those others, her grandfather slipped away to speak to the owner of a bar only minutes away. Her grandfather, then unable to return to their table.

I knew in my heart something was wrong before you could even be considered late. There was a chill in the air and a tightening in my chest, and I smiled for her because there was nothing else to do, but I knew. My darling, I knew.

It's been a few days now, and while it's been a reality for far too many of our friends, I still can't believe you were arrested in a raid, however small. I can't believe it was only your ability to trade decades of goodwill, an unimaginable amount of money, and the career you loved so much that has allowed you to be close to me now.

Why are you close to me now?

I know why, because it is the same reason I can't leave you, but there is something I can do. There's something we can do. We can apologize to your family and thank them for all they've done for us, and then we can move away. We should move away. We can live our lives as we have chosen, but we should do it alone. Maybe we can find others somewhere new, but it should always be people who are taking the same risks for all the same reasons. Our loved ones should never have to suffer because we made the choice to be selfish.

Please, Peter.

I love you too much to know how to do this any other way.
Yours, Edgar

Alex doesn't know how Elijah made it through the entire letter without breaking in two, but Alex watches him crumple now and is gentle when he pulls the letter from Elijah's hand. There's nothing to say, not right now, so he only pulls Elijah into him and wraps them up together while they absorb this latest chapter.

Maybe the most important one.

Because that had been the missing piece, the answer to their biggest questions. After all those small steps forward, however quietly brave they might have been, Peter and Edgar had to have had a reason for ending up where they did, away from the family with a once open secret locked up tight again. And it was Edgar who pulled them back into the darkness after wanting the world to see them for so damn long.

Alex has to admit he hadn't seen that one coming.

There's still more to read, of course, and Alex thinks they'll get back to that soon, but Elijah's breath is still ragged, and as much as Elijah has promised to be patient with Alex upstairs, Alex will be at least as patient here. The hot cocoa becomes cold, but they barely move.

When Elijah finally does, Alex starts to untangle them. "Talk, read, or sleep?"

Anything else seems close to impossible.

"Would you have done the same thing? Would you have wanted to leave everything behind?"

Alex thinks about it for a second, then he nods. "I'm not sure it's a whole lot different from what you asked me before, about whether I'd cut off my family to protect my kid. Edgar just did it the other way around—suggesting that they cut themselves off—but the motivation was essentially the same."

"Protecting my mom," Elijah huffs.

"And in this case, it was definitely to protect your grandparents too, but yeah. He'd already begun to cut himself off when he wrote the letter."

"What do you mean?"

Alex shrugs. "Edgar had called them 'our family' before, but in that letter—"

"He used 'your family' instead."

"I don't think he ever stopped loving them, but I'm sure he wished he could."

Elijah groans. "And somehow we all ended up together almost 30 years later, assuming my memory's legit."

"I'm gonna guess it is," Alex says. "I don't think this broke them up, I just think it was the reason everything changed."

"Only one way to find out."

They turn back to the box, and while there's no direct response to Edgar's plea, they do find a note written by Peter after he's broken the news to James, telling his son that they've decided to move to San Diego, and that it will be better for everyone if they keep some distance between them for a while, the world unsafe for people like them, and maybe for anyone who dares to love them anyway.

Tear stains on the paper make Alex certain James reread the note more than was probably good for him.

But James must have agreed, or maybe Annie convinced him it was okay to let them go, or maybe Edgar and Peter just refused to leave it up for debate at all, because it becomes clear when they've left, setting up a whole new life for themselves without family close enough to help them rebuild.

"This picture, the one that caught our eye before," Alex says, holding it up now as they marvel again at whatever secret is being shared between the two men. "It's from after they moved, so your grandpa probably didn't take it."

"Guess they did find new friends," Elijah mumbles.

Alex looks at him carefully. "You're upset about that."

"I—maybe? I don't know if that's the right word."

"Do you want time to think of a better one?" Alex asks.

"It's just messy. All of it." Elijah shakes his head and takes a deep breath. "I get why they had to hide in those early days, and I get why they were so careful as they let more people in. I get that they *thought* they had to take all those same steps backward after my great grandfather was arrested. It scared the shit out of them, having my mom that close when it happened, and knowing it could be even worse the next time would have been terrifying. But I hate it. I hate it because it wasn't just the two of them anymore. They had a *family*, and whatever else we read now, we already know it was never the same again after they left."

"The whole world was kind of a mess those days," Alex says,

though he doesn't even know what point he's trying to make.

"Sure, and other people stood up and fought and weren't lucky enough to have anyone to support them through it. My great grandfather and Uncle Edgar ran away from their support. They could've had it all."

"They could have, but maybe that wasn't such an easy thing to believe back then. I'm not sure it's easy to believe now."

Elijah absentmindedly rubs a hand over his stubbled jaw. "We have to believe it. What else is there?"

Alex doesn't answer, mostly because he doesn't have one, but he aches anyway. "We've already agreed, at least a couple of times now, that the quiet ones weren't cowards—just victims. You haven't changed your mind about that, have you?"

"No, but now we know that their decision to be quiet made my grandparents and my mom victims, too."

"And you."

Elijah's eyes flare with something both indignant and weary. "Me?"

"You lost out on being part of their story, too. And that hurts you."

The flare dies when Elijah blinks and looks away for nearly a minute.

"Okay, so now what?"

Alex nods toward the coffee table. "Now we read the rest of it, and you try to remember what you told me before—that there aren't any good guys or bad guys here. Everybody made the decisions they thought were right at the time. I married

Cassidy, and Peter and Edgar ran away, and your grandpa never told you about them, and you sold me some books at a garage sale one morning, and maybe some of that was a mistake and maybe some of it wasn't. The problem with anybody's story is that you don't often know the end at the beginning."

"So, we just keep reading."

"We just keep reading."

The written birthday and holiday greetings seem to stop after that, though it becomes clear that James never fully let go, visiting them each year on his birthday. Alex looks down at the paper he holds.

Edgar, my love, I know we put up such a fight about these visits from James each year, but I'm so glad he uses his birthday as a reason to force our hand, asking for something from us on the one day we can't help but agree to give it. These days are always a chance to remember what we had and what could someday be again, if only the world dares to turn upside down. He still doesn't understand why we had to leave, but he continues to respect our wishes. He has always and will forever.

Laura hasn't asked about us in a while, and Annie no longer cries. But James. Oh, James. I hope he never stops spending his birthday at our side, and I know how selfish I am for taking it away from anyone else, but it's all we have. It might be all we ever have.

Peter

Elijah just nods, and they move on, even though there's not much more to see. Newspaper clippings about progress made by, and plenty of harm done to, the gay community. A couple of pictures. Small notes. Collected bits of what seems to have been an increasingly lonely life, even the new friends they'd made seemingly kept at a safe distance, whatever risk Peter and Edgar had thought they were willing to take when they moved to San Diego quieting over the years and leaving them at home with only each other more often than not.

Always in each other's arms because they had nowhere else to go.

Alex hadn't expected them to find wedding bands in the box, but they're in there too, identically simple, and saved in an envelope with vows written to each other for a wedding nobody else would attend. One that wasn't yet legal but must have served as a secret act of resistance, as though their whole lives hadn't already been so much of that. Maybe it was pointless, or maybe nothing like that ever could be, and Alex just wants to cry.

But the first decade passes, then another, and it's clear from the handwriting alone that Peter is so much older now, each shaky word on the page leaving something raw to rattle in Alex's chest. Elijah had said Edgar was a lot younger, and maybe that's obvious too, a little more energy in everything he has to say. And just a little bit of the fight he'd left behind a while ago. They breeze past the births of Elijah's brother and sister, then through the year Alex was born, and then they pass Elijah's birthday too, one celebrated in a note from Edgar, and maybe just enough to finally change his mind.

Peter, we should go see them. All of them.

I know I'm the one who did this, the one who took you away from your family, and I will carry all the blame for that for the rest of my life, and likely for so many years after you're gone. But there are three of them now, three great grandchildren you should be able to hold, and while I wouldn't have been surprised to find that James and Annie don't want us anywhere near, James has never stopped inviting you home. Inviting us home, really, though why he continues to love me, I will never understand.

So, please, let's go see them, so your youngest great grandchild can rest in your arms. If only for an afternoon, let's be a family again. Let's remember something good. We deserve something good.

Edgar

"He held me when I was a baby?" Elijah whispers, tears clinging to his jaw until their stubbornness loses out to gravity and they fall into his lap.

"Here," Alex rasps, holding up a picture they must have missed on their first quick run through the box.

An elderly man, maybe around 80, with Elijah's same curls, even if they're thin and gray, and Elijah's same broad shoulders, even if they're curved forward now, both age and the innate desire to protect a baby curling his entire body around a much smaller one. The baby is looking up at him with blue eyes, a gummy smile, and the kind of peace little ones can offer better than anyone else on the planet.

"Oh my god."

Alex leaves him with the picture for a few minutes, breaking his earlier promise just long enough for Elijah to have this moment alone, and taking their mugs back into the kitchen to wash them far more thoroughly than is probably necessary. But then he returns to sit close to Elijah again, and he holds his hand while he sorts through the last handful of things left in the box, and Elijah clings to the picture.

"There's not much after that."

Elijah's voice is barely there. "Don't need anything else right now. I want—can we go to bed? We don't—it doesn't have to be anything else, just—I want to sleep. I'm so tired and I just want to sleep."

"Of course," Alex says, careful when he lets Elijah go, and maybe even more so when he picks up the piles and puts everything back in order, the lid back on the box when he's done.

After that, he locks up and turns off the lights while Elijah grabs his duffel bag, and then they head upstairs together, most of the comfortable desire between them replaced by emotional exhaustion tonight. Alex lets Elijah duck into the bathroom first and he uses the time to get changed, Elijah doing the same when they trade places. And once they're in bed together, Alex only leans in for a single kiss, almost too innocently, before Elijah closes his eyes.

Anything else Alex might have said will have to wait, pushed aside by years and years of grief.

Chapter Thirteen

"**Y**ou better not try to make me a morning person," Elijah grumbles, Alex failing when he attempts to sneak out of the bedroom for the second day in a row.

He laughs and walks over to the bed to give Elijah a kiss on the forehead. "Wouldn't dream of it. And you won't be spending the night here tonight anyway. You have to work."

"Ugh, the night before Thanksgiving. When everyone wants to get drunk off their ass before they have to deal with family all day tomorrow."

"Well, I understand the temptation," Alex says. "This will be my first holiday without Cass and Elena by my side."

"Mmmm, then you should come see me tonight."

"At the bar, or after you go home?"

"Both," Elijah answers.

"Okay."

"Yeah?"

"Did you really think I was gonna say no?" Alex chuckles.

"I don't know. I wasn't great company last night."

Alex glances over to where the picture of Elijah and Peter rests on the nightstand. "Something something, for better or worse, in good times and bad."

"Just the sight of wedding rings was enough to have you reciting that shit when the sun's barely up, huh?"

Alex grabs a pillow and swings it at Elijah's head, then backs away toward the door. "Take your time and let yourself out whenever you're ready. I'll see you tonight."

And it's just that easy, as hard as it is to say goodbye at all, Alex grabbing coffee and something small to eat in the kitchen before he packs up his work bag and heads to the office for what he assumes will be a half day for everyone. He doesn't actually hear from Elijah, and maybe that's a good thing, a little space after two emotional nights, and he runs a couple of errands after lunch, mostly to keep his mind on anything else. Once he's home again, there's time to take a late afternoon nap before he catches up on a couple of shows, changes clothes, fixes his hair, packs a bag, and makes the drive to the bar.

Elijah hadn't been kidding about people wanting to drink before the holiday, the place more crowded than it probably is on any other Wednesday, but Alex takes quick note of one table open next to the wall, such an easy place for him to hide, and a single open stool at the far end of the bar, where Elijah stands now.

Watching him. Waiting for him. The Edgar to his Peter, except for all the ways Edgar and Peter hadn't quite figured out the balance of fear and hope, and Alex so badly wants to.

He slides onto the barstool, and Elijah smiles. "Hey, handsome. Decided to step out of the shadows?"

"Seems like a good night for new adventures."

"Kinda got a jump on that a couple nights ago, didn't we?" Elijah points out just before he ducks his head, though it does little to hide the pink in his cheeks. "No, wait, listen, I don't mean—that sounds terrible, and I—you don't have to prove anything to me. Adventures or—I need you to know I can be plenty patient."

"Still want you to be," Alex says, reaching across the bar to tip Elijah's chin upward until he can smile at him again. "But I want a lot of other things, too."

"Okay, that's—yeah. You wanna start with dinner and a beer?"

"Yeah, that sounds perfect."

The next few hours are full of all the expected chaos in a crowded bar, but Elijah is as attentive as he can be, and Alex isn't demanding much of anything anyway. There's plenty of time to get tipsy and sober again, so after Alex's plate is cleared, Elijah brings over another beer and a shot of the good tequila.

"Body shots with the cheap shit are gonna have to wait for another time," Elijah teases. "Unless you want me to find someone here for you."

"Nah, you're my only someone."

When the shot is gone, Alex goes back to the beer and enjoys the view, Elijah such a natural behind the bar, flirting with everyone in a way that doesn't threaten Alex at all, laughter erupting everywhere and the music overhead the perfect complement to the fun being had. And then slowly, just as Alex thinks he's getting the slightest bit impatient, more people leave than come in, the noise softening around them, and all the space to breathe leaving Alex ready to gasp for a little more. Eventually, a couple of the other bartenders are gone too, and Tyler nudges Elijah's shoulder with his own.

"You guys should get out of here," he offers.

"I'm not gonna stick you with closing again," Elijah argues, though he's apologetic when he glances toward Alex. "We're okay."

Tyler just laughs. "Sure. But also, I've already got family crashing at my place, and I am *not* in a hurry to get back there, so how about we pretend you're doing me a favor? Just clean up your shit and go. I'm totally fine, I swear."

Elijah blushes again when Tyler winks, then he turns to grab Alex's empty glass and take care of as much as he can at his end of the bar, disappearing into the back a minute later.

"Thank you," Alex says.

Tyler shrugs. "That guy has had my back more times than I can count. This is really the least I can do."

Alex gets up then, sliding a tip across to Tyler, whether he'll be happy to accept it or not, and he uses the next couple of minutes to stretch his legs and make his way toward the door. Elijah isn't all that far behind him, nodding goodbye to the handful of customers left before he presses his hand to the small of Alex's back as they step outside. He thinks maybe

Elijah will take his hand as they walk to their cars, but he never does, and Alex hasn't decided whether he wishes he had.

"You're okay to drive?" Elijah asks once they've reached the parking garage.

"I am, yeah. Promise. See you there?"

There's a moment in which Alex wonders whether Elijah will steal a quick kiss before he turns away, but just as with his hand, he never gets quite close enough, and this time Alex is sure it's better this way. His entire body tingles with all the ways he wants to be touched, and there's no reason for him to get a hint of that relief now.

When they close Elijah's front door behind them though, relief happens everywhere, all at once, even while Alex just wants and wants and wants and can't begin to know how to chase each new thing.

"You should've never come to the bar tonight," Elijah says, his mouth hot at Alex's neck, Alex's body slammed tight against the door. "I just wanted to quit my job and do this instead."

"Glad you didn't quit. And now you've got all night to do this."

"Gonna make me do all the work?" Elijah teases.

Alex's hand fists around Elijah's hair until he can tug him away and kiss him, splitting the difference between reverent and obscene in a way he wouldn't have thought possible. Elijah's hands seem to land in one place, then another, and another, Alex distracted with the need for him to stay still, even while he wants Elijah to keep moving.

Alex scrapes his teeth against Elijah's lower lip. "Fuck, I—I still don't really know what I'm doing. I've touched you, but that wasn't—you knew, but I—I'm gonna need—"

"Patience."

"Yeah."

"We're doing a terrible job with that right now."

"Yeah," Alex whimpers, Elijah's thigh so solid and exactly where he didn't know he needed it to be.

"Can I take you to my bedroom?"

It means all of this will stop long enough for them to move away from the door and down the short hallway, but there's a bed there, and maybe no need for clothes, and Elijah will be so damn patient, and Alex will learn. In the end, he supposes the question is entirely rhetorical, but he answers anyway.

"Please."

They don't end up letting go of each other all that well, which has them tripping over Poe a little, and apologizing with loads of promises of long walks and treats in the morning, but they make it into Elijah's room and Alex is pushed against that door too, Elijah so much gentler this time around. He leans in for a kiss, slow enough for the rhythm of it to carry Alex far, far away, only to bring him back when Elijah's fingers catch the hem of Alex's sweater and he begins to pull it over his head. Once it's gone, Elijah's lips crawl along Alex's jawline, his breath warm at Alex's ear.

"Now it's your turn," he murmurs.

Alex nods when their heads are still close enough for him to feel the scrape of Elijah's cheek against his, and he shivers with it, taking another second or two before he manages to untuck Elijah's shirt and fumble his way to the top button, nervous as he works his way back down. He makes it there though, focused when he pushes the material over Elijah's shoulders and pulls it free from each arm, trembling as his fingers trail over one tattoo and then another. Then it's Elijah who reaches forward, fingertips almost painfully light as they dance over Alex's bare skin, chasing goosebumps an impossible task when more appear than he could ever touch, Alex finally taking the cue and brushing his hands over Elijah until he knows what his goosebumps feel like too.

It's so different, somehow, from when they'd kicked everything aside in Alex's bed, all of that on a whim and everything so intentional about the way they're exploring now. They continue to kiss while they begin to map each other's bodies, learning about a dozen unspoken wishes while they swallow the sounds that get passed between them. Then Elijah's fingers trace the skin just above the waistband of Alex's jeans, and he catches Alex's moan before he smiles against his mouth.

Alex pulls just far enough away to pout. "You can't laugh at me. You already know what I sound like when you touch me like that."

"Oh, I am definitely not laughing at you, sweetheart. And I don't care what we've done before, that noise you just made might be the best thing I've ever heard," Elijah says, unfastening Alex's belt before he works his way past the button, then the zipper, his knuckles dragging against the length of Alex's cock on the way down, another damn moan impossible to hide. "Should I keep going, or do you want to catch up?"

Words get caught in his throat, but Alex knocks Elijah's hand away and returns the favor, clumsy and unpracticed, and going one step further when he pushes the pants all the way down, leaving Elijah in nothing but his boxers, something he's already seen in his own bedroom, but even more stunning when he's been given more explicit permission to look tonight. And they're still standing so close, helping themselves to as many kisses as they can while they undress, everything almost unbearably slow around them by the time Alex's jeans join Elijah's on the floor.

"You're so—" Alex trails off because he doesn't know what he was going to say anyway, but when he wraps his arms around Elijah and meets his open mouth for something tender and intimate, Elijah seems to know.

"So are you," Elijah tells him. "And I want you to remember we can always stop. It doesn't matter what we did or didn't do the other night, okay? We'll keep going slow and I'll keep being patient, but if it's ever—it won't change how much we both want this if you ever need to stop."

"You too?"

Elijah's hand slides over the side of Alex's face and into his hair, holding him still while he smiles. "Yeah, me too. I can always stop this, too."

He walks them over to the bed then, pulling the covers back and encouraging Alex to lie down before he crawls over him, Elijah's weight pushing him so perfectly into the mattress, their bodies quick to shift against each other, and the cotton of their boxers a wonderful, terrible tease. Without thinking, Alex's arms wrap around Elijah's body, one of his legs curling over the back of Elijah's too, wanting him impossibly closer while Elijah sucks at his neck and makes Alex squirm, everything inside him ready to claw its way out.

"M'not gonna stop. I never knew it could be like this—didn't know I could have this," Alex confesses. "Please, I—please show me everything. I want to feel everything."

Elijah kisses Alex deeply, grinding against him just enough to relieve and ramp up the tension between them at the same time, and when he eases away again, his blue eyes are dark and honest and curious.

"Have you thought about this?"

Alex frowns just the slightest bit. "You're worried I'm not sure what I want?"

"No, sorry, that's not what I meant. I'm pretty sure you're sure." Elijah huffs out a little laugh and rolls his hips. "It's just—have you actually imagined how this will go? Because there are options here, and if you've thought about this, can you tell me what you—I mean, I like it all and I—anything. It can be anything."

It's overwhelming, a conversation like this, not because

Alex isn't willing to have it, but because the mere mention of *options* has his mind spiraling. Alex has absolutely thought about it, and he's absolutely imagined at least a couple of ways this could unfold, and it might be impossible to answer Elijah's questions when he's imagining a few more, his cock aching with each drag of Elijah's body against him.

"So much," he mumbles, though he isn't sure what it's in response to. What has he thought about? What does he want now? How much is Elijah already making him feel?

Elijah smiles against Alex's mouth. "How about this—is there anything you know you *don't* want to try?"

"No."

"Okay. I can work with that."

And then he does.

Elijah starts with another kiss, long and almost lazy, belying the heat between them and the buzz beneath Alex's skin. When he's ready to move on, he only makes it to the line of Alex's jaw, nuzzling there as he sucks the skin just below it, then just below that, and just below that. He wriggles free from Alex's hold and kisses his way to one nipple, and eventually the other, the pressure from his lips and teeth and tongue perfect enough to have Alex whimpering and clutching at Elijah's shoulders.

"I—fuck."

"Didn't know that either?" Elijah asks.

Alex doesn't bother to respond, the arch of his back probably doing that for him, and after Elijah has played around long enough, he lets his hands lead him further down Alex's body. He's quietly captivated by Alex's ribcage and his belly button and then the line of dark hair that disappears beneath the waistband of Alex's boxer briefs, but when he could pull those away, he doesn't, skipping over the material entirely and kissing the inside of Alex's thigh when he finds bare skin again.

"Seriously?" Alex growls, everything about it weakened by the weightlessness behind it.

Elijah doesn't respond with anything Alex can hear, his mouth too busy against Alex's legs—down one and up the other—until he's satisfied and hovering just above where Alex wants him. Then he drags his tongue over Alex's still-covered cock, from base to tip, his smile wicked when he uses his hands to help keep Alex's hips pinned to the mattress.

"You okay?" Elijah asks.

"M'never gonna last. Want this so much."

"So do I. And I'm gonna go slow for both of us, okay?"

Alex moves beneath him, some sort of argument and agreement all in one, and it's easy enough for Elijah to catch the waistband he's been teasing and drag Alex's boxer briefs away, kissing Alex's hip before he goes far. Elijah smoothly removes his own boxers too, and then he's on top of Alex again, both gentle and not when he has them wrapped up in each other, Alex surrendering to the sensation of his naked body pressed to Elijah's, a hundred points of contact leaving him unable to decide which one might be his favorite.

Elijah kisses him, maybe only to check in before whatever happens next, and Alex misses the weight of him when he's gone, Elijah stretching across the bed to reach for his nightstand. Alex is curious, though not enough to turn his lust-heavy head, trusting that Elijah will have anything they need.

He thinks it's been true so far.

There's no other check-in kiss now, Elijah stopping to bite Alex's side and hold him still against the bed and lick a stripe along the inside of his thigh, and then he nudges Alex's legs further apart and settles there. His gaze flickers upward as he slides a hand over Alex's shin and silently encourages him to bend his knee, Alex breathing past the inherent vulnerability of baring even more of himself, Elijah nodding and kissing right next to where his fingers still rest before he finally lets him go. The click of a plastic bottle cap comes next, then Elijah wraps his hand around Alex's cock and whispers reassurances Alex can barely hear, stroking him slowly while he begins to rub the lube in small circles over his hole, the pressure nothing until Elijah takes him in his mouth and slides a single fingertip forward. Alex is overwhelmed, probably obviously so, but Elijah is practiced and confident and is already playing his body perfectly. Elijah's wicked tongue won't be enough to get him off when it's this goddamn gentle, and Alex isn't naïve enough to think it's Elijah's goal, so he lets himself relax into the distraction being offered while Elijah works him open.

Seconds or minutes or hours pass, and one finger becomes two after Alex has stopped telling time, Elijah's mouth still a tender devastation when Alex registers that his hips have gone in search of more. The moment Elijah eases away from him, Alex whimpers at the loss, and Elijah raises his head and stares up at Alex with a smile that knows too much, using more lube to stroke himself before he tucks his other arm under Alex's body and helps give them both a better angle as he guides himself deep, Alex arching away from and into it all at once.

"You still with me?" Elijah asks, holding himself still, his lower lip suffering for his attempt at control.

"It's a lot," Alex says, his hand landing somewhere at Elijah's side.

"It is, yeah," Elijah agrees. "Do you want me to stop?"

"No, it's—god, please don't. It's just a lot."

Elijah's careful when he leans over Alex until he can kiss him again, one arm still around Alex's waist as he begins to rock into him. Their tongues drag against each other almost lazily, but it's the perfect counter for the way Elijah becomes more deliberate, Alex's entire body steadily giving itself over to him and each stroke filling him up when he's ready for more. It's still so close to being too much, but Alex wraps his arms around Elijah's back and grabs almost mercilessly at the idea of more.

There's a responding growl from Elijah and he stops kissing Alex long enough to swallow it whole. "You feel so good like this."

He breaks away from Alex's embrace then, rising until he

can press his palm to the back of one of Alex's thighs, giving himself more room and a better view. Elijah nearly slips all the way free of Alex's body before rocking forward again and again, his eyes a beautiful and almost frightening dark blue, and his chest rising and falling in a rhythm that might've held Alex's attention any other time. For now, there's nothing to do but clutch at the sheets around him and arch his back again when Elijah finds something inside him that brings him dangerously close to a sob.

"Oh my god—oh—" Alex cries out. "Oh—fuck."

"Trying to, sweetheart."

Alex thinks he's doing just fine, but he still wants Elijah's body closer, needing to be grounded by it for reasons he doesn't fully understand, and he reaches for him as well as he can while he tries not to go wholly dizzy with pleasure.

"Come back."

Elijah groans, his hips stuttering as he falls forward to do as Alex has asked, holding himself up by one forearm, his hand cradling the side of Alex's face. "Didn't really go anywhere."

And maybe he didn't, but everything is so much better now anyway, Elijah still able to take everything Alex thinks he could possibly offer and then give it all back over and over again. It gets harder to speak, the two of them sweaty and breathless, Alex clawing at Elijah's back again as they rock together, increasingly sloppy and loud and needy. And when Elijah leans down for a messy kiss, their mouths open against each other as much as they manage anything else, his stomach rubs against Alex's cock just enough to drive him crazy, Alex reaching down to stroke himself as soon as Elijah moves far enough away, suddenly bold and eager to get himself off while he encourages Elijah to do the same.

"It's good," he pants. "You can let go. We can both let go."

Elijah's cry is one of pure relief, and Alex imagines his must sound the same, the two of them coming so soon after one another that it's almost impossible to know where one moan ends and another begins. After a few seconds, another wave hits one of them, and then they're both boneless and shaking and Elijah does his best to roll to Alex's side, still landing half on top of him as if Alex would ever mind at all.

"I—god, Alex, I—"

"I know," Alex says, a laugh bubbling inside him and breaking into something utterly wrecked on its way out. There's just so much happening and he's feeling it all at once, Elijah immediately rising with concern, though Alex tugs him right back down and refuses to let him go. "No, no, I'm okay, I just—I *didn't* know. And I kinda can't believe I was lucky enough to have you be the one to show me."

Elijah kisses him, a simple and perfect thing, before he rolls away to get them both cleaned up, Alex far too enamored by the sight of Elijah's lazy post-sex stumble to be frustrated by his absence for long. Still, he's grateful a few minutes later, when they're a little more recovered and a little less messy, and Elijah crawls back into bed with him, the covers pulled around them until they're comfortably cocooned there. They kiss again, Alex's tongue sweeping into Elijah's mouth just one more time, and then Elijah's fingers dance over the hair on Alex's chest until he can press his palm against a heartbeat that has slowed to something subtle.

"Don't think it was luck that got us here," Elijah muses. "Just think you needed to be ready—you needed to *want* to know."

"But now what?" Alex asks. "Now that I know what I want, and it can't be that easy, can it? To just—have it forever?"

"They had it, though," Elijah says, and Alex doesn't have to ask who *they* are when his heart has been beautifully crowded by them for weeks now. "All those years together, with so many things they *didn't* get to have—they still had this. And it might've been the only thing that was ever easy. The nights when it didn't matter whether the rest of the world knew anything about them. Nights when they got to hold each other and love each other and commit a hundred acts of wonderful, private defiance. Way back then, they still had this, and all of it happened when they were ready to want it."

"So maybe that's where the luck comes in. Maybe if I'm lucky, the person who waited for me to be ready will want that same kind of forever."

Elijah nuzzles into Alex's neck, his breath warm where Alex's skin is just beginning to cool. "Mmmm, maybe so."

Chapter Fourteen

They wake up a couple of times in the middle of the night, bodies that should be fully sated somehow not. Those moments are sleepy ones, slow and lazy and messy, and then they close their eyes again, sure of things that have probably been true for a while now. And when they finally get up to share a shower and a secret or two, it's Thanksgiving.

Everything Alex wants to say about that sticks to the roof of his mouth.

"I honestly can't figure out which one of us should ditch our own family to crash the dinner at the other's," Elijah jokes over a late breakfast at his kitchen counter.

"I mean, my family is still half hysterical about my divorce, though that should be finalized next week, so maybe it's a great time for them to freak out about something new."

Elijah sets down his coffee and tilts his head. "How do you feel about that?"

"My family always needing something to freak out about? I'm pretty used to it by now, though I wouldn't mind if my sister could figure out a way to take the heat off me for a bit."

"Alex."

Alex's eyes fall closed, because he knows what Elijah was really asking, and he's not all that sure he has a good answer, his divorce something that has been a long time coming, even before he knew that was true.

"I think I'm good?"

"Okay," Elijah nods. "And you know you can talk to me if you're not, right? I don't want you to think you have to keep anything to yourself, just because it's about Cassidy."

And yeah, he does know that, and his gratitude is sort of overwhelming, both Elijah and Cassidy somehow wholly accepting of someone they haven't met, even in these early days, when everything could be an uncertain disaster. Alex is sure there will be some problem at some point, somewhere down the road, because even while Elijah and Cassidy insist there are no bad guys, they're all gonna make mistakes, but things are good right now, and he's not about to take it for granted.

"Yeah, I know," he promises, falling into a kiss that might prove he means it.

He packs up his things not long after that, and heads home to get ready to spend the rest of the day at his parents' house with more people than should probably fit into a space like that. Elijah will be at his mom's, with both siblings and their families too, but they've agreed to check in with each other throughout the day, and Elijah's already asked Alex to spend the night again. It will make four nights in a row, and Alex thinks maybe he's supposed to stop and breathe and step aside and let some time pass between them, but there's no part of him that wants anything but exactly this, so he's agreed, his bag packed and in the back of his car when he leaves to see his family. His body is sore, but it feels like a sigh of relief.

The day is exactly what Alex expected, or maybe even a little bit better, when almost every question he's asked is very pointedly about Cassidy and Elena, his family rarely making the effort to ask much about how he's feeling or what he's been up to. He doesn't think he would've been bothered by the slight on any occasion, but Alex definitely doesn't care now, when he can keep his relationship with Elijah tucked away for another time.

Mostly, anyway. His sister has a close eye on him all afternoon, doing her best to insert herself into as many of his conversations as possible, her instinct for a story almost better than Alex's own. Her presence succeeds in making their relatives fawn over her as much as they've already been going on about the other lovely ladies in his life, and Alex assumes that was at least half of Gabriela's plan, but the twinkle in her eye suggests she isn't interested in talking about anyone but him. Still, as much as she might be there to make him squirm, he knows she won't push for more in front of an audience, and it's his saving grace for at least a couple of hours, until they've finished their dinner of turkey, tamales, and mole, and she very literally bumps into him when she lands on the couch next to where he's been sitting.

There's music playing as loudly as it always is when their family gathers, but everyone is quiet as they let their food settle, a drink still in nearly every person's hand, Gabriela taking a slow sip of her own cocktail before she artfully lifts an eyebrow.

"You've been checking your phone a lot today," she says.

"My daughter isn't here," Alex shrugs. "You're surprised I'd want to make sure she's having fun with her mom today?"

It's bullshit and they both know it, Alex absolutely texting Cass earlier to wish them both a happy Thanksgiving, but thoroughly distracted by someone else the rest of the time.

"That excuse might work for mom and dad. Maybe even with abuelita if she's busy enough in the kitchen. But there's no chance that the smile on your face has anything to do with your daughter. Or your ex-wife, for that matter."

"Cass and I are getting along really well."

"Not my point and you know it," Gabriela chides.

Alex rolls his eyes. "Okay, but I'm smiling, so that's good, right?"

"Probably extremely good," his sister agrees. "And I look forward to hearing all about this person whenever you're ready to spill."

Her carefully neutral choice of words is hard to miss, and Alex looks away for a minute, wondering just how many people figured out his whole life before he did. And as much as he thinks the fact that everyone else seems to know should make the public confirmation of it less of a disappointment, Alex kind of doubts that will be the case.

"Not sure the rest of the family will be as happy about it."

It's her turn to shrug. "Maybe, maybe not, but I think it's about damn time. Cassidy and Elena know?"

"They do," he says.

"Then everyone else can go through me. I'm happy as hell for you."

His phone chirps with a new text and his sister just laughs.

Call me when you can get away for a min

Alex's quick frown is enough to leave Gabriela quiet.

You okay?

Don't know. It's about the books and stuff. About them

He looks at her, holding up the phone. "I've gotta—it'll just be a quick call."

"Go," she says. "And if you need to bail before dessert, I'll cover for you."

Alex hurries up from the couch and ducks into a bedroom to make the call, and Elijah answers almost immediately, out of breath when his hello follows the sound of a slammed door and a couple of cars whirring past him.

"You didn't wander into traffic, did you?" Alex asks.

"No, I just—I ran outside to talk to you without an audience."

"Okay, what's up? I thought you weren't gonna bring up anything about Peter and Edgar today?"

"Yeah, and I didn't," Elijah says. "My *mom* did."

Alex nearly gasps, shaking his head like it'll help clear up anything. "Wait, like, just right there at the dinner table? 'Please pass the turkey and also I have something to tell you about your great grandfather and the man who isn't actually your uncle'?"

"No, Alex. This is—fuck, it's a lot and I—" Elijah pauses, still catching his breath though he's been outside for a minute now. "I'll fill you in on most of it later, but I just had to tell you because I really don't know if I'm okay right now. I can't—I didn't think—"

"Shhhh, okay, Elijah, listen to me," Alex urges. "You sound like you're about to hyperventilate. Just take a couple of deep breaths first. I'm not going anywhere."

There's silence for several seconds, other than another passing car, but then he hears Elijah exhale. "Yeah, I'm—I'll be okay. I will. How much longer do you think you'll be at your parents' house?"

"I can probably get out of here pretty soon, actually. I think my sister knows about us, or at least knows there's something to know, and she'll help me out."

"Sounds like you've got stuff to tell me, too," Elijah huffs. "But yeah, I—shit, okay. If you can meet me at my place in like an hour or so?"

"Sure," Alex agrees. "You wanna give me the bottom line here, or should I just wait for the long version?"

"No, I—you don't have to wait, it's—it's Uncle Edgar. He's still alive."

Alex is at Elijah's front door 57 minutes later, his sister having helped distract from his whirlwind of goodbyes right after she'd pulled him close and whispered in his ear, "I want to meet this guy, so just tell me when we're on for dinner."

Elijah throws the door open and ushers him inside, Alex crouching down to say hello to Poe while Elijah locks up behind him. As soon as he's standing again, he studies Elijah and closes the distance between them, his arms wrapped around him as they hug for a very, very long time. Alex doesn't think Elijah is crying, and maybe he's not even that upset, but he's been thrown off balance again, one surprise after another kicking him sideways over the past couple of months. When Elijah finally starts to back away, they thread their fingers together and crumple onto the sectional, Poe quick to lie down where he can keep an eye on Elijah and whatever might be wrong.

"So," Alex starts.

"So," Elijah echoes. "Your sister knows?"

Alex laughs in spite of the wild day it's been. "Really? You want to do this backwards?"

"Your drama will be much faster to tell than mine."

"Okay, yeah, that's true because there's really almost nothing to tell," Alex says. "I was smiling too much, she saw right through me, and she wants to have dinner with us. Your turn."

"Dinner? I'm in."

"Your turn," Alex repeats, squeezing Elijah's hand.

"Yeah, all right. Like you said, I wasn't going to bring anything up, but I guess the few times I called my mom to ask questions was enough for her to know she had to sit me down for a much bigger conversation. She said she was waiting because she knew we'd see each other today, so she didn't bother telling me anything over the phone, even once she realized I must have found the books and the Poe box."

"So, she knows *everything*."

"Everything," Elijah confirms. "Some first-hand, most of it from my grandpa."

Alex nods. "Okay, go ahead."

"She confirmed the stuff we pieced together about their early years. While my great grandfather was working at the firm, Uncle Edgar was some kind of warehouse worker or stock boy or something, and he picked up a little extra cash for running errands."

"Including deliveries and pickups."

"Yep. They met, and I guess it was a whole big love at first sight kind of thing, but it was about a year or so before Uncle Edgar got the idea to pass the same couple of books back and forth. They were as careful as they could be for the next several years. Gay in the 1940s, from two drastically different social classes, and while Uncle Edgar was an adult, he was actually closer to my grandpa's age than to my great grandfather's, which might've been fine on its own, but probably looked like one more perversion in their case."

"Did she know anything about the attack on Edgar?" Alex asks.

"Nothing that we didn't already know or assume," Elijah says. "He got jumped and beaten and left for dead. A couple of other workers found him and may have saved his life."

"Okay, did she say anything about when your grandpa found out?"

Elijah smiles, a softly sad little thing. "Pretty soon after he left for college. He wasn't really that far away, and he went home unannounced one weekend. Saw them, but they had no idea he was there, so he quietly left again. Then he privately freaked out for a little while before he realized this was the man who had loved him and cared for him and treated him with so much respect, and he made the conscious decision to give nothing less in return. Took him a whole lot longer to actually *say* anything about it, but they got there eventually."

"And then your grandpa met your grandma, and they had your mom—"

"And my great grandfather and Uncle Edgar became more interested in the growing movement around them, they finally started living together, and they engaged with some of the community, at least having occasional dinners with other gay couples. They were still careful about everything then, but with time, they got more comfortable, too. My mom remembers seeing them pretty regularly when she was little, obviously without understanding their relationship, but still—they were family. Which was wonderful for all of them until my great grandfather and Uncle Edgar started acting as messengers for the movement, something my grandpa didn't actually find out about until the arrest."

They're still holding hands, but Alex pulls away now to turn toward Elijah, fingers brushing against his face until Elijah's fully facing him, their foreheads falling together. He's doing okay, Alex thinks, but it won't hurt to breathe for a minute, patience as important here as it has been anywhere else.

Eventually, he steals a quick kiss and sits back again. "We never got your grandpa's take on that—or your mom's, obviously. Does she remember much of it?"

"Yeah, she was 8, so she remembers that the three of them were having lunch when her grandfather had to go 'run an errand,' and then he just didn't come back," Elijah explains. "She was nervous, maybe just because Uncle Edgar was visibly worried and hurried them out of there, and she knew something must be wrong because they weren't getting ice cream, but she doesn't think anyone said anything to her after that. She went back home to her parents, and she saw her grandfather and Uncle Edgar one more time after that, and then the visits and lunches and everything just stopped."

"And your grandpa?"

"My mom definitely doesn't remember anything about his reaction at the time. And she was just a kid, so once my great grandfather and Uncle Edgar moved, she kind of didn't worry about them one way or the other. Asked about them a few times, maybe, but then it was just a new reality—they weren't around anymore, and she had other grandparents on my grandma's side to still see often enough," Elijah shrugs.

"It wasn't until she was older, in college, that she eventually started asking about them again, and my grandpa told her about everything that had happened. And she never knew whether he'd ever been mad at them for the arrest, or for the fact that she could've been caught up in that mess, because by the time she was hearing about everything, he was just incredibly sad about it, missed them terribly, and certainly wasn't mad at them at all."

"And he told her the truth about their relationship?" Alex asks.

"Yeah, he told her, and asked her to keep the family secret out of respect for a decision he hated, but that they had made. My great grandfather and Uncle Edgar refused to risk any more harm to my grandpa, my grandma, or my mom, even once any significant danger was long gone."

Alex nods, his head heavy. "How did you end up at a birthday party in San Diego?"

"Well, we read about my grandpa's annual trips to visit them and Uncle Edgar's change of heart," Elijah says. "As my great grandfather got older, and he couldn't really argue a reason to keep everyone apart, even if they weren't going to introduce Uncle Edgar as anything other than that, my grandpa pushed for a few family visits. Apparently, the time my great grandfather held me as a baby and the memory I have of the San Diego trip weren't the only two times my whole family was with them, but more often, it was just my mom and grandparents who went down there."

Elijah gets up then, and heads into the kitchen to make them a couple of drinks, and while Alex thinks he's still full from dinner with his family, he takes the glass when it's handed to him, Elijah taking a long sip of his and ending with some kind of sigh.

"Okay, so there was a little bit of a reunion, some wounds at least slightly patched, and then your great grandfather died," Alex says. "So, what happened then?"

"I remember hearing about it, but my brother, sister, and I were in school, so my mom and my grandparents went to San Diego for the funeral without us. And I don't know—I'm not sure they would've taken us anyway."

"Small service, with just the friends they'd made in the community?"

"Basically, yeah," Elijah confirms.

"And then Uncle Edgar?"

"He stayed in their house alone for a long, long time—probably part sanctuary, part solitary confinement," Elijah says. "My mom and my grandparents continued to visit, maybe even more than they had visited when my great grandfather was still alive, and then eventually my mom and grandpa helped Uncle Edgar move into an assisted living facility about seven years ago."

"In San Diego?"

Elijah snorts. "Yeah. They tried to move him closer again, but he refused and getting him to agree to leave the house at all was damn near impossible, so that was the compromise.

They continued to visit there, then my grandpa died, and now it's just my mom."

Alex's eyes go wide. "Wait, what? She still goes?"

"On my grandpa's birthday, my great grandfather's birthday, and on Uncle Edgar's."

"Wow."

"Yep."

They both pause to drink, and Alex gives Elijah a few extra seconds before he goes ahead and pokes at what he assumes is the most tender of all of Elijah's wounds, raw now in a way that it hadn't quite been throughout the rest of his life. It's the obvious question, and Alex thinks he could probably come pretty close to guessing the answer, but he takes a deep breath and keeps his voice as soft as possible.

"So, why didn't she tell you? You said before that your parents didn't say much of anything one way or the other about Peter and Edgar, and that they seemed to outwardly approve more when you liked girls, but if your mom knew everything about them, *and* she knew about you—that's quite a choice she made."

Elijah's jawline tightens before he seems to become conscious of it, working it free of whatever hold the past, however understandably, has on him. Then he looks skyward, his lip caught between his teeth, and Alex waits him out. He hadn't wanted to be left alone the other night, and Alex won't leave him alone now either, but he can't push too hard when there's a chance of breaking things they've barely built. A minute passes, then another, and maybe even more, but then Elijah leans forward to set his glass on the coffee table and Alex does the same, welcoming Elijah into his arms when they both fall back against the cushions again.

"She said she—it was a mistake—she was—" Elijah's voice cracks fiercely and while he could probably go on, Alex won't make him explain if he doesn't want to.

"Want me to give it a try?" he offers.

"Please."

"She was scared," Alex starts. And honestly, he probably doesn't need to finish when that's the beginning and end of it all, but his arms are around Elijah and neither one of them seems eager to be anywhere else, so he goes on. "For years, she'd kept Peter and Edgar's secret because your grandpa asked her to—because years before *that*, your grandpa had sworn he was going to treat his father with nothing but the love and respect that had been shown to him—but that's a hell of confusing thing to do when the secret itself is a whole lot of love tied up in guilt and fear and shame. Then when you were little, she was making trips to see Peter and Edgar in San Diego after they'd basically exiled themselves there on her account, which gave her a chance to *witness* the love and guilt and fear and shame, and a lonely life she would have never wished on her own kid. And maybe she always knew you weren't straight, or maybe your grandpa said something to her, but you were just a little kid when Matthew Shepard was murdered, and that's just one story that had to have hit her hard. It would've been so nice to believe that the world had changed from when Edgar was nearly beaten to death, but what was she going to think, watching the news, and then looking at you? So, she was scared, maybe sometimes selfishly so, and she let your grandpa keep you close because she didn't know how to, and he'd already devoted his entire damn life to loving two men the world wanted to hate."

"Alex," Elijah breathes.

"Mmmm, I'm still right here. Not going anywhere."

He means for it to reassure Elijah, but Alex thinks maybe he needs to remember it too. That while their time together has been driven, and occasionally even halted, by somebody else's love story, they aren't inextricably tied to faded ink and tear-stained pages.

"Things *have* changed, though," Elijah argues. "And she's had so much time to tell me, but instead I got loved under unspoken conditions that I only occasionally met. Even in the last two years, after my grandpa died, she could've *told* me."

"Look, I don't know her at all. Maybe we've finally stumbled upon the one bad guy in all of this," Alex says, his mouth warm where he brushes a kiss against the top of Elijah's head. "Or maybe she's one more person who made wrong decisions for what might have been all the right reasons. And I know I just said she might've been selfishly scared, but we *all* have been—Peter and Edgar and Cassidy and me and your grandpa who stayed quiet out of respect and you who walked away from me because you needed to make sure *I* was sure—we all hurt somebody somewhere." Alex feels Elijah start to growl, but he goes on. "I'm not really a betting man, but if I was forced to put some money down, I'd guess she's thought about telling you many, many times. Each time she considered it, she probably came up with some good enough reason to wait, and I'm sure that became an easy pattern to fall into. But then your grandpa died, and she put you in charge of cleaning out the house, knowing full well that those books were still there, so I'm pretty sure she was ready to tempt fate after a lifetime of dodging it."

"Guess I got lucky it was you who stopped by my garage sale that morning," Elijah murmurs.

"See? Fate."

Elijah finally turns in Alex's arms, stuck somewhere between a laugh and a frown. "You're not a betting man, but you really believe in fate?"

"How else am I supposed to explain how I was lucky enough to land in your driveway before all the other good-looking single guys in the neighborhood?"

Alex is on his back before he can really figure out how he got there, but he can't possibly care long enough to try, Elijah's body so strong and sure on top of his. And maybe the abrupt shift from where they were just a minute ago should feel stranger than it does, but the way Elijah is kissing him now makes Alex think there's some kind of catharsis coming, a way to wrest back control when it's felt like so much of it might have been stolen from him years ago. Their hands end up everywhere somehow, pushing and pulling without getting anywhere at all, and neither of them seems worried about just how desperate they sound, both left breathless when Elijah finally braces himself over where Alex lies.

"This—is this okay?" Elijah gasps. "It's—I'm sorry."

"No, don't—it's perfect," Alex answers, rising onto his elbows to chase another kiss. "You gonna take me to bed again?"

Elijah slips away, very, very, very slowly crawling down Alex's body. "Soon. Just give me a few minutes here first."

It's a lot later when they're half-asleep and curled around each other in Elijah's bed, a sliver of moonlight cutting across the duvet they're buried beneath, Elijah's hand combing through Alex's hair and bringing him so close to the edge of something.

Somehow, Alex still finds the strength to ask the question that has felt inevitable since he'd called Elijah sometime between Thanksgiving dinner and dessert.

"When are we going to San Diego?"

Chapter Fifteen

The answer, as it turns out, is in a little over two weeks.

Alex and Elijah spend most of Thanksgiving weekend together, Alex going back to his house only when Elijah goes to work, like maybe there's a chance he can pretend he wants to be home at all. He does find the time to text his sister a thank you, and an invitation to go out to dinner sometime after the holiday chaos. Elijah lets his mom know that they want to visit Uncle Edgar, and she doesn't hesitate to give them all the information they need.

The delay has more to do with work schedules and the fact that Alex has Elena for a week, so they look at the calendar and figure out a Saturday night Elijah can get someone to cover for him at the bar. Technically, there would be plenty of time to drive down to San Diego, see Uncle Edgar, and drive back, but they're both prepared for the visit to wring them out a little, so they decide to book a hotel room for the night and make plans for a nice dinner—a getaway that really isn't going to be much of one, Nora agreeing to keep Poe with her while they're gone.

Elijah comes over for dinner with Alex and Elena the Tuesday after Thanksgiving, and after she's in bed, the two of them talk more about what Elijah's learned while they do the dishes side by side.

"It's been a few months since my mom was last down there, but she was careful to warn me that he's unlikely to talk to us."

Alex takes the wine glass handed to him and begins to dry it. "Because he's unwilling or unable?"

Elijah shrugs. "Maybe some of both? Apparently, there's nothing specifically wrong with him, but he's obviously very old and his entire body is just sort of done. The nurses help move him from bed to a chair and back again, but he doesn't show an interest in much of anything. He's not belligerent, just tired."

"The love of his life died over 20 years ago, and he never made it all the way back to that peace they'd once had with your family," Alex sighs, reaching for another glass. "He stayed in their home as long as he could and now he's probably just—unsettled? Unable to let go?"

"Yeah, unsettled is probably accurate," Elijah agrees, turning off the water and pulling the dish towel from Alex to dry his hands, bringing him close enough to kiss at the same time. "And I'm so torn about my mom visiting him—about what that does to both of them."

Alex tilts his head. "How so?"

They lean back against the countertop, pinkies linked as Elijah tries to explain. "They're both living with the consequences of the mistakes they made—decisions they made for each other—and it can't be easy to sit in a room so full of memories and what ifs. You and I know neither of them were ever the bad guy, no matter how I feel about the ways their choices have messed with my head, but I'm not sure either of them knows how to forgive themselves, and seeing each other must trap them in the past every time."

"It's a matter of knowing how to let go of what's already happened so you can make whatever happens next a little bit better."

"Yeah," Elijah nods. "Which means there might be hope for my mom and me if we can just give it a little while longer, but for someone like Uncle Edgar, there's not much time left for *next*."

"And a whole damn lifetime of what might have been."

Elijah goes home that night, leaving Alex with Elena for the next few days, the finalization of Alex and Cassidy's divorce something acknowledged over a late-night phone call that winds up being more emotional than Alex would've liked it to be. He, Elijah, and Elena hang out most of Saturday together, all three of them indulging in an enormous breakfast before they walk off the meal by spending several hours at the zoo. On Sunday night, Alex takes Elena over to Cassidy's, and he tells Cass about the plan to spend a night with Elijah in San Diego, though he lets her assume it's entirely romantic and not at all bittersweet. Monday and Tuesday, Elijah stays with Alex, and then they spend the rest of the week texting and talking when neither of them is too busy with work, both packed and ready to leave for their short road trip on Saturday morning, as soon as Elijah has had enough sleep from the night before.

They both ignore the fact that he was never likely to get any rest anyway.

Elijah texts once he's given up, and Alex tells him he's ready to be picked up anytime, offering to drive but not at all surprised that Elijah would rather focus on traffic than stare out the window at whatever they're leaving behind. Miles roll by, and there's music from somebody's playlist, though Alex doesn't think either of them could name a single song they've heard. Their hands are linked between them, and the connection seems at least as important as any conversation they could have, except that there's something that's been on Alex's mind for a while now, and while the timing is probably all wrong, Elijah catches him thinking too hard.

"You're allowed to talk," Elijah teases, soft and sweet. "I won't get spooked by the sound of your voice."

"Mmmm, no, I know. But you don't know what my voice might say."

Elijah shoots him a quick look, his eyebrows high. "Well, now you *have* to talk."

"What about the spooking?"

"Probably impossible."

Alex's gaze wanders elsewhere, like there's actually any way out but through, and he's still somewhere around his side mirror when he talks. "Are you guys still planning to put your grandpa's house on the market after the new year?"

"Yeah. I've got most of it ready. Might have another garage sale weekend, but don't worry, I'll wear my 'Property of Alex Ramos' hoodie those mornings." Elijah squeezes Alex's hand, but everything's a little too tight in Alex's chest, and it takes him a second to smile at the joke. Elijah squeezes another time to acknowledge the delay. "No, seriously, what's up?"

"What if you didn't?"

"What if I didn't what?" Elijah asks.

"What if you didn't put the house on the market? What if you bought your brother and sister out of their share?"

"Come on, we've already talked about this. It's silly to move into a house that big when it's just Poe and me."

"But—"

"But I have all those incredible memories there. Yeah, I know," Elijah sighs. "And not to be spectacularly cheesy or anything, but the memories will stay with me long after the house belongs to someone else."

"No, that's not—" Alex shakes his head and finally looks at Elijah again, Elijah's focus back on the road. "I was going to say, but what if it wasn't just Poe and you? What if maybe it was me, too?"

Elijah's gasp is far too loud in the quiet car, no matter how much he tries to swallow it down after it's long gone, and now Alex is the one who's spooked, about to scramble to take it all back, a shoulder pressed to the car door and his hand pulling away from Elijah's until Elijah is grabbing for anything else to hold, the sleeve of Alex's henley an innocent victim to his grip.

"Don't you dare freak out on me now. I swear to god, Alex, I will pull over if I have to."

"To leave me on the side of the road until someone takes pity on me?"

Elijah scoffs. "To kiss you senseless, even though you're being an idiot right now."

"Okay, if I don't freak out, does that mean we're gonna talk about my offer to live with your dog?"

"You really like my dog that much?"

"I love your dog," Alex says, his voice low enough that it might be hidden by the hum of the road. He isn't sure whether he wants it to be, but Elijah lets it go either way.

"What about your house, though?" Elijah asks. "I mean, either one is pretty big for us, but two seems incredibly excessive. And if one of them has to go, shouldn't it be the house that's already mostly empty?"

"Okay, yeah, it's not the most logical move, but it feels right. I'm still living in the shadow of a life I built with someone else, and it's not—I don't need to escape it. It's fine. But if you and I could be together in a place that kept you safe before you really understood why—a place where a little piece of queer history was damn near built into the foundation and painted onto the walls—it seems worth it to do everything a little bit backward. It seems worth it to live in their shadows instead." Alex takes a deep breath and finds Elijah's hand again, his own trembling as it gives away his secrets. "And I—I'd obviously want to see how Elena feels about it all, though if you haven't noticed, she's kind of a fan of yours. I'm pretty sure she'll trade the house for the chance to be closer to you."

"Jesus, Alex, I—what about Cassidy?"

"Also a big fan of yours, which should probably terrify me more than it does. Not inviting her to move in, though."

Elijah can't quite elbow him while their hands are still tangled against the console and he's keeping his eyes on the spots of traffic around them, but the attempt is a decent one, and it's exactly what they both need before Alex squirms away with a laugh.

"You know, Poe loves you too, but I'm not totally sure how he feels about all your sass."

"Pretty sure my *sass* is one of the things he loves the most about me," Alex bites back. "But yes, I definitely need to talk to Cassidy too, and if I sell it, she'd get half the proceeds."

"But then with some of your half, and with the money I have in savings, we could—"

"Yeah. We could," Alex murmurs. "If you want."

"I want."

"And the 9-year-old with me half the time?"

"I'll take her at 9 and 10 and 11 and—"

Alex damn near giggles. "Okay, okay, I got it."

But then Elijah changes lanes and slows down just noticeably enough, his attention turned to the signs up ahead, and Alex finally starts to read them too. His heartbeat kicks up again, and he takes his hand back.

"We're almost there," Elijah says unnecessarily.

They're quiet after that, Alex looking anywhere but at Elijah, afraid that he might become more of a distraction than a comfort. There's nothing particularly interesting around them, just the same array of buildings found in any place like it, and it takes them another ten minutes—stoplights as bad here as anywhere else—before they land in the parking lot of the care facility, and neither of them moves for a minute when Elijah parks.

"You know, when we first started reading their story, I thought I was so much like Peter," Alex says.

"Why?" Elijah rasps, anything they're about to do leaving him shakier than he probably wants to be.

"He was scared. Kind of fascinated by what he felt, but he would've kept it inside him, tucked into little corners of himself that nobody else could see," Alex explains. "It was Edgar who first suggested they write in the books, because maybe Peter had already resigned himself to the smallest kind of happiness, just seeing Edgar when the world tilted the right way for him. It was Edgar who pushed for more, who seemed brave and ready and eager to embrace what they were told they couldn't have. Peter lived passively, not wholly unhappy with his son at home, but not with any genuine passion either."

Elijah nods, his exhale a shaky one. "And now?"

"Edgar ended up being the one who wasted so much time—then and now—terrified of doing everything wrong and hurting the people he loved, unable to see that his own so-lution was the biggest problem of them all. And I spent most of the last 20 years hiding in my marriage and he's spent that same time hiding after Peter died, and it's just—this is your family's story, but I feel so much of it inside me, too."

"That's because it is," Elijah says, leaning across the con-sole for a long kiss, one inexplicably intimate in the middle of a parking lot, everything both cold and warm under San Diego's confused December sun. "Yeah, it's my family, but the story is mine and yours and ours, and it belongs to millions of people we'll never meet."

"Everyone who's ever hidden from something good?"

Alex doesn't get an actual answer to that, but he doesn't need one either, and he shifts easily when Elijah comes back with a question of his own. "Did you know, way back at the very beginning, that marrying Cassidy was a mistake? That you weren't being honest with yourself about what you really wanted?"

"Mmmm, no, I don't think I could have, really," Alex muses. "It would've meant pausing long enough to have a much big-ger conversation with myself, and whether I wasn't ready for that, or whether I just thought everything happening was sort of an imperative, I never—I did what I thought was inevitable, I guess."

Elijah nods slowly and looks toward the sliding glass door waiting to open for them whenever they're ready. "I'm not sure he stopped to have those conversations either, or he would've remembered how hard he fought for love way back when it seemed impossible."

"So, what now? What happens today or tomorrow or ten years from now?"

"I never, ever want to forget that fight," Elijah says, his voice low. "But I need to make sure he knows it's okay that he did."

Alex watches him sit with that for a minute, Elijah almost visibly affected by his own words, then nods toward the building. "You ready?"

"I don't know."

"Careful, you're starting to sound like me," Alex warns.

"That's not the insult you think it is."

"Okay, come on," Alex says, twisting to pull the faux Edgar Allan Poe collection from the backseat, everything put carefully back inside where they'd found it, except for the picture of Peter and Elijah that Elijah's kept for himself. They plan to leave the book with Edgar when they go, knowing they're likely to get the entire collection back again soon enough when Alex can't imagine anyone else will lay claim to it once Edgar's gone. "If we stall much longer, it's gonna get really hard to go inside at all."

So, they open the doors of the truck and slam them again and are silent until they get inside, the sliding glass doors sighing their impatience behind them. The man at the reception desk is perfectly pleasant when he checks them in and asks them to take a seat in the waiting area, and they're not there long before they're greeted by the nurse who arrives to take them to Edgar's room but wants to talk to them first.

"You're Peter's great grandson," she says to Elijah, and Alex doesn't miss that she—Natasha, according to her name tag—isn't really asking.

"Elijah," he replies with a nod.

"You look just like Laura and James," Natasha tells him. "And from what I've gathered, they both looked just like Peter."

"Sounds like you've gathered a lot," Elijah says. "You've taken care of Uncle Edgar for a while?"

"Since he moved in, yeah. And Laura told you he doesn't really talk? I don't want you guys getting your hopes up too much."

"Yeah, my mom said he sleeps a lot, and even when he's awake, conversations are basically one-sided."

"Exactly," she agrees.

"Okay, but—" Elijah's frown is quick, but the furrow of his brows remains strong. "You mentioned that I look like—I mean—Uncle Edgar's memory is okay, right? He's not confused?"

Natasha's eyes are kind, her smile soft. "He won't mistake you for Peter. First, his memory is probably far too intact for his own damn good. And second, I mentioned that you'd be visiting today, and he reacted to your name. Pretty sure he knows exactly who you are."

"Reacted how?"

Her eyes get even softer, though the smile is gone. "Edgar

has always been—conflicted, I think. Your name carried a lot of weight, and I think he might have curled under it a little."

"I'm too heavy for him, but you're still—" Elijah shakes his head, frustrated, and he looks out the glass doors like maybe he needs the fresh air on the other side. When he doesn't continue, Alex does his best to finish for him.

"You're still okay with us visiting with him today?"

"I'm very okay with it," Natasha promises, her stare gentle when she levels it on Elijah. "I don't actually think *you're* heavy at all."

She turns to lead them through the corridors that will take them to Edgar's room, and Alex hears everything Natasha didn't say—that the past was the heaviest thing of all, Elijah's name something that contained so many memories in a single breath. His birth had been the breaking point, after all. The moment Edgar finally tried to turn everything back around for their last chance at filling up an empty life he'd made them live for too long.

Alex presses the Poe collection into Elijah's hands just as they reach the door and Natasha knocks, a courtesy more than something requiring a response of any kind.

Then they step into the room and meet the man whose idea to express his love in the small space left next to other people's words, an idea from nearly 80 years ago, might be the only reason they're standing here now. It's absolutely the only reason Alex is here at Elijah's side.

Edgar is asleep. Natasha leaves them.

"Alex?"

"I'm right here," he says from just over Elijah's shoulder. "Not going anywhere unless you want to be alone with him."

"No, I—please."

Elijah steps closer to the bed then, two chairs already set up for them there, and he drops into one, the book resting in his lap. Alex follows easily, his eyes settling into a slow back and forth between Edgar and Elijah, one currently at peace and one very much not, though the rest of their lives have usually been the other way around. Elijah sets the book onto the mostly bare nightstand and lets Alex take his hand, no matter how much it might shake, their fingers threaded together atop the armrests pressed between them.

"You think your mom has talked to him about you?" Alex asks. "Or do you think he just remembers your name from when you used to visit?"

"Honestly, I have no idea. I can't—I still haven't fully wrapped my head around the fact that my mom was holding on to this my whole life," Elijah admits. "After those family visits when I was a kid, only one of which I even remember, she put a pretty swift end to any sort of honesty with me, but I don't know—maybe that still needed somewhere to go. Maybe she had to have those conversations with someone."

"And this room might have become one hell of a confessional for both of them."

Elijah turns his head toward Alex, something of a crooked smile pulling at his mouth. "And here I was working on forgiving them for the choices they made. You think they've just needed forgiveness from each other?"

"My family will be the first to tell you that I'm not one to be talking about the absolution of sins when I don't seem to be properly sorry for committing them," Alex snorts. "But I think they probably need all the forgiveness they can get, and for the last couple of years, they've only had each other."

"And only my grandparents before that."

"A family full of people who loved each other so much and did it far too quietly for far too long."

They fall silent for a bit, Edgar's soft snoring the only notable sound, but then Elijah squeezes Alex's hand to get his attention, like Alex hasn't been focused on him all day.

"I get why Edgar would think he needs my mom to forgive him," he starts. "I mean, hell, that goes all the way back to the day of the raid. But why do you think my mom would need that from Uncle Edgar? What does she think she's done to him?"

Alex frowns and catches his lip between his teeth for a few seconds, trying to buy himself the time to piece together the explanation in his head. He knows so little but thinks maybe he's figured out just a little bit of this.

"She kept the wrong legacy alive," he murmurs.

"The wrong legacy?"

"It's like we already said. They fought—all of them," Alex answers. "Edgar fought for ways to be with Peter, even after he was almost killed. Peter fought to bring him closer, even when the neighbors might have been watching. Both of them fought to find others like them, and then they fought to get all the way out of the margins they'd been born into, helping the community rage against a whole world that might have wanted them written out of the book altogether. And James fought too, first to embrace their love even if he didn't understand it, then to bear witness to it, long after Peter and Edgar made it so much harder to see."

Elijah sighs. "But then there were all the secrets."

"Then there were all the secrets, yeah. Or just the one, maybe, surrendered and renewed over and over again. And what hurts so much is that everyone's decision to keep Peter and Edgar's relationship a secret was always motivated by a desire to protect the people they love. Edgar didn't want Peter to risk losing his career or his son, Peter didn't want Edgar to be in physical danger, James didn't want to put either of them at risk, Peter and Edgar didn't want to put James, Annie, and your mom at risk, and then your mom—she protected them until they stopped demanding it, but then she thought she needed to protect you from all the same things."

"And the world around them wasn't getting any worse. Hell, you just came out to your daughter in the middle of a pizza parlor," Elijah huffs. "But the more love they let in, the more they ended up hiding from it, and everyone followed their lead. Everyone kept the secret."

"Instead of remembering to fight."

"Which would've been the right legacy," Elijah says. "Fighting to get away from a lifetime of hiding places."

"And onto the middle of the page."

Elijah scrubs his free hand over his face, but his grip immediately tightens around Alex's hand when there's movement in the bed, Edgar's head rolling against the pillow until he very slowly blinks up at them. He says nothing, and it seems like maybe it takes him several seconds to drag himself all the way back from sleep, but he gets there eventually. Edgar offers Elijah the very faintest nod, and then whether he actually catches the sight of it or whether he just senses that there's something more to find if he continues to look for it, Edgar turns a little further and his gaze lands on the Poe collection, the spine facing him and so easy for him to read, though Alex imagines he must have memorized every detail about it long ago.

Alex clears his throat, and Elijah begins to talk. "Um—I—hi, Uncle Edgar. I'm Elijah and I—I met you a really long time ago, when I was just a little kid. And I'm sorry it's taken me so long to visit, but I—I'm glad I could be here with—this is—I'd like you to meet Alex."

"It's an honor to meet you, sir," Alex says with a shy smile. Edgar's eyes are red and watery, but he doesn't cry, and Alex wonders whether it's an indulgence better saved for when his audience is gone, or whether such tangible grief is something he denied himself long ago. "And thank you for sharing your story with us, even if you never wanted it to happen that way."

Elijah nods. "Yeah, we—my mom told me you asked my grandpa to take all the books away after my—after Peter died, but you—they changed my life, and you deserve to know that. I think maybe it's easy to remember how much didn't go the way you wish it had, or to blame yourself for the ways it all went wrong, but all your love was too big to stay a secret forever, and I will always be grateful for the pieces of it I got to know."

Edgar seems to track everything Elijah says, but doesn't respond, nor does he react much more than someone might if they were reading the back of a box of cereal, except that there's the quick lift of an eyebrow here and there, a silent invitation to say a little more. Alex brushes his thumb over the back of Elijah's hand, maybe to keep himself grounded as much as to soothe the man sitting next to him, and then he exhales, slow and steady.

"Reading everything you and Peter wrote to each other—it sort of feels like your life was the inverse of mine," Alex tells him. "You were so open and brave, and you let yourself love honestly, and you only tucked that all back inside when you thought you might be hurting anyone else with that love. I spent 20 years never knowing how to let any of the truth out in the first place, loving the way I was supposed to because I wasn't courageous enough to believe there was any other way. And I'm so, so lucky that I have the time to finally do it right, and I'm sorry that you keep looking back, but none of it's really that simple anyway. All the mistakes I've made are always going to be part of my story, and all your mistakes will be part of yours, but we get to keep all the rest of it too. All the joy and the love get to be ours, too."

There's another glance toward the nightstand, and Elijah's free hand moves to the cover of the book, fingertips brushing over the embossed title there. "Do you want me to open this for you?"

Edgar doesn't say anything, but there's something about the way his eyelids flutter shut that answers for him. He's seen plenty and isn't ready to look again now, but maybe there's still time for that another day.

"We'll leave it here for you when we go," Elijah promises. "It's the story of how much you've loved my family, and how much they've loved you, and it's yours again."

"There's so much happiness in there," Alex adds. "Your happiness."

Elijah looks to Alex, cautious maybe, and then he turns back to Edgar. "I want you to remember it and I want you to remember me, too. Everything you gave to my great grandfather and to my grandpa and to my mom—that all helped get me here, to where I could—where I could fall in love and know it was okay. Your honesty made it so much easier to recognize how to hold on to mine, and to know it was—"

"Good."

It's only because they're both already so focused on Edgar that they catch the word as it falls from his mouth, an interruption neither had expected. They're both breathless when they watch Edgar's eyes fill up with tears, ones that finally spill over when he nods toward where their hands are still joined against the armrests, clinging to each other in here because they haven't stopped shaking. And Alex wouldn't be able to let go anyway, stuck on Elijah's quiet confession and how much it hasn't surprised anyone in the room at all.

"Loving him is very good, yeah," Elijah whispers, pulling a tissue from the box he'd pushed aside with the book. He finally moves away from Alex only long enough to help wipe away some of Edgar's tears, but then he sits back and curls an arm around Alex's shoulders, tugging him close enough to press a kiss to his temple before he rests a hand over Edgar's wrist. "Thank you."

Chapter Sixteen

They stay a while longer, telling Edgar a little more about how the books brought them together, sharing all the lightest parts of the past couple of months because Edgar's had too much sadness of his own to carry the weight of any of theirs now. Elijah talks about his brother and sister some, and has a lot to say about his grandparents, and then Alex chimes in with anecdotes about Elena, and they don't miss the new glow in Edgar's eyes, still watery yet remarkably clear.

Once Edgar drifts back off to sleep, Elijah's hand still gentle on his arm, Alex and Elijah nod to each other and carefully slip away, finding Natasha soon after they wind their way back to the reception area.

"You guys were in there for a very long time," she notes. "I'm guessing everything went well?"

"It did, and we're—" Elijah trails off and attempts to clear his throat. "Thank you very much."

Natasha shakes her head. "I should probably be thanking you. I've known Edgar for so long, and I think maybe he really, really needed this visit from you."

"I think maybe we really, really needed it too. And if it's

okay—" Elijah starts, Alex's immediate nod putting a small smile on his face before he continues. "—I think we'd love to come back and see him again soon."

She digs a business card out of her pocket and hands it over. "I know your mom has all my info, but I wrote my cell number on the back just in case you need me when I'm not here. You're welcome back anytime."

They say their goodbyes and head back through the sliding glass doors to the truck, so much lighter without the Poe book and all the heaviness that came with it. It started raining while they were inside, and the gray feels kind of perfect—not at all bad, but a silent reminder that today was more tender reunion than celebration, life too complicated to pretend otherwise. They climb into the truck and fall back against their seats, wrung out and on the verge of too much of something there's probably no name for. Alex isn't sure either of them has fully stopped shaking, and maybe that's why Elijah hasn't bothered to start the truck, or maybe it just seems like a good time to stare out the windshield for a while, hundreds of droplets racing each other down the glass.

"Hey," Alex murmurs, still looking straight ahead because, as much as he's learned over the past several weeks, he's somehow enough of a coward to avoid eye contact now.

"Hey," Elijah echoes. "You okay?"

"I am, yeah, I—of course. But I—I didn't—I—"

"You don't have to say it, Alex."

He doesn't. He knows that. But the words keep knocking

against each other in his mouth, and it has nothing to do with any sense of obligation at all. It's that he wants to say them, almost desperately, but he's held on to them for so long because he's still so new to wanting and each small syllable tastes sweet on his tongue.

"Please," he says instead, mostly because it's the first sound to make it all the way out.

Elijah turns his entire body toward him, the movement visible from the corner of Alex's eye, and Elijah's hand lands against the far side of Alex's face to help turn his head. Neither of them has buckled up yet, and it's almost too easy to meet Elijah in the middle, Elijah's fingers so gentle where they stay at Alex's jaw.

"Please what, sweetheart?"

Alex sighs, an exhale Elijah is close enough to feel. "Please love me."

The rain taps out a beautiful rhythm as they kiss, the first touch almost nothing at all, familiar and chaste. They don't back away from it though, not even when they both know they're in the middle of a San Diego parking lot with a hotel reservation only a few miles from where they sit, Alex opening easily when Elijah wants more, their mouths such a warm contrast to the chill inside the truck. It lasts forever, or maybe Alex just wants that to be true, but then Elijah slows and smiles against him.

"I love you," Elijah says. "And I love you enough that—I don't—you don't have to say anything. It's okay. I know."

"No, you can't—don't let me keep taking from you. Not like this."

Elijah kisses him again, quick and needy. "Okay. Then tell me."

"I love you. I think I have for a while."

"Mmmm, and will you still love me if I tell you I don't want to go to the hotel?"

Alex chuckles. "We can have an early dinner if you want. I'll still love you, even if you're hungry already."

"No, that's not—I mean, you can keep saying that you love me because I like hearing it, but no—I don't want to go out to dinner, and I don't want to stay in San Diego at all."

"Okay, yeah, we—" Alex is confused, maybe from their visit with Edgar or the unexpected rain or the kissing or the I love yous or the idea of them not sticking to any of the plans they'd made, but ever since he walked back to Elijah's that second morning, he's not sure he could've denied the man much of anything. "You just want to go home?"

"Please. Any of them. Anywhere."

Alex smiles into another kiss. "See, this'll be much easier when there's just one home to choose from."

Elijah ducks away, almost shy about it when he rolls his eyes and finally gets the truck started, steering them onto the freeway within minutes. They're nearly as quiet on the drive back as they had been on the way down that morning, but their moods have shifted and Alex hates that he's struggling to find the words to describe how he's feeling now. There's nothing wrong, obviously, the two of them looking different pasts in the eye and coming out all the better for it, but they left a lot behind in Edgar's room, far more than a faux Poe collection, and while Alex understands Elijah's desire to avoid restaurant and hotel crowds on a San Diego Saturday night, he hasn't figured out how best to handle the solitude they're about to share.

The sharpest edges of their grief have been dulled, but Alex's skin tingles with the subtle scrape of a thousand other things, and he senses the same restlessness in Elijah already. The same need to tether themselves to something more solid than a love story that never really belonged to them, and personal promises they haven't had time to believe in. And when Elijah pulls into Alex's driveway, neither of them has spoken about how they're supposed to get from one fragile place to another, but Alex aches with the need to figure it out.

He's the one to grab their unused duffel bag from the backseat, maybe just to keep himself busy with something that doesn't require a steady hand, his keys tossed to Elijah to open the front door.

Elijah seems to understand enough to let them in without a word.

It's not until the door is locked behind them that Elijah presses the keys back into Alex's hand and holds him there. "You okay?"

"Yeah."

"Are *we* okay?"

Alex doesn't bother to answer aloud as they kick off their shoes, and he just barely nods before he takes Elijah's hand and leads him upstairs, past the mostly empty walls he might not need to fill with new pictures after all, and into his bedroom like a couple of decades of lies don't linger in the sheets. He closes the door behind them unnecessarily, but maybe he needs their entire world narrowed to something small tonight, their bag dropped to the floor before Alex presses Elijah against the wall.

"We're gonna be good," Alex tells him, his fingers light where they brush over the sleeves of Elijah's flannel, up and down until he stops to help remove it entirely. Elijah's t-shirt is next, and once it's on the floor, Alex has a perfect view of the deep breath Elijah takes before he kisses away the crease between Elijah's brows. "I think I just really need to feel you right now."

Elijah fists the back of Alex's henley, the roughness of his touch a counter to his gentle kiss. "I need it too. I think it feels like I've been floating away ever since we left."

Since we left could mean the moment Elijah picked Alex up that morning, or perhaps when they said goodbye to Edgar in San Diego, but Alex doesn't ask Elijah to clarify when the precise length of time doesn't matter, and Alex has brought them upstairs to solve that problem anyway. They kiss again, a little more intent behind it, and then Alex lets Elijah undress him. As soon as everything's gone, Alex works to finish the favor, and then they're wrapped up in each other, maybe more comfortable than they ever have been, sure of this even when so many other things still feel brand new. And then Alex finally pulls away, okay with the distance only because he knows he isn't going far and won't be alone for long.

He clings to Elijah's hand again, a timid curve to his smile when he leads them to the bed. "Come here."

The command isn't necessary when Alex has already pulled Elijah halfway there, but he might be searching for boundaries that belong to him more than they're likely to be Elijah's, driven by how intensely he wants things he's never had before. Then Elijah agrees whether Alex needs him to or not, and after Alex stacks pillows against his headboard and pulls the covers away, he checks again, just in case Elijah will change his mind.

He won't, and Alex thinks they both know that.

Alex lets go of Elijah only to crawl onto the bed and get settled there, and then his eyes trip down Elijah's body and back up again when he reaches for him, Alex still at least a little bit stunned that he gets to have this so easily, and every part of him alive with that reality when Elijah comes close.

"You're so fucking beautiful," Elijah murmurs, cautious as he straddles Alex's thighs.

Alex's hands are quick to bracket his waist, both thumbs brushing perfect arcs over Elijah's skin. "Sit. Just—sit."

His voice is so low, and the way Elijah's blue eyes blaze dangerously dark suggests he likes the sound a lot, his lower lip caught between his teeth when he rests on Alex's lap. Alex hasn't stopped watching him when he lifts a hand to the side of Elijah's head, and it's incredible to see the way Elijah nuzzles into his touch, seeking and finding without question. Then he finally releases his oft-abused lip when Alex arches upward to coax it free with the tip of his tongue, teasing Elijah open for a kiss that lasts just short of forever.

Their lips are exceptionally tender, and it contrasts beautifully with the rougher scrape of their skin, every touch gentle while their hands remain strong, their bodies needy while they patiently give and take, and scream about how much they love each other while saying nothing at all. And when Alex eases away from their kiss, he doesn't go far, his lips opening against Elijah's neck while he brings them back from whatever daydream they'd just shared.

"I asked you to let me move in with you," Alex says. "I didn't—I just sort of invited myself."

"You've got me in a hell of a position right now, and I've got no truck to pull to the side of the road," Elijah groans, the vibration in his throat an unfamiliar but welcome taste on Alex's tongue. "But I'm not above pushing you onto the floor if we need to have a serious talk about this."

"No, I—today was a really emotional day, and I—did we get carried away? Did I get carried away?"

"Halfway to San Diego wasn't the first time you'd thought about it."

Elijah's not really asking, but Alex looks at him and shakes his head anyway. "No."

"And we're kinda naked together in your bed, so I'm guessing you're not suddenly *opposed* to the idea of living with me?"

"No."

The room is so quiet, and it makes Alex's whimper seem loud when Elijah rolls his hips forward, a wicked grin on his face before he leans forward to bury it against Alex's temple, the continued motion between them a slow and steady thing.

"I'm overwhelmed too, but I haven't been carried anywhere I didn't already want to go," Elijah whispers. "So, Alex, please, will you move in with me?"

Alex's hands have been almost lazy as they skate over Elijah's back, his touch light where it dances along his spine, but then Alex's fingernails begin to etch something across the expanse of his skin, and he's ready to catch Elijah's moan in his mouth, chasing it with his tongue by the time he finds himself holding on to Elijah's hips again. They kiss for as long as either of them can when they both want Alex to give his answer to a question that doesn't require one, and he's breathless and at least a little bit gone when his lips crawl across Elijah's collarbone.

"Yes, I—god. Yes, I want to move in with you. So much," Alex says, and Elijah shivers, a long and stupidly sexy thing that gets passed along to Alex, his bare skin warm and wanting so much more, a portion of his heart grounded while the rest of it remains in danger of being lost to the sky. "Still really need to feel you, too."

Something mischievous flashes in Elijah's eyes when he looks down to where they're still pressed together, the tips of their cocks wet for a while already, but Alex guides Elijah's chin back up and buys himself another few seconds with a filthy kiss before he twists to the side, stretching for his nightstand from beneath Elijah's curious stare. When he returns with what he needs, he kisses Elijah again and runs one hand around the curve of his ass to pull him that much closer, then Alex drags his fingers back over Elijah's thigh until he can tear at the condom wrapper, Elijah waiting and left surprised when he never feels Alex slide it over him.

It makes sense, of course, Elijah's assumption that Alex would get them ready for Elijah to kneel between Alex's legs or to flip them over and let Alex be on top or maybe lie side-by-side with Elijah's chest tight against Alex's back while Elijah's fucks him so, so slowly for so, so long. It's the way it's been since that first night, when Alex couldn't have fathomed how to tell Elijah what he wanted, and Elijah had made the decision to take Alex apart by rocking into him again and again and again.

But it's not what Alex wants now.

"You don't just need to feel me," Elijah realizes, taking the lube from Alex so he can pour it onto Alex's fingers before he rises up onto his knees, one on either side of Alex's waist. "You need to feel me *around* you."

Alex remembers Elijah telling him that he likes it all, and because there's nothing to suggest that's changed, Elijah's words are only barely past his lips before Alex pulls him down to him again, his tongue chasing the way each letter must have tasted before they'd become something he could hear. While they kiss, Alex spreads his legs a little further apart, Elijah's own position widening naturally in response, and their mouths are still open against each other when Alex curls his hand around Elijah and starts with one slow stroke, then another, the rhythm against Elijah's cock more notable than the pressure.

"Is it only me, or do you still need this too?"

"Need it, yeah," Elijah says. "And I want it from you. For you. With you."

With fingertips that are still plenty slick, Alex slips his hand between Elijah's legs to stroke him there instead, surprisingly sure when he begins to work Elijah open, his own body reacting loudly when Elijah's head tips backward on a long, beautiful exhale.

"Tell me more," Alex rasps. He keeps moving, an easy back and forth as unhurried as the way his lips brush across Elijah's chest, occasionally pulling his fingers away to tease Elijah before pushing into him again, the building tension between them delicious and maybe important. "Tell me if I make you feel as good as I feel when you're inside of me."

Then he starts to go a little faster or harder or deeper even, still careful and trying to lean further back against his pillows, intent on doing everything he can to watch Elijah while Elijah watches him. Alex smirks when he catches Elijah's breath hitching at random, but his expression falters, and Alex becomes some kind of pathetic when he adds a second finger and feels Elijah's body adjust to it eagerly. It's different, being the one to touch Elijah like this, but Alex is so fucking turned on, he thinks maybe he's operating on instinct alone when he does something new with his fingers, twisting them or crooking them or whatever it is that suddenly makes Elijah gasp.

"Again," Elijah begs.

Alex doesn't stop, and for as long as he can, he gives even more, his grip on Elijah's waist tightening, and both of them too worked up to be able to wait much longer. He moves quickly then, enough lube poured into his hand to make each stroke of his cock obscene, Alex unsure where to look when he wants to see it all.

Elijah gets impatient after another few seconds, and Alex manages a clumsy nod, and however much Alex is still nervous about any of what happens next, Elijah is confident enough for both of them, straightening and shifting far enough forward that he can lower himself onto Alex.

Then they wrap their arms around each other, and everything makes such perfect sense.

Alex shivers. "Fuck, I—this is—"

"One more thing you didn't know?" Elijah finishes, grinding against Alex's lap before he starts to rise and fall again. "It's okay, I've got you."

And Alex knows he does. He's known it since the morning Elijah wouldn't let him walk away from his garage sale without explaining why he'd bothered to go back, and since he asked for Alex's number after hearing about an old book's margins, and since he called after Elena's bedtime to talk about a love story that might have belonged to strangers. It was obvious when Elijah asked Alex to meet him at the bar, and when he asked Alex why Cassidy left, and when he refused to kiss Alex after too many tequila shots.

Even after Alex got lost for a couple of weeks, Elijah had him when they first came in each other's arms, and he hasn't let go since.

The control is all his right now, and he braces himself on Alex's shoulders as he takes him deeper, everything about it both fast and excruciatingly slow, a long moan keeping him company on the way down. Each time he reaches Alex's lap, Elijah doesn't stay there long, rocking to fill himself over and over again, Alex's hands on his hips to help however he can. It's everything Alex had dared to want and a little too much too, his body still shaking with the sensation of having Elijah so tight around him, and it doesn't help—or maybe it very much does—that Elijah's cock leaks where it rubs against Alex's stomach, Elijah still content with his languid up and down while Alex is so close to surrendering to a few different things.

For one, Alex wants to promise Elijah that he's got him too, for tonight or for the rest of their lives, but the words get mixed up somewhere along the way.

"I'm—feels so—I—I love you," he stutters.

"I love you, too," Elijah says. "I'm so far beyond in love with you."

The gentleness of their exchange should probably keep the roll of their hips just as measured, but it appears to kick-start Elijah instead, and Alex chases the reminder that this is all part of the story they get to write together, all the twists and turns ones they'll share. Elijah rises a little higher this time, his body sinking back down the next second, and Alex reads him perfectly, his thrust timed to meet Elijah there, both of them crying out at the unexpected pleasure.

"I—fuck—" Elijah cries.

"Keep going," Alex pants. "Whatever you need—tell me."

Even as he makes his demand, Alex sort of wishes he could turn it on himself, his own thoughts everywhere at once because he needs so, so much, still aching from too many years of things he'd never had, and he isn't sure how to beg for all of it now. He's tempted by a recklessness he doesn't know, but their moans are punctuated by the frenetic slap of skin on skin, and Alex thinks maybe he's being introduced to it here.

And then Elijah's hooded eyes meet his, and he reads Alex as well as he always has. "No, you tell me."

"Christ, baby, I—"

"Anything."

"I want to know what it feels like when you—I want you to come like this—while I'm still inside you."

Alex is close to confessing so much more when he catches the look on Elijah's face, his teeth digging into his lower lip like he has to hold back several fantasies Alex isn't ready to hear. He should know he doesn't have to bother, though—Alex wants to hear it all.

Would probably *do* it all.

But neither of them says anything more for now, Alex wrapping the fingers of one hand around Elijah's cock, his thumb sweeping over the tip and his other hand pushing through Elijah's curls until he can hold him there. Alex thinks he'd love to kiss him again too, but he can't when he's rapidly losing all semblance of control, his body desperate for everything else they can give each other before it's all over.

When Elijah's rhythm starts to break into a hundred heartbeats another minute later, Alex notices immediately. "Yes, please—come for me."

And just before he does, Elijah stares down at Alex, his cheeks flushed and his mouth falling open, and Alex swears he'd stare back forever if he weren't so fucking turned on by what Elijah was about to do, looking down between them just in time to catch the mess spilling over his chest and stomach. Then he releases Elijah's cock surprisingly quickly, one arm winding around Elijah's back while his other hand is still fisted in Elijah's hair, and Alex thrusts into him without a care in the world, every sound from the back of Elijah's throat one of abashed desire.

Alex does his best to muffle his cry against Elijah's body when he finally shudders, his hips jerking once, then twice, then a third time before they crumble into each other, their chests heaving. And Alex knows he needs to get up once they've caught their breath, but Elijah reaches for his face first, a hand on either side of Alex's head when he curls forward to kiss him, the intimacy of it almost enough to keep him there for a lifetime.

He lets go, though, peeling himself away from Alex and falling sideways onto the bed, and Alex stumbles away to clean himself up until he can return to Elijah's arms, sated and silent and maybe half asleep once they've piled the covers on top of them. Alex isn't sure how long they lie there, Elijah's fingertips tracing any number of patterns onto his bare skin, but his eyes have been closed for a while when he feels a warm sigh at the back of his neck.

"I know I probably did this family introduction thing a little backward, but I—" Elijah sighs again, and Alex turns in his arms to wait for the rest. When it takes another minute, tears blinked away as they appear, Alex kisses him, as tender as he can be when Elijah needs help finding the right thing to say. "I think there's someone else I'd like you to meet soon. Someone I need to get to know a little better, too."

Alex smiles and presses it to Elijah's cheek. "I would love to meet your mom."

Epilogue

The fog whispers good morning when Alex steps onto the back deck, the coffee in his hand having said the same just a few moments ago. Poe is the only one to mostly ignore him, trotting outside for a couple of minutes in the yard before going back to comfortably snoring at the far end of the living room couch. After closing the door behind him, Alex sits down in one of the patio chairs and takes a sip from his mug, and he thinks he loves it all—the fog, the patio, the coffee, and the dog—though not quite as much as he loves the man sleeping upstairs in their bed.

In their room. In their house, just a few streets over from where Alex had lived once upon a time.

He's still a little stunned that so many of the things he'd wanted, through all the years he'd had no idea they were possible and then the months he was afraid they were, are now his without question. And it's not that everything is perfect, all the best stories are far too complicated for anything like that, but he's grateful for the changes he's given himself permission to embrace. He's grateful two of the best people in his life told him he's never been the bad guy, and that he's always allowed to take something for himself.

Alex coughs a little, too many emotions making it difficult to swallow, and then he thinks back to the night they'd driven back from San Diego and had first talked about him meeting Elijah's mom. They'd made plans easily enough afterward, promising to grab takeout from a Chinese restaurant near her house on their way over a couple of nights later, but it hadn't been the cute kind of dinner someone might have expected after watching too many rom-coms. Life rarely follows those scripts closely, and Alex, Elijah, and Laura had clumsily conversed and distracted themselves with cashew chicken, veggie egg rolls, and wonton soup in lieu of anything more meaningful. All three of them had hoped there would be other chances to be more honest later, of course, even in the shadow of opportunities lost long ago, and their relationships with her have grown in their own wholly different ways since that first night, Elijah scrambling to recover anything left behind by time's implacable claws, and Alex building something next to the remains.

It's all about as solid as Alex thinks it can be, both fulfilling and flawed.

His relationship with his family is both of those things too, except there's a distinct dividing line between the two. Alex is so much closer to his sister now and finding more time to see her no matter how busy they are, but he's barely tethered to everyone else, the conditions to their love ones Alex isn't all that concerned with meeting. They still talk, his relationship with Elijah not enough to sever the ties to his parents, abuelita, tías, and tíos permanently—his cousins don't seem to care much either way—but it's not all that comfortable to be around them, and he isn't interested in wasting that kind of effort. He and Gabriela will build a new legacy if it comes to that.

He, Elijah, Cassidy, and Michael are already working on building something special to pass along to Elena. Cassidy and Michael will be doing the same with their baby boy, born a few months ago, just after Elena's 11th birthday.

Their baby boy. *That* was an interesting conversation, Cassidy telling Alex about her pregnancy before sitting down with Michael to tell Elena, and then it became an argument between Alex and Elijah, because neither of them had thought to talk about whether they'd have kids before they'd moved several steps beyond where a discussion like that might have fit in.

In hindsight, most of the blame for the fight rested fully on Alex's shoulders, even allowing for the fact that there don't have to be good guys or bad ones, too much of his past colliding with too much of his present again. He was trying to reconcile his feelings about the mother of his child having a second one without him, and why that made him feel left out of something that hadn't belonged to him for a while. And then he swung wildly in the other direction, assuming that Elijah must want that from him now, a baby or the promise of a future that didn't already exist before the day they'd met.

So, he'd picked a fight about something they didn't actually disagree about at all, Elijah more than happy with the way things were, their family of three all he's asked for.

Alex takes another sip as his thoughts, as they often do, wander to Peter and Edgar. Reflecting on this wonderful little life he and Elijah have built will lead him there every time.

"I always knew you would force me to be a morning person," Elijah grumbles from behind him.

Alex turns to find him just inside, leaning against the door-frame with a tired smirk. "Oh, come on, I already know Tyler let you leave early last night, so you had time to get plenty of sleep. Grab some coffee and come sit with me. The fog is pretty."

"You're pretty," Elijah says, so soft this early. "And I really do need some caffeine."

He leaves, however momentarily, and as Alex looks to the backyard again, he wonders what Peter and Edgar's mornings were like all those years in San Diego, when they might not have had as much to look forward to in their day as Alex and Elijah do now.

Really, so much is different now, but at least they'd had time to tell Edgar about it. To thank him over and over again for the gift he'd given them, and to promise him they would never take it for granted.

They'd made an effort to visit him every few weeks after that first trip, just for a few hours on Saturdays, Elijah giving up some of his morning sleep then too, and not about to complain about being tired. Natasha was there to greet them every time, and they bothered her as little as possible, happy to sit quietly at Edgar's bedside, telling him all about their new life together, whether he was sleeping or not. And though he never talked much, even while wide awake, he'd offer a few words when he felt like he had something important enough to say. Usually, it was in response to something funny about Elena, or maybe a quiet confession Alex and Elijah felt safe enough to share, but every now and then Edgar would react to their retelling of some of the best moments of his difficult past, the smallest smile accompanying his whisper as he chimed in with a secret they hadn't yet heard.

Once, they brought Elena with them to San Diego, mostly because both Edgar and Elena had asked, and Alex and Elijah weren't eager to deny either of them a request like that. It wasn't lost on them that she was only about a year older than Laura had been the day Peter had been arrested, and they weren't sure whether the sight of her would truly sting or soothe, but while Edgar didn't talk at all that day, he'd motioned for her to sit on the edge of his bed, and he reached for her hand as she told him story after story after story.

Then there was the beautiful sunny day, about five months after they'd first met him, when Alex and Elijah walked into Edgar's room to find the Poe collection on his nightstand, just as they'd left it there for him on that rainy mid-December afternoon. Edgar's eyes were wide open, and maybe as clear as they'd ever seen them.

"Yours again," he said.

It was goodbye, or the closest they were ever going to get from him, and they both knew it, their tears waiting until they were back in Elijah's truck, the book in Alex's arms. They got the call from Natasha four days later.

Elijah's fingers comb through Alex's hair and bring him back to the crisp morning, and Alex tilts his head back to smile up at where Elijah's standing behind him, a mug in his other hand.

"Good morning again," Alex says.

"Don't think you actually said that the first time," Elijah huffs, a sarcastic little sparkle in his eye. "Maybe we should both go back to bed and start over."

"Mmmm, or we can start over with a shower after break-fast."

"That works too," Elijah agrees, moving to sit in the chair next to him. "We reminiscing this morning?"

"We are."

"Anything in particular?"

"Nah, just some of everything, I guess," Alex answers. "I love you a lot, you know."

Elijah nods, the way he bites his lip doing little to hide his smile. "I do know, and I love you, but are you okay? Seems like maybe you wandered pretty far down memory lane."

"I did, but I'm okay," he promises. "Or I will be by the time the coffee is gone."

Alex takes another sip as if to help make his point, and Elijah does the same, both of them quiet for a while when

Elijah reaches for Alex's hand and pulls it to rest against his thigh. It's immediate, the way Elijah begins to play with the ring on Alex's finger, a habit stumbled upon during a rough night and now a reliably easy way for them to find a moment of calm. Alex closes his eyes and lets himself get lost in the sensation of Elijah's touch and the smooth metal against his skin, wedding bands they wear because when they were first exchanged decades ago, they'd never been given the chance to be seen by anyone at all.

He and Elijah had recited their vows to honor each other, but there was no small amount of love set aside for the couple who should have been able to do the same just as loudly.

"What do you want to do today?" Elijah asks after another minute. "When you're okay again."

"Other than the shower I already suggested?"

"Other than that, yeah," Elijah laughs.

Alex thinks about it, then tips his head to the side. "We could go for a walk around the neighborhood."

"A walk, huh?" Elijah says, suspicion lifting a single eyebrow. "Not looking for any garage sales, are you?"

"Would it really matter if I were? Pretty sure the biggest flirt around here already managed to con me into buying some used books. What else could I possibly need?"

"Oh, I'm the biggest flirt?" Elijah snorts. "That's cute coming from the guy who couldn't resist telling me to keep the vinyls and buy a record player before he came back to see me again on day two."

"Okay, mister 'I have plenty of charm all the time.' Please, tell me more."

Alex pushes up from the patio chair and hurries to take his mug into the kitchen before Elijah can respond, though he's really only succeeded in trapping himself inside, Elijah right behind him when he reaches the sink, his voice low against Alex's ear.

"I want to go for a walk with you this morning."

"Okay," Alex says, turning in Elijah's arms so he can read the secret forming in Elijah's eyes. Something else is on his mind, and Alex knows it won't go unspoken for long. "What else?"

"I want to call out of work tonight," Elijah murmurs. "It's a Saturday night—won't be hard to find someone to cover for me."

"Okay," Alex says again. "Why?"

"I want more memories. Good ones. We were never going to be able to change any of their story, but we're still writing ours."

"Okay," Alex smiles, one last time, because he already knows the answer to his next question. "Where are we going?"

"San Diego."

Acknowledgements

It's the most predictable way to open these acknowledgements, but I cannot start anywhere but with immense love and appreciation for my wife, Natalie, who never stopped encouraging me to chase this dream. She was supportive when I ignored her for all of November 2022, sneaking off with my laptop to fuel myself with a bagel and coffee while I wrote my first draft. She listened as I went on and on and on about ideas I'd barely formed, a small smile on her face and well-timed questions on the tip of her tongue. And then she handed me stacks of sticky notes with scribbled reactions to the version I finally let out of my grip, patient (and reliably hilarious) about the parts of the book she was never going to love.

My kids. Ah. Sometimes it can be quite a reality check to get opinions from children, but then they come through with some of the simplest support, and when their confidence in me never wavered, it made it a lot easier to move forward. "Margins? That's a good title." "You wrote 10,000 words? I think the most I've written is 500." "Alex and Elijah? They sound very nice." "They're trying to figure out some secret notes about a really old story? It's like a mystery! Or historical fiction!" "Wait, they're in love, right? Does that mean they kiss?" Amelia and Oliver, your reactions to this book may change as you get older, but I will never forget the way you helped me through the creation of it. I love you both!

Oh, yes, the creation of it. Well, I had a lot of help with that, and while writing about Alex, Elijah, Peter, and Edgar required putting words onto a page, putting my overwhelming gratitude into words for *this* page seems incredibly insufficient for how I feel about Zahli, Nina, Rowan, and Frida, my international beta crew. They took a big chance when they agreed to read this book, promising to offer criticism when they'd only ever offered me praise, and if there's anything wrong with the book now, the fault is all mine. All four of them were thoughtful and serious and gentle and so tolerant of any breakdowns I had along the way, and thank you will never be enough.

Is it time for the speed round? Okay. My mom, Kandi, obviously, and for a hundred reasons. I've thrown her for quite a few loops in my lifetime, and she's navigated them as calmly as anyone ever could. Apropos of nothing, I hope she continues to buckle up. My sister, Kari, who has spent years listening to me talk about fictional characters as though they're close personal friends of mine. At least Alex and Elijah are my own? My dad, Larry, who died a very long time ago, but would be so proud of me today. My in-laws, especially Emily, who has always been willing to discuss (in detail!) the m/m scenes that make my wife leave the room with her fingers in her ears. LJ for their immediate reaction to Alex, and for never making me feel like I am too much in their texts and DMs, even when I am definitely too much in their texts and DMs. Dr. Hernandez for being unabashedly excited and ready to attend book signings long before I could wrap my head around the idea of them. Zahli, wholly separate from the beta thing, for being the F to my A.

To say I'm grateful to Garrett Leigh would be a hell of an understatement. She created a gorgeous cover for me. I'm still (affectionately) dizzy about it.

My mutuals. Yes, them. Hi, everyone.

I'm sure I could go on forever and still forget so many important people who helped make this happen in some special way. Friends and family and strangers on the internet. Days or months or years from now, I'm going to wake up in a cold sweat and realize I left you off the list, so I'll just apologize for that here. And hey, I'm already working on another book, so I'll have another chance to remember you then.

Seriously, I'm not known for my ability to express my feelings, and I won't pretend to have mastered that now, but thank you. For anything and everything. Thanks.

About the Author

Landry Brennan wrote her debut novel, *Margins*, after the fictional characters she's read about for years finally left room in her head for a couple of her own to make their voices heard. Plenty of others have tumbled in since, loud about it more often than not, so she's back to work on other love stories celebrating the beautifully complicated flaws and dreams so many of us recognize in ourselves.

When she's not writing, Landry is hanging out with the friends who live in her computer, watching hockey, drinking coffee, planning a road trip, or spending time with her family.

Landry lives in the Pacific Northwest with her wife, Natalie; their twins, Amelia and Oliver; and the family's black lab mix, Charlie.